BOOK TWO

DANGEROUS FOOD

CLARK SELBY

Quantum Discovery
A LITERARY AGENCY

Dangerous Food

Library of Congress Control Number: 2024923001

ISBN
978-1-964982-80-9 (Paperback)
978-1-964982-81-6 (eBook)
978-1-964982-79-3 (Hardcover)

This Book is dedicated to the men and women, who Serve to Protect our Freedom, the CIA, FBI, U.S. Military and Police Officers, and for my wife, Karen Serene Selby who helps with all of my books.

Table of Contents

CHAPTER ONE

The wheels of the 737 hit the runway hard as it landed at the airport in Des Moines, Iowa and CIA Agent Tom Parker and FBI Agent Bob Barker grabbed for the arms on their seats as the 737 bounced back off of the runway. Than settled back on the runway again. This time the wheels glided smoothly down the runway and the 737 was soon parked at the Jetway.

Tom and Bob picked up their luggage and headed for the Hertz Rental Counter and were soon on their way to their Ford Explorer.

They found their vehicle in the Hertz Parking Lot. They loaded their luggage in the back of the big black vehicle and were on their way to Ames.

The drive to Ames up I-35 didn't take them long; they exited off of I-35 and drove toward Iowa State University. Arriving at the University they asked direction to The School of Veterinary Medicine to find Dr. Logan H. Price.

Dr. Price was one of the people in America with the most knowledge of mad cow disease. They needed his help in the worse way and maybe the people in America needed his help in the worse way. The hope was that Dr. Price could help them since maybe he was one of the only people in America that could help in this matter.

They found Dr. Price's office and went inside and were met by a young man who told them that Dr. Price would be with them in a few minutes. About five minutes past before another young man opened the door and brought in a wheelchair containing a very sick looking late seventy year old man, Dr. Logan H. Price.

Tom and Bob didn't know that Dr. Price had been confined to a wheelchair.

Dr. Price greeted Tom and Bob and explained that he had recently been involved in a car accident and injured his spinal cord and could no longer walk.

Tom asked if they could go somewhere that they could meet in private. Dr. Price said that they could go into his office and directed his helper to take there. Than Dr. Price asked his helper to leave so that he could meet privately with Tom and Bob.

Dr. Price begins by stating that he understood that some how the Government of the United States needed his help. Than he said "OK gentlemen, how can I help you?"

Tom said "Dr. Price, I am Tom Parker with the CIA and this is Bob Barker with the FBI and the reason that we are here is because you are the leading expert on mad cow disease in America."

Dr. Price said "Well I don't know that I am the leading expert on mad cow disease in America, but I have spent a lot of time studying the disease."

Bob replied "Dr. Price we are here because we believe that you are the most qualified person on the disease that we have in America. I might also add that we are here on direct orders of the President of the United States to seek your help."

Dr. Price replied "Gentleman I will do everything I can to help you, what is it that I can do for you and the President."

Tom said, "The CIA has reliable information that terrorist plan to introduce mad cow disease into America's beef supply. Our problem is we don't know how or where they plan to do this. We don't even know if it is possible for someone to do something like this."

Bob said, "What do you think Dr. Price is it possible for someone to do such a thing?"

Dr. Price replied "I am sorry to say that with enough knowledge of the disease and the ability to introduce diseased brains, spinal cords or nervous-system tissues into the cattle food it could be done."

Dr. Price thought for a moment and said, "Gentlemen we could have a major crises in our food supply here in America if someone could do such a thing! I think you are going to need someone other than me to help you because of my physical limitations and I am going to suggest that since it seems that time is of the essence. I would suggest that my associate Dr. Shane Smith that worked with me on my studies be brought in to help with this problem.

Tom said, "Dr. Price we are at your mercy, so if you think your associate is the man to help us with this job let's get him in here."

Dr. Price picked up the phone on his desk and paged Dr. Shane Smith to please come to his office.

Only a couple of minutes went by before they heard a knock on the door and in popped Dr. Shane Smith.

Dr. Shane Smith was in his early thirties, well built; about six foot two in height and 180 pounds with light brown hair and brown eyes. His face and arms were tan from working out in the sun. He was dressed in Khaki's and with the epaulets on his shirt he looked like he was wearing a military uniform. He didn't look like what Tom and Bob expected that a University Professor would look like.

Dr. Smith said, "Dr. Price, did you need me?"

Dr. Price replied, "Yes, Dr. Smith I need you as well as these men are going to need your help!"

Dr. Price continued, "Shane, I want to introduced you to Tom Parker, he is with the CIA and Bob Barker is an FBI Agent. They are here to see us about a potential problem with mad cow disease. Apparently the CIA has picked up information that terrorist maybe trying to destroy America's supply of beef by spreading the disease into America's cattle."

Dr. Smith said, "Gentleman, how do you do." as he shook hands with both of the men. "It sounds like we could have a major problem if such a thing happened."

Tom spoke, "Dr. Smith, this could be major problem for America. As you know the cost to the beef industry would be enormous and the potential loss of human life could be very high. This could be a disaster."

Dr. Smith said, "Mr. Parker, what can we do to help?"

Tom replied, "Dr. Smith we need to find out who could do it and how it could be done and what we can do to stop it".

Dr. Smith said, "This doesn't seem like something that would appeal to terrorist since it would take so long for any results to show up."

Bob Barker answered, "Dr. Smith, we believe that this is one of the appeals to this plot, just think of what it would take to destroy the millions of cattle in this Country and the cost of trying to treat people that could contact the Disease. This could set the country's economy in a tailspin and the health of the people for years."

Tom Parker added, "Dr. Smith the other problem is that our information indicates that the terrorist are working with scientists to try to develop a new strain of BSE and to have it penetrate the entire carcass of the cattle, not just the spinal cord, brain and spleen. BSE, I think that's what you scientists call mad cow disease, a super acting strain that would be deadly within a few months not years as it has been in the past."

Dr. Smith replied, "That could be a disaster for the cattle industry in America and everyone who ever eats meat. It's hard to think of all of the potential problems with our food supply without beef. We could see Mc Donald's without hamburgers. That's unthinkable. Personally I don't think I could make it without a great steak once in awhile."

Tom said, "Now that you begin to see why the President is worried if a terrorist organization could carry out such a plan."

Dr. Smith said, "What do you think Dr. Price and I can do to help stop this threat to America."

Tom Parker replied, "We need you to come to work for Homeland Security and head up this investigation to stop this threat. You are going to need a team of experts to help you and perhaps go to England to talk with some of the folks that have been working on the problems caused by mad cow disease there. Do you know anyone in the UK that you trust that is knowable on this disease?"

Dr. Smith said, "We do know people in the UK that we have worked with on other projects in the past and at least one of them has been involved with the problem that the mad cow disease has caused in England. I would need to confer with Dr. Price concerning me being away from the University. He's my boss and right now we are pretty short handed here."

Dr. Price said, "Mr. Parker, Dr. Smith and I need a few minutes to talk about this problem and how we can help. Would you mind giving us about an hour to go over a few things by ourselves?"

Tom replied, "Of course not Dr. Price. We'll just take a look around Campus and come back in about an hour."

Tom and Bob left Dr. Price's office as Dr. Price was telling Shane to sit down and to talk about this problem.

Dr. Price begins, "Shane I see this as a three prong problem. First, the problem of deciding if a super strain of mad cow disease could even be developed that could not only work faster but have the ability to effective the whole carcass. Two, determine who in the world has the ability to develop such a product; and three, how can we stop them from introducing a super strain of mad cow disease into the beef supply in America."

Dr. Smith replied, "Logan, I agree with you this requires a tremendous effort on several fronts to stop this type of terror."

Dr. Price said, "Shane, I don't know how you can turn down helping on this problem. I know that you have a lot of projects here at the University, but they will just have to be put on hold. This is going to have to take priority over everything else. There is too much at stake, the damage to the food industry and the potential health threat for American's is too great an issue to not do everything we can to help stop this plot."

Dr. Smith replied, "Of course you are right Logan, we are going to have to help stop this threat. Do you think you could put together a team to look into the potential of developing a super strain of mad cow disease here at the University? The Government surely has some folks in the US Department of Agriculture and the United States Department of Public Health that could help or has already been looking at this problem. You know these Government Agents play their cards pretty close to their vest."

Dr. Price said, "Shane, it could be Tom and Bob are just trying to check their own Departments to see if they are on the right track or they really need our help."

About that time a knock came at the door of Dr. Price's office and Tom stuck his head in and asked if they could come back in.

Dr. Price replied, "Come on in gentlemen."

Tom and Bob entered the office and sit back down on the chairs they had been sitting on earlier.

Dr. Price spoke, "Dr. Smith and I have discussed the situation and agree that we will do everything to help you that we can in this matter."

Tom said, "That's good news we need to get started right away on this project."

Dr. Smith replied, "What we would propose is that if it is agreeable that Dr. Price and a team that he assembles look into the possibility that a super strain of BSE, mad cow disease could be developed. I would put together a team to try to find out who in the world would be capable of developing this super strain of mad cow disease and if it was developed how it could be introduced into America's food chain."

Tom said, "Dr. Smith, we have directions from Secretary of Homeland Security Ridge to give you what ever you need to get started on this project. In fact we need to return to Washington DC tonight with you if at all possible for a meeting tomorrow morning regarding this project.

Dr. Smith replied, "All right, I guess if you can give me a couple of hours to close up my house, pack my clothes and make arrangements for someone to look after paying my bills. I can be ready to leave."

Dr. Price filled out the University form putting Dr. Shane W. Smith on unpaid leave from the University effective the first of next month.

In the meantime Shane was busy making arrangements with his friend Jake Johnson to look after his house and to pick up his mail once a week from the Post Office. Shane decided that he could pay his bills using his computer and the Internet regardless of where he might be in the world.

Shane than packed his clothes in a couple of suitcases and his notebook computer in his oversized briefcase. He asked Jake to ride with him in his new Black Thunderbird back to the University to meet Tom Parker and Bob Barker. Jake would than take the T-Bird back to Shane's house and park the car in the garage and put the cover over it. God, Shane loved to drive his new T-Bird and hated to think how long it might be before he drove it again. He had no idea how long he might be gone or where he might be going.

Tom and Bob were waiting for Shane when he arrived at the University. They loaded his luggage in the back of the Ford Explorer where their luggage had been stored.

Shane thanked Jake and told him that he appreciated him taking care of things while he was away. As Jake was getting into the T-Bird, Shane told him please drive my baby carefully.

Jake laughed and said, "In your car I will be able to out drag all of the student's cars and most of the cops in town."

Shane replied, "Sure you will."

Shane went in the office to say goodbye to Dr. Price. Shane and Logan Price had been together since Shane was a freshman at the University. In fact Logan had known Shane since he born. Shane's father, Dr. John Paul Smith was Logan best friends and his roommate when they had gone to the University. Shane's dad was a veterinary too; his veterinary practice was in Western Oklahoma and ran a large Black Angus Cattle Ranch that had been Shane's grandfathers. Logan had stayed at the University to do research and never had any interest in having a private veterinary practice. Logan and John Paul continued to be very close.

So when Shane started attending the University John Paul had asked Logan to look after his son. Shane had lived with Dr. Price and his wife, Molly while he was a student and developed a father-son relationship. Dr. Price and his wife never had any children so Shane became like a son to them.

Shane told Logan to take care of himself and to give his best to Molly and tell her he would see her soon and that he was sorry that he did not have time to tell her goodbye.

Shane leaned over and gave Logan a hug and reminded him not to over due himself.

Shane said, "We are going to really need your help with this potential danger to America. Don't try to do everything by yourself we've got lots of good people at the University that can help you with the research and help take care of you."

Shane turned and walked out of the office door and as he was about to close the door he turned around and said, "I will call you when I can. I have my cell phone with me if you need to get in touch with me call me."

Shane got into the back seat of the Ford Explorer and Tom started the SUV and pulled out of the parking space and headed toward Interstate 35. When they reach the interchange with I-35 Tom pulled onto the southbound ramp headed to Des Moines.

About an hour latter they reached the Des Moines Airport. Tom pulled the SUV into the Hertz Parking Lot. They unloaded the luggage from the back of the vehicle and started walking to the terminal. Bob pulled out his FBI identification and his tickets and showed it to the United Ticket Agent. He told the Agent that he and Tom Parker had a reservation on the next flight to Chicago with connections to Ronald Reagan National Airport in Washington DC. He also told her that they needed another ticket on the same flights for Dr. Shane W. Smith.

The ticket agent checked her computer to see if seats were available on the flights that Tom and Bob were on. She advised them that it was no problem and asked how they wanted to pay for the ticket and if this was to be a round trip ticket or one way.

Bob took a credit card from his billfold and said, "To make it a round trip ticket since he was sure that it would be much cheaper than a one way ticket."

The ticket agent asked to see Tom and Shane's identification papers. Tom showed her his CIA ID card and his tickets. Shane handed her his USA Passport.

She said, "You were lucky to be able to get another seat on both of these same flights. Although I guess since 9-11 your chances are a lot better than they would have been before 9-11 since there are a lot less people traveling now."

The flights to DC went without any problems and although it was getting late Shane was not feeling too tired. However, Tom and Bob were beginning to feel the effectives of a long day.

Bob said, “I will get our car while you fellows pick up the luggage and I will meet you as close to the terminal as I can get.”

Soon they were on their way into Washington DC they told Shane that they made a hotel reservation for him at the Park Hyatt Hotel and would drop him off there.

By the time they got to the hotel it was almost one am as Shane was getting out of the car they told him we will pick you up at ten o'clock in the morning. We guess it is, already morning? But we will be back after you at ten.

Shane registered at the desk and was informed that his room and all other expenses in the hotel were to be charged to the FBI. He just needed to sign for his charges.

Shane tipped the bellman and as soon as the door was closed he begin taking off his clothes for a quick shower and to fall into bed. He knew that ten o'clock would come very soon.

The next morning Shane took another shower, shaved and got dressed as soon as he could. Just as Shane was finishing his breakfast in the hotel restaurant Tom and Bob appeared at the entrance of the restaurant.

Shane said, “Good morning Tom; good morning Bob. You are a little bit early aren't you, it's only nine.”

Bob said, “Well welcome to Washington, our meeting with Secretary Ridge has been moved up to nine-thirty.”

Tom said, “I am glad that you are ready to go because if we are lucky and the traffic is not too bad we may make it on time. But that doesn't mean that the meeting will” start on time.

Bob replied, “No meeting with any top official in Washington ever started on time. But God help us if we were ever late! I would say that the average wait for these meetings for us peons is about two hours based on my twenty plus years of working in Washington.”

Shane said, “Well that might be a good thing it would give me time to organizing my thoughts to talk about our problem.”

Bob replied, "That would be something new in Washington someone thinking about what they were going to say before they started talking. Doctor they might put up a monument to you just for being unique!"

Tom and Shane laughed at Bob's comment.

Bob said, "Well we better get going."

With that they started out to their car and Bob got into the drivers seat and Tom got in the right front passenger seat and Shane took a seat in the back of the car.

In a few minutes they arrived at one of the several huge government building somewhere in Washington and Bob showed the security guard at the entrance to the parking lot his FBI ID and the guard had the security gate raised to let them into the lot.

They exited the car and went inside of the building through a door that was marked for employees only. Once inside the building they showed their ID's to the security guards. Tom and Bob each took out their weapons and place them on a table in front of the metal screening device. Each of them passed through the device without any problem, than the security guard handed them back their weapons.

Bob explained to the guards that Dr. Shane W. Smith was with them and they had an appointment with Secretary Ridge at nine-thirty.

Shane took everything out of his pockets and passed through the metal detector without any problem. The guard returned the items that Shane had removed from his pockets to him and directed him to a security desk. At the security desk they asked Shane for his ID. Shane gave the guard his passport. The guard made an ID tag for Shane with his name and a picture of him copied from his passport. She told Shane that when he was ready to leave that he should turn in his ID tag and she would return his passport.

Bob said, "We need to go or we are going to be late."

The three of them approached the nearest elevator just as it arrived at the first floor and the door opened. They got in and Bob pushed the 8th floor. The elevator soon made its way up to the 8th floor and the door opened. They left the elevator and walked to the first door on the right from the elevator.

When they entered the office they were in a high tech security enclosure. A security guard using a speaker system requested them to place their ID's into a steel drawer on their side of the enclosure. He than pushed a button and the drawer slide inside the security enclosure. After checking their ID's he allowed one of them to enter the general office area one at a time.

They approach the receptionist desk and the receptionist said, "Hello Tom. How are you Bob? It looks like you have company, for his sake I hope he's not working with you two."

Tom replied, "No, it looks like he is going to be working for you."

The receptionist said, "In that case I better introduce myself. I am Sue Barrett."

Sue offered her hand to Shane and said, "Your name is?"

Before Shane could answer Tom said, "Sue, this Dr. Shane Smith with Iowa State University."

At the same time Shane extended his hand to Sue and said, "Hello, Sue I am glad to meet you."

Than Sue gave them the news that Bob had predicated, Secretary Ridge had been called to a meeting at the White House this morning and would be late for their meeting.

Bob said, "Well how long do you think it will be before our meeting?"

Sue replied, "Normally when he goes to the White House he is back around eleven. That's my best guess, but he did call and say that you needed to wait because he wanted to have this meeting as soon as possible."

Sue than said, "Please go on into conference room "A" and have a seat and I will have someone bring you in coffee and some rolls. I know that you guys are always ready for coffee. Is coffee all right for you Dr. Smith?"

Shane responded, "Certainly."

Tom led the way to conference room "A" and the three of them sit down at the very long conference table to begin their wait for Secretary Ridge. Only a short time past before another young woman entered the room with a silver tray with coffee and donuts.

Bob said, "Rita, I see you are on coffee duty today."

She replied, "It seems like I am on coffee duty everyday around here. So who is your new helper?"

Bob said, "This is Dr. Shane Smith and I believe that he will be joining your staff today."

She said, "That will better for him than working with you two. I am sure that you would get him in trouble if he was working with you guys."

Shane said, "I can see that you two have a certain reputation around here. But that reputation seems to be a little questionable."

Rita replied, "You can say that's for sure! Very questionable."

With that remark Rita left the conference room. Tom poured the three of them coffee and asked who wanted a donut besides him. Both indicated they would have a couple of donuts. Than each of them begin enjoying their coffee and donuts. Tom and Bob just begin to relax for a few minutes. Shane was busy thinking about what he might be able to offer to the meeting with Secretary Ridge.

An hour and a half past when Sue Barrett came into the conference room and told them that Secretary Ridge was enroute back to his office and should be with them in 15 to 20 minutes.

Just before eleven Secretary Ridge came into the conference room along with five other men and two women. The large conference table was soon filled up.

Shane recognized Tom Ridge by seeing him on TV. Shane had no idea who the other folks with him were. He was soon to find out.

Secretary Ridge begin by shaking hands with Shane and telling him that he was glad that he had agreed to help them with their problem. Secretary Ridge begins the meeting by introducing Dr. Shane W. Smith from Iowa State University and than proceeded to introduce each person at the table.

They were; Dr. Charles Stairs, Department of Public Health; Dr. Robert Ford, Department of Agriculture; Don Johnson, Homeland Security; Tracy Darling, Presidential Advisor International Affairs; Ted Jones, Assistant Director FBI: Ron Parsons, Assistant Director CIA; Betty Cohen, FDA.

After the introductions Secretary Ridge said that he would turn the meeting over to Dr. Smith.

Shane begins by say that he wanted everyone to know that he and Dr. Logan Price would do everything possible to assist Homeland Security with the potential threat posed by mad cow disease.

Shane said, "Dr. Logan and I have spent the last three years studying and working on a cure for mad cow disease. Based on our conclusions so far the best cure for mad cow disease is to never let the disease get started in America. In other words the best cure for it is prevention."

Than Shane continued, "I think that it is important for us to approach this potential problem by understand a little about mad cow disease without trying to make everyone an expert on the subject although many of you here may already have a great deal of knowledge on BSE. Here is my list of twenty facts about mad cow disease, kind of mad cow disease 101:"

1. I would guess that the most important fact to date is that we know that there has never been a confirmed case of mad cow disease in the USA.
2. I am sure that everyone here knows that mad cow disease is brain disease that affects cattle. This disease at first causes cattle to have difficulty walking and than a short time latter they die.
3. Mad cow disease is known as Bovine Spongiform Encephalopathy or BSE.
4. If you examined a cow's brain that had BSE under a microscope you would find that the brain would look like a sponge with holes throughout the brain.
5. The cause and spread of the disease is caused by feeding Cattle by-products from slaughter cattle that had BSE, such as brains, spinal cords and spleens used to add protein to feed pellets. Even though these by-products are made into pellets by cooking them at a temperature of 140 degrees Fahrenheit this temperature is not high enough to kill the disease.
6. Although the FDA restricts using such products in food supplied to cattle in the USA. There still could be a potential problem

due to not enough inspections of facilities that manufactures or distribute such food products.

7. Earlier this year when one cow in Canada was found to have mad cow disease over twenty countries banned beef being imported from Canada. Canada is losing eight million dollars a day by not being able to export beef.
8. BSE has only been found in cattle that are more than three years old.
9. Earlier this year when twenty-five cows in Germany were found to have BSE. Germany destroyed 400,000 older cattle.
10. The result was that beef consumption in Germany dropped 50% since November of last year.
11. We know that mad cow disease has been confirmed in the UK; Germany; Spain; Portugal; Belgium; Denmark; Ireland; Denmark; Luxembourg; Liechtenstein and France.
12. Humans get a disease from eating beef that had BSE called variant Creutzfeldt-Jakob disease or vCJD. This disease causes a person to have mood swings, numbness and uncontrolled movements of the body and death usually occurs within 18 months after contacting the disease. This disease is related to Creutzfeldt-Jakob disease or CJD which affects only older people but the vCJD can affect younger people. The regular CJD is normally fatal in about four months. This disease affects about one older person in a million. But either one of these diseases is 100% fatal. If a super strain of BSE could be developed that could penetrate the total carcass of the animals the death rate for humans could be staggering. Beef would be totally out of the food chain in America. It would be too risky for human consumption.
13. It is now estimated that at least 132 people in the European Union has died from eating beef from cattle with BSE.
14. BSE has an incubation period in cattle from two to eight years and in humans up to thirty years.
15. There is a lot of controversy between scientists as to what type of test for BSE is better and how many animals should be

tested. The European Union now test about one out of every four cows and the USA test about one in 5,000. However, the USA contends that they actually tested a larger percentage of the thirty-five million cattle slaughter each year in the USA.

16. The fact is that there is no known cure for BSE or vaccine to prevent BSE at this time. Nor to the best of my knowledge a vaccine that is ready for testing by anyone in the USA.
17. The beef industry in the USA is a multi-billion dollar industry yearly.
18. Hundreds of thousands of America's are employed in the beef industry.
19. Billions of dollars are earned in exporting beef annually.
20. Any threat to America's beef supply by spreading mad cow disease would be devastating to America's economy and could cause serious health problems and death for millions of people over a long period of time in America.

Shane continued, "You can understand by my brief explanations of mad cow disease if terrorist could develop a super strain of BSE and introduce it into the USA we would soon have a very dangerous food. Dr. Price and I see that we will need a three-point effort to stop this potential threat to America's beef supply."

"First, we must do research to see if there is a Q and D method of development of a super strain of BSE, sorry I mean quick and dirty way of developing a super strain of BSE. If it is not possible to develop such a product quickly than it might take years to develop it or it may not be possible to develop it at all. No one knows since no one has ever been interested in doing such a thing we have only been interested in treating or preventing the disease."

"Second, we must find the people that are trying to develop a super strain of BSE and stop them."

"Third, find how the terrorist plan to introduce the disease into America's beef supply and stop it. As well as safeguarding the cattle supply from any future attempts of introducing BSE into America."

Shane than asked Secretary Ridge to please take over the meeting.

Secretary Ridge said, "I am sure that everyone in this meeting understands that this entire subject is Top Secret. Any leak of this threat would send panic throughout America. Believe me the last thing that the President needs at this time is another crisis. Right now I want to ask CIA Director Ron Parsons to bring this committee up to date on what the CIA has learned about this threat to America. Ron."

Ron Parsons begin, "About two weeks ago one of our operatives that penetrated one of the al-Qaeda cells picked up this information during a meeting that they were having about getting money to scientists that were working on the development of the super strain of mad cow disease. The money was needed to pay the scientists and provide equipment and supplies for the work. What was not discussed was who or where these scientists were working. Our operative is trying to find out where the courier that was taking the money was going. So far no luck in obtaining this information. He did confirm that the courier left with the money."

Ron Parsons added, "The cell leader was quite pleased to tell the men at this meeting that the surprise American's would soon be getting in their hamburgers would just kill them."

Secretary Ridge said, "Folks that is a chilling thought we must pull together to stop this diabolic plot against America. Dr. Smith, the President wanted me to convey to you that all of the resources of the Department of Homeland Security; the FBI; the CIA; the FDA and any other government agency are at your disposal to foil this threat to America."

Dr. Smith replied, "I will personally do everything possible to bring this threat to a complete stop and with everyone's help in this committee I am sure we can do it."

Ron Parsons said, "Tom Parker will be your liaison with the CIA. You can work with him on anything you need from the CIA and beginning right now he is assigned to you full time."

Ted Jones stated, "I guess you can figure out that Agent Bob Barker will be assigned full time for your FBI liaison and support."

Secretary Ridge stated, "The other members of the committee that are here representing their departments will provide liaison for you with their departments. You may feel free to call on them for what ever support you may need from their departments."

With this Secretary Ridge closed the meeting and asked Shane to meet with him in his private office.

The private meeting with Secretary Ridge was short. Shane was given the following items:

1. A Homeland Security ID Card;
2. A nine-millimeter pistol with multi clips of ammunition and a leather shoulder holster;
3. Two credit cards with his name on them, an American Express Card and a MasterCard;
4. Various government forms including a Homeland Security Employee Handbook;
5. A diplomatic passport complete with a picture that somehow had been taken when he came in the office this morning;
6. A worldwide cell phone with satellite hook-up;
7. Phone, fax and email numbers for each of the committee members present at this mornings meeting.
8. A Global Positioning System (GPS) device;
9. Digital camera system;
10. A compact high speed computer with printer and Internet System;
11. A lapel pin with a personal worldwide tracking system that the military could pin point his location anywhere in the world;
12. Ten thousand dollars in US one hundred dollar bills;
13. A large leather briefcase that had hidden compartmentsto carry all of his new equipment:

Secretary Ridge told Shane that he was appointed as a Homeland Security Agent effective today and given a classification as a GS-071-15 with a salary of $124,783 a year.

Than Secretary Ridge asked Tom Parker and Bob Barker to come into his office to be witnesses as he gave Shane his oath of office.

Secretary Ridge took a Bible from his desk drawer and told Shane to please place his left hand on it and raise his right hand and repeat after me:

"I, Shane William Smith do solemnly swear that I will faithfully execute the office that I am about to enter, and will to the best of my ability, preserve, protect and defend the Constitution of the United States of America and defend America against all enemies both foreign and domestic, so help me God."

Shane repeated the oath of office.

"Congratulations Special Agent Smith and welcome to service with the Department of Homeland Security." Secretary Ridge said as he shook his hand and uttered. "Good luck."

Bob and Tom also congratulated him and shook his hand.

Now it was time for Shane to get to work.

CHAPTER TWO

Shane packed his newly acquired equipment into his new extra large briefcase and said goodbye to Secretary Ridge.

Tom Parker and Bob Barker waited for Shane to get his new gear packed and than Tom asked, "Where would you like to go now boss?"

Before Shane could reply Secretary Ridge said, "Dr. Smith if you need to use an office or a conference room I can have someone make arrangements for something for you."

Shane responded, "Thank you Mr. Secretary, but I think my hotel room will do just fine for now. I have to have time to gather my thoughts and assembly a plan to combat this terrorist plot."

Secretary Ridge again shook Shane's hand and said, "Good luck Dr. Smith, I would appreciate a written report weekly on any progress that you make in order for me to report to the President and call me if I can help in anyway. Don't forget to use the committee members for any help that they or their Departments could provide."

Shane, Tom and Bob left the Secretary's office and returned to the Park Hyatt Hotel. Shane told Tom and Bob to have lunch or take care of anything else that they might need to do while he gathered his thoughts and put together an action plan. One of them should call him back in about four hours to check on what he might need for them to do next.

Shane returned to his room and began turning on every light in the room. Perhaps the lights would shed some light on this problem and the approach he should take.

Suddenly the enormity of the task that he had just accepted hit him. What do I do now?

Shane thought, I have to do what my father and Dr. Price taught him about solving complex problems. The first thing that he needed to do was to break down the task into its smallest pieces. He knew that it would be impossible for him to tackle the task in its entirety. He thought that his mind or no one else's could handle this problem in its entirety.

Shane's methodical mind began arranging the segments of the complex problem into little boxes.

Box 1) Who was capable of providing the research necessary to develop a super strain of mad cow disease or as Shane had now named it SSBSE?

Box 2) Who could help Dr. Price in America check out the possibility of developing a SSBSE Disease or would Dr. Price require international help?

Box 3) If a SSBSE Disease could be developed, where could it be manufactured into feed pellets?

Box 4) If the feed pellets were made outside the USA, how could the terrorist get them into the Country?

Box 5) If the terrorist could get SSBSE into America how could they get the pellets dispersed into America's cattle herds?

At that point Shane stopped. He decided that he needed to devise a plan to answer the questions posed in these five little boxes next he decided that if they could be successful in answering the questions in these boxes than they could stop the threat.

He thought about the boxes and decided that until he solved the problems in boxes one and two that the other three boxes would have to wait. Who could develop SSBSE? Was it possible that any scientist in America could be a party to such a deadly project that could bring death to so many Americans? He didn't think that a super strain of mad cow disease could be developed that would penetrate the normal cuts of meat of the cattle, but he didn't know that for sure. One thing he thought that he knew was that no one had ever tried to do such a thing.

Shane ran the names and faces of all of the scientists that he could think of in America that had the capability of working on such a project. Shane decided that no scientist in America would be involved in such a project.

Shane called the Assistant Director of Agriculture, Dr. Robert Ford and asked if he would serve as the Chairperson of a sub committee to investigate anyone that could be a suspect for the development of the SSBSE Disease in America.

Shane suggested that Dr. Ford ask Dr. Charles Stairs from Public Health and Betty Cohen from the FDA to serve on his sub committee?

Next Shane requested Dr. Ford to contact Dr. Price at Iowa State University with anyone the sub committee could provide to help with the research necessary to find out if it was possible to develop the SSBSE.

Shane came to his own conclusion that it was highly unlikely that any America scientist would be involved in this plot.

With that assumption Shane concluded that any scientist that might be involved in such a project had to be from some other country, but which one? Shane concluded that because Europe had been hit the hardest of anywhere in the world with mad cow disease the terrorist must have recruited a scientist or a team of scientists from somewhere in Europe.

Shane realized that he needed to contact Dr. Clive Browning in England as soon as possible. Shane took out of his new briefcase his newly acquired worldwide cell phone. Although it was five hours latter in England than it was in Washington. Shane figured that he could still get Dr. Browning. Dr. Browning was one of the workaholics in veterinary medicine research in the world. He was a close colleague of Dr. Price and shared a lot of the same work traits.

Shane had first met Dr. Browning when Shane was a freshman at ISU. Dr. Browning was in Ames to work with Dr. Price on a new improved serum for cowpox. Dr. Price and Dr. Browning spend six months on the completion of the new serum.

Shane had the opportunity to help by serving as the "go for" when the two scientists were working on the project. Even though Shane was only a freshman at the time the two scientists treated him as if he was part of the research team. In a way he was part of the team even if it was go for this and go for that. Shane had the chance of being involved in a real live research project and was present when the project reached a successful conclusion.

As Shane was thinking back to the good times they enjoyed during the project as he heard Dr. Browning answer the phone after about ten rings.

Dr. Browning answered, "Dr. Browning here."

Shane said, "Hello Dr. Browning, this is Shane Smith calling from America. How are you?"

Dr. Browning said, "Shane how is Logan? Is he all right?"

Shane replied, "Dr. Price is OK, he is about the same as he has been for the past few months."

"I was afraid that he had taken a turn for the worse after his accident." Dr. Browning said.

Shane told him, "No he is stable, but it doesn't look like he has any chance of ever being able to walk again."

Dr. Browning replied, "I am very sorry to hear that." He paused than continued, "Is there some other problem that you are calling about? You know you never call unless you have a problem on some project that you need help on."

Shane said, "Well I guess you know me too well Dr. Browning. I do need your help."

Dr. Browning laughed and said, "OK, what can I do to help you and Dr. Price?"

Shane than grew very somber and replied, "Dr. Browning this is a top secret project for the America Government."

"Oh you got one of those easy big money research grants have you my boy! Good for you!" Dr. Browning said.

Shane answered, "No, I am sorry to say that it's not that kind of project, this project is much more sinister."

"My God, Shane what have you gotten yourself into?" Dr. Browning said.

"Dr. Browning the CIA has uncovered a terrorist plot to introduce a super strain of mad cow disease into America's beef supply one that could even penetrate the normal cuts of meat used in America. We don't think that's possible but who knows for sure. The Government asked Dr. Price and me to help with the problem." Shane answered.

Dr. Browning, said, "I can't believe that such a terrorist scheme could possibly work and it would take years to show any results."

Shane replied, "That was my first response, but after rethinking the concept, that if instead of taking years to cause death to cattle and people it took only a few months. By thinking about the plot in this context. Than the concept of developing a fast acting super strain of BSE would make sense to terrorist. It could be devastating to America and the whole world."

Dr. Browning replied, "Shane I must admit if such a super strain of BSE was developed it could be a devastating plot for America. So what can I do to help?"

Shane replied, "I need you to begin assembling a list of scientists in Europe or anywhere else in the world that you know that might have the knowledge to develop this super strain of BSE or as I now call it SSBSE."

Hearing Shane's words, Dr. Browning said, "All right Shane I will begin working on a list of scientist that I know that might have the ability to do this type of research."

Shane replied, "I will certainly appreciate any help you can give me. We also need to think about who might be willing to be a party to such a plot as well as having the ability to pull off the development of a super strain of mad cow."

Dr. Browning said, "Shane I believe that we need to include in this list where each of these scientists live and work. As well any other information that we can get about each one of them. Shane I am going to need my associate's help in compiling this list, is this going to be a problem?"

Shane replied, "Of course not you can use your associate to help and anyone else that you can trust one hundred percent. We need to get this list as quickly as possible because we already know that someone is working on this research. Time is not on our side."

"Shane we will begin working on the list tonight." Dr. Browning said.

Shane replied, "Thanks Dr. Browning, I will look forward to hearing from you soon. I will give you my new worldwide cell phone number, its 101, 201, 555, 7272. I may see you very soon in England."

Shane than called Dr. Price to tell him that the Director of Agriculture, Dr. Robert Ford would be calling him to offer his help in putting together a team of scientists to do research on the super strain of mad cow disease.

Shane told Dr. Price that he had just spoken to Dr. Browning to enlist his help in providing a list of scientists in Europe that had the ability to do the research on developing the super strain of mad cow disease. Shane also told Dr. Price that he had named the disease SSBSE to cut down the number of words used to describe super strain of mad cow disease. Dr. Price said that was a good idea.

Dr. Price asked Shane, "How Dr. Browning was and Shane had to tell him that he hadn't even asked about his health. However, Shane told Dr. Price that Dr. Browning had asked about how he was doing. Shane explained to Dr. Price that he had brought Dr. Browning up-to-date on his condition.

Dr. Price told Shane that he called Shane's dad to tell he what was going on. Dr. Price told Shane that his dad said that if he could be of any help in any way on this problem to let him know. Shane said that he appreciated that and told Dr. Price that with all of the gadgets and equipment that the Government had issued him he now felt like James Bond after a visit with Q.

Dr. Price told Shane not to start thinking and acting like Bond because he had been trained as a scientist not a spy.

Shane assured him that indeed he wasn't James Bond or anyone like that but he did have CIA Agent Tom Parker and FBI Special Agent Bob Barker assigned to help him with the investigation.

Dr. Price told him that that was good news and he was happy that Shane had these two men looking after him.

Just as Shane was about to tell Dr. Price that he needed to go. Shane heard a knock on the door. Hearing that he told Dr. Price that there was someone knocking on his door and he had to go.

Shane opened the door and Tom Parker and Bob Baker were waiting on the other side of the door. Shane told the two men to come on in.

Tom Parker asked Shane, "If there was anything that he could do right now?"

Shane asked him, "If he could contact CIA Headquarters and find out where in the world that the agent was when he picked up the information regarding this plot against America. Shane said that might give us a clue as where the scientist or scientists were working to develop the SSBSE."

Tom told Shane, "That he would try to get this information from the Assistant Director of the CIA Ron Parsons."

Tom decided that he might have a better chance of getting this information in person so he left the hotel to go to CIA Headquarters.

Shane told Bob Barker that it would good if he could see what kind of arrangements he could make for them to go to England. So that they could meet with Dr. Browning regarding a list of scientists in Europe that he was putting together that might be involved in the research on SSBSE.

Bob told Shane you don't understand Washington do you. Right now you've got the "Juice" you can get anything you want in this town because they need you.

Shane said "Well use some of my "Juice" and get us to England as soon as we can. I almost know that the scientists that could be working on this project have to be from Europe."

Bob said, "I will go to work on that right now. I'll go back to the office and make arrangements for us to leave as soon as you are ready."

Shane told him that would be great and that he would be ready to go whenever their transportation was ready.

In less than two hours both Tom and Bob were back in Shane's room. Tom told Shane that the information about the terrorist plot came from a CIA Agent in Indonesian. Tom told him that the CIA didn't think that the work on SSBSE was being done anywhere near

Indonesian. Because the carrier delivering the money needed for the project had been gone for several days. Shane was inclined to believe that was right because he was sure that the scientists needed for this project almost certainly came from Europe.

Bob told Shane that they had a plane that could be ready to take them to England in one hour after they called the pilots to advise them that they were on their way to Andrews Air Force Base. Shane asked how soon Tom and Bob could be ready to leave and was surprised when they said that their bags were in their cars.

Shane said, "It will take me about ten minutes to pack up everything."

Bob said, "I'll call the pilots and tell them to get the plane ready."

Bob told Shane that Tom and him would take Tom's car and park it at CIA Headquarters and be back to pick him up in front of the hotel. Shane began picking up and packing all of his things. He checked over his recently acquired equipment and repacked it back in its briefcase. He pushed the pin on his personal id button into the buttonhole of his sport coat and attached the fastener firmly onto the pin. In a few minutes he had everything packed and left the room.

Shane checked out of the hotel at the front desk and went out to wait for Bob and Tom to pick him up. Shane had not been waiting but a few minutes when Shane saw Bob's car pulling up in front of the hotel.

They loaded his suitcases and briefcases into the car and they set out for Andrews Air Force Base.

When they arrived at Andrews they were directed to one of the large hangers where they were to meet their pilots. Bob drove their car into the hanger and one of the pilots came up to the car and said that he was Captain Tony Martinez and would be in charge of their flight.

Bob parked his car in an empty space next to the wall of the hanger and was told by Captain Martinez to please gather up their gear and follow him over to the plane. They did as they were instructed. Captain Martinez told Bob to leave the keys in the car and it would be safely stored while they were gone.

When they reached the plane Captain Martinez told them that they would be flying on a Gulfstream V to England. Their gear was soon stored in the luggage compartment of the plane by one of the ground crew.

Captain Martinez told Shane, Tom and Bob to go ahead and take seats inside the plane and they should be ready to leave just as soon as the copilot was back with the latest weather information. No sooner than they had taken seats in the plane when First Lieutenant Brent Wheatley came onboard.

Captain Martinez introduced himself and Lieutenant Wheatley to them and said that it should be a smooth flight tonight to England. He said that we are going to have a good strong tail wind for almost the whole trip and that would help speed up the trip. He estimated that from wheels up to wheels down would be about six hours.

Tom Parker introduced himself; Bob Barker and Shane to the airmen each of them shook hands with the airmen.

Captain Martinez told them they had some sandwiches and plenty of soft drinks and bottled water in the galley. He said that this is a self- service flight so for them to help themselves to anything that they wanted to eat or drink. The last thing he said was buckle up your seat belts and we will be on our way.

With that he turned and went up to the cockpit and closed the door. They could soon hear the roar of the engines and the plane began taxing out to the runway. A few minutes latter the Gulfstream began screaming down the runway and lifting almost straight up into the night sky. A few minutes latter the plane leveled off and Captain Martinez announced over the intercom that they would be holding this altitude for some time until they burned off some fuel than they would climb to a higher altitude and pick up more speed.

As the plane headed east to England Shane began to get acquainted with his two new associates. Shane asked Tom Parker if he used to work for Elvis. Tom told him no and if he had he would not be flying to England with him tonight.

Bob said, "Tom did have something in common with the man that worked for Elvis, they were both Colonels."

Tom told Shane that was true that he had been in the Army and was a Colonel when he retired after putting in his twenty years. Tom had been a Green Beret and had seen action in Vietnam and during the Gulf War. During his military career he spend a lot of time working with the CIA as an Intelligent Officer and when he retired from the Army he moved over to the CIA.

Tom had been a highly decorated solider including a couple of purple hearts. Tom was not one that wanted to talk about his war experiences. Shane knew other combat veterans that had been in a lot of fighting and they never wanted to say anything about their experiences. They just wanted to forget it or at least put it out of their mind as much as possible.

Tom had never married although he confessed that he had intended to get married but before he got back from Vietnam his girl married somebody else.

Bob said, "Tom never got over her."

Tom laughed and said, "I guess you're right because I haven't found anyone else that was like her, but I'm still looking."

Shane also found out more about Bob Barker by asking Bob, "Do you do "The Price is Right" besides being a Special Agent for the FBI? Are you like the fellow that used to MC "The Gong Show" that claimed he carried out executions for the CIA."

Bob said, "No, he had been with the FBI since he got his law degree and was never on TV.

Unlike Tom, Bob had been married to his wife Virginia since they were collage students and had four children. The oldest was a boy 18, a girl 16, another girl 14 and his youngest a boy age 11.

Tom said, "You guys messed up on that last one didn't you, since the rest of the kids were all two years apart?"

Bob said, "Yeah we did, because we were stopping at three. Surprise!"

Shane realized that he had not eaten since breakfast and missed dinner last night he decided to grab a couple of sandwiches and cokes. After he finished his lunch, dinner or what ever this was. He reclined his seat back and was soon fast asleep.

The Gulfstream began climbing and picking up speed and than leveled off and continued winging its way to England. As Shane dreamed about his problem he hoped that many of his questions would be answered in England.

Shane was soon awake as he heard Tom and Bob talking about how good the coffee tasted and how beautiful the sunrise was this morning.

Tom asked Shane if he wanted a cup of coffee. He sure did. It was an awful short night Shane thought and when he looked at his watch it was two o'clock in the morning in Washington and seven in the morning in England.

A few minutes latter Captain Martinez announced over the intercom that they would soon begin their descend and be landing in Manchester, England in about an hour. Shane thought that he should get shaved and cleaned up before they landed. He went into the bathroom and begin his clean up by washing his face and as much of the rest of him that he could in such a small space with a wash cloth. He brushed his teeth; shaved; put on fresh deodorant and aftershave lotion; and finally combed his hair. Well he guessed he was ready for the day. He didn't know it yet but he was about to have a life-changing event this day.

Shane, Tom and Bob peered out the windows of the plane suddenly as they begin to descend lower and lower through the clouds they begin to catch glimpses of some of the most beautiful countryside in the world the green fields and small hamlets of England. Shane always thought when he was landed in England that he felt like he was coming home. He knew his ancestors had come from England from somewhere near York but he didn't know exactly where, maybe that's why he felt like he was coming home he didn't know any other reason for his feeling. It was a long ways from Western Oklahoma.

Soon after that Captain Martinez landed the plane and taxied to the terminal for transit private planes. At the terminal they were met by custom and immigration officers that immediately cleared them for entry into England. Captain Martinez said that they would remain with the plane and wait for them until they had finished their business in England. He said if we are not here at the plane the attendants in the transit lounge would knew where to reach them by phone. He assured Shane that they would be standing by to leave whenever he was ready. Shane got the number for the transit lounge and thanked

Captain Martinez and Lieutenant Wheatley for their help and a very smooth flight.

After getting out of the plane CIA Agent Billy Gene Murphy greeted them and said that he had a mini van and a driver for them to use during their stay in England. Agent Murphy introduced them to Harold Chester who would be their driver. Harold loaded their luggage into the rear of the van and asked if anyone needed to use the water closest before they left for Doncaster everyone said that they were all right and ready to get started.

They thanked Agent Murphy for his help and told him that if they need anything else that they would give him a call. Tom had his telephone number. They loaded into the van with Shane sitting in the front passenger seat and Tom and Bob in the rear seats. Harold started the van and cleared security at the airport gate and found his way onto the M62 Motorway headed east.

Harold didn't do much talking nor did anyone else in the van they were trying to get accumulated to the time change. In fact all three of them went back to sleep and remained that way until Harold turned the van onto the M1 Motorway traveling south and at that point the three of them kind of woke up do to the change in speed of the van.

A few miles latter Harold exited off of the M1 onto eastbound M18 and before much longer he was leaving the motorway and entering into Doncaster. Shane begin providing directions to Dr. Browning's laboratory and after several turns on different streets they arrived at their destination.

Shane exited the vehicle and went inside the laboratory and was greeted by a beautiful young woman that Shane guessed was in her early thirties. She had beautiful tanned skin, shoulder length raven black hair, dark brown eyes and was dressed in what looked like a safari outfit and he wondered who she was and what she was doing in Dr. Browning's laboratory.

She spoke in a very soft pleasant English accent and said, "Hello love, how may I help you?"

Shane was so taken with her presents in Dr. Browning laboratory that he had a hard time replying. Finally he said, "I am here to see Dr. Clive Browning."

The young woman replied, "And whom should I say is here to see him?"

Shane said, "I am Dr. Shane Smith from the United States."

Than she said, "You are the fellow that I am doing all of this work for then."

Shane said, "Well I don't know about that."

She replied, "Just a moment and I will tell Dr. Browning that you are here."

Then she left the reception area through a door directly behind the counter and entered into the laboratory.

Dr. Browning came through the same door that the young woman had gone out of and he said to Shane, "You said that you would see me soon but I didn't expect you quite so soon."

With that he came from behind the counter and shook Shane's hand and than gave him a big bear hug.

Shane had forgotten how big a man that Dr. Browning was and how strong he was. Dr. Browning was almost six feet six inches tall and weight almost three hundred pounds. He had a ruddy complex like someone that had spent too much time at the pub.

Just then the young woman came back into the reception area and Dr. Browning turned to her and said. "You have not met Dr. Shane William Smith before have you love?"

She replied, "No Father, I have never had the privilege or the pleasure."

Dr. Browning than told Shane, "This is my daughter, Dr. Elizabeth Victoria Browning."

Shane was really taken back because he never knew that Dr. Browning had ever been married or had a daughter.

Dr. Browning read Shane's look of surprise and said, "Shane you didn't know that I had a daughter and until the last few months neither did I. It's a long story better taken up over dinner or at some other time. I know you have more important things on your mind."

Just for a moment Shane was not so sure that he had more important things on his mind than Dr. Elizabeth Victoria Browning.

However, Shane caught himself and said, "Dr. Browning how much progress have you been able to make on the list of scientists?"

Both Dr. Browning's begin to speak at once. Than the senior Dr. Browning said, "Lets make this easier for all. Let's just make it Clive, Elizabeth and Shane since we are all doctors."

Shane and Elizabeth both agreed, except Elizabeth said, "I might forget and call you Father."

Clive said, "Well I don't think Shane will answer to that."

Clive than said, "Shane early this morning I received a call from an official from the Home Office in London and he said that the Prime Minister's office had called him to request that Elizabeth and I assist you in every way that we could. It seems that the President of the United States had call to request the United Kingdoms help with this potential terrorist threat. They seemed to know that you would be arriving here this morning."

Shane replied, "I guess that doesn't surprise me much since I flew here in a US Air Force plane with a CIA Agent and an FBI Special Agent. It looks like everyone thinks this threat is real and they are really concerned."

Clive said, "Well the chap from the Home Office certainly gave that impression. Elizabeth why don't you get the list of scientists that we have put together so far?"

Shane said, "Before we look at your list let me bring in my associates that are working with me."

Clive said, "Certainly."

Shane went to the door and asked Tom and Bob to come in. When they had made their way into the office Shane introduced everyone to each other.

Shane asked Elizabeth, "Please go over the list that Clive and you have prepared." Elizabeth began by saying that they had only begin working on the list late last night and were sure that it was a long way from being complete and that they had not had time yet to check the location of any of the scientists on the list. Than she begin reading the list:

Dr. Anthony Hinson, UK	Dr. Kathleen Fraser, UK
Dr. Gene Carlson, UK	Dr. David Allen, UK
Dr. Robert Alstatt, UK	Dr. Donald Darmstaedter, Germany
Dr. John R. Weichmann, Germany	Dr. F.R. Ybarguen, Germany
Dr. Bernard Woolwine, France	Dr. Amos Treadway, France
Dr. Chandler Townsend, UK	Dr. Barbara Tripplehorn, UK
Dr. Donald Sunderberg, Belgium	Dr. Paul Summerhill, The Netherlands
Dr. Lucas Sturtevant, Switzerland	Dr. James Saxon, Jr., Switzerland
Dr. Tom Rogers, UK	Dr. Jarod Phillips, Denmark
Dr. Charles Bentley III, UK	Dr. Ben Lairmore, UK
Dr. Richard House Sr., UK	Dr. Larry Davenport, UK
Dr. Arden Borland, The Netherlands	Dr. Roland Nelson, UK

Elizabeth said, "So far this is the list of names and the countries that the scientists work in that we consider have the ability to carry out the research required to produce the SSBSE."

Clive added, "I am sure that there are others that could do the work that we have not thought of yet, but these people would be the most likely since we know that they have been involved in working on a cure for mad cow disease. Many of them have been in contact with us in the past when we were having so many problems with the disease here in England. The Home Office said that after we had our list assembled that they would help check out all of the scientists located in the UK."

Shane said, "That would certainly help since we need as much speed as possible in investigating this terrorist threat."

Tom spoke up, "I will contact CIA Headquarters and request that they have our agents located in each of the other countries check out the rest of the people on the list."

Bob said, "The FBI would be checking on everyone on the list being prepared by Dr. Price that is located in the USA."

Shane thought about the progress that they were making and said, "I think we need to sit tight here in Doncaster until we begin to get feed back from the Home Office, the CIA and the FBI. What does everyone else think?"

Tom was first to reply, "I believe that it is the only thing that makes sense at this point since we have no idea where this research maybe going on."

They all agreed that it was the only logical thing to do and Clive suggested that Elizabeth make arrangement for rooms at the local hotel for them. He told Shane that he should stay at his home while he was in Doncaster. Shane agreed.

Clive then said, "The Home Office suggested that he should consider going to America to work with Dr. Price on the research to see if it was possible to develop a super strain of mad cow disease."

Shane said, "He thought that was a very good idea and that when they flew back to America that he could go with them on their plane."

Elizabeth made arrangements for rooms for Tom and Bob at the White Swain Hotel. They decided that they could go to the hotel and work out of their rooms and since it was only a short walk from the laboratory they could send Harold and the van on his way. They unloaded Shane's gear from the van and brought it into the laboratory.

They had the driver drop them and their luggage of at the White Swain and registered and moved into their rooms. Tom had gotten a copy of Elizabeth's list of scientists and contacted CIA Headquarters to ask them to check out the scientists located outside of the UK. He explained to the CIA that the Home Office was checking out all of the scientists on the list in the UK.

Shane was very interested to here about Elizabeth since in all of the years that he had knowing Clive. Shane had never heard of her. Clive said that it was a long story but he would give Shane the abridged version.

Clive had met Elizabeth's mother, Frances when they were both students at Cambridge. She was studying English Literature and him Veterinary Medicine. They fell in love and got married and after a few years they grew apart and divorced. After the divorce he moved to Northern England she moved to London. Elizabeth was born after their divorce and his ex wife didn't tell Clive that she was going to have a baby and didn't tell him about Elizabeth after she was born.

His ex wife told Elizabeth that her father had died serving in the military. Elizabeth must have gotten some of his genes since she always loved animals and when she grew up she wanted to be a veterinary. She got her degree and before she had been practicing very long her mother became very ill with breast cancer. After she found out that she was not going to survive the cancer she told Elizabeth of her father and how to get in contact with him.

Clive said that he received a very strange telephone call one-day and Elizabeth told him about her mother's illness and that she was his daughter.

Clive told Shane that he went to London to see about Frances and to meet his daughter. He said that he stayed with Frances until she died and after the funeral he asked Elizabeth to come back to Doncaster with him and work on research. He told Shane that Elizabeth loved working with him and they had become very close after only a few months.

Clive said that it was hard to believe that neither Frances, nor he had married again but the true was that they never could love anyone else. Before Frances died they were remarried and Clive forgave her for not telling him about Elizabeth. Although they had only a short time together before she passed away they had a lot of happy days together and were very much in love. They finally realized that they had been in love with each other all of their lives.

Frances told Clive that she named Elizabeth after her favorite poet, Elizabeth Barrett Browning, but because she knew that Clive's favorite woman in English history was Queen Victoria she gave Elizabeth, Victoria as her middle name.

Just as Clive finished telling Shane about his newly found daughter, Elizabeth returned from telling Tom and Bob how they could walk from the hotel to the laboratory and about various places for them to eat in town. She also pointed out all of the local pubs.

Clive said, "Elizabeth why don't you take Shane to the house and get him settled into the guest room."

Elizabeth replied, "All right father, will you be along shortly?"

Clive said, "No, I will be home in about an hour maybe two. I want to go through my collection of calling cards to see if I can find any other names of veterinarians that we may have missed. People that might be capable of conducting the research on SSBSE."

Elizabeth asked Shane "If he was ready to go to the house or if he needed to do anything else before leaving?"

Shane told her, "No, I am ready to get out of these clothes and into a shower and maybe lay down for awhile. After that I will be ready for a long conversation."

Clive said, "Shane my boy, you are looking rather tried. Go take a rest and I will see you latter."

Elizabeth helped Shane load his luggage into the Land Rover and drove him to her father's home. Arriving at the house Elizabeth helped Shane carry his luggage upstairs to the guest-room.

She gathered up some guest towels and face cloths for Shane. Next she turned on the shower for him as she explained that in this old house it takes awhile for the water to get hot or even warm. Shane thanked her for her help.

He started taking off his clothes it felt like he was taking off a layer of skin since it felt more like peeling off skin instead of taking off clothes. Had he been only two days in these clothes, Shane thought that it felt like he had them on for a month.

The shower felt wonderful, Elizabeth had the temperature set just prefect. Just like he thought she was, just perfect. Shane began to feel better as the water from the shower continued to breathe new life into his body.

Shane finally turned off the shower and proceeded to dry himself off. He again began feeling tried. He put on his blue bathrobe and went into his bedroom and climbed into bed. He was soon fast asleep. Just as he was falling asleep he thought of the whirlwind these last three days had been and than about Elizabeth.

Shane was awaking by someone touching his shoulder. He opened his eyes and heard Elizabeth say, "Shane, father asked me to see if you wanted to meet him for dinner? He is on the telephone waiting for your answer."

Shane asked, "What time is it away?"

Elizabeth replied, "About nine in the evening."

Shane said, "Well since I am awake I do feel hunger. Please tell him that I would be glad to meet him for dinner."

Elizabeth left the room to finish her telephone conversation with her Father and to see where they should meet him.

Twenty minutes latter Shane and Elizabeth were in the Land Rover heading back into town to meet her father for dinner. Clive had told Elizabeth to meet him at the Ox Yoke Inn for dinner at nine thirty.

They were going to be a little late but if fast driving could have gotten them there on time than Elizabeth was doing her best.

Shane asked, "Elizabeth do you always drive this fast?"

She replied, "I don't know do you think we are going fast?"

Shane replied, "Well I guess it is a matter of opinion, it would not be too fast if we were in the Indianapolis 500."

Elizabeth just laughed and turned a square corner at almost fifty miles an hour. Soon they pulled up in front of the Ox Bow Inn. Clive was waiting for them in the foyer of the restaurant.

Clive gave Elizabeth a hug and he asked Shane if it felt better or worse. Shane was not sure after his quick dressing and his ride to the restaurant, but he did say that after the nice shower and resting awhile he did feel much better. Now he was hunger.

When they entered the restaurant several towns' folks spoke to Clive and Clive returned their salutations. After a very short wait a waiter showed them to a table seating Elizabeth between Clive and Shane.

Clive said, "I think we should have a drink to celebrate having Elizabeth joining our little research team. I have told her all about the time I spent in Ames doing research with Dr. Logan Price and you.

Elizabeth knows all about you so I guess you will have to be on your best behavior and besides you will have to remember I am her father."

Shane said, "I certainly think we should have that drink to welcome Elizabeth to our team, except that being a Freshman "go for" didn't qualify me much as a member of the research team when you were in Ames."

Clive laughed and said, "Well you were an excellent "go for" and a very willing student and I love you a lot my boy!"

Clive ordered a bottle of French Champagne and after the waiter had poured each of them a glass of Champagne. He proposed a toast, "This is a toast to my lovely daughter Elizabeth and my dear friend Shane may we be successful with our currant problem and may our friendships endure today, tomorrow and forever."

Shane quickly replied, "I will drink to that, and Elizabeth I certainly want to welcome you to our research team." With that Shane leaned over and kissed Elizabeth on her left cheek and whispered, "Elizabeth I really do want to welcome you into my life."

Clive said, "Well I think we better order dinner so we can get a few minutes rest before we have to get started tomorrow."

After they finished the Champagne and their dinner Elizabeth drove Shane to her Father's home. During the trip Elizabeth confided that she really liked Shane and told him that her father had spoken so highly of him that before she met Shane she had been a little jealous of him. She said that she was afraid that her Father was disappointed that she was a daughter and not a son. Shane told her that he didn't believe that for a minute because he could see that Clive just beamed when he introduced her to people and when he looked at her. Shane thought that Clive was very proud of her.

Elizabeth thanked him for the kind words and told him that I think I like you a lot more than I ever thought that I would.

Shane thought to himself that he might be able to go farther than just liking Elizabeth he thought he might be falling in love with her. Shane had never fallen in love with anyone.

Clive was right morning came quickly and as Shane was still lying in his bed he could hear the shower running in the bathroom and thought I have to get up. After another few minutes past he heard the shower being turned off.

Shane got out of bed and found his blue robe and some clothes to wear for the day or for how many other days he might have them on. He checked to see if the bathroom was available. It was. Shane was soon dressed and had his bags repacked. He went downstairs to find Elizabeth with coffee and toast ready for him. She had some English strawberry jam that Shane liked so well on the table.

Shane said, "Good morning Elizabeth, you look wonderful this morning and breakfast looks pretty good too. Well not as good as you."

Elizabeth replied, "Shane are you flirting with me?"

Shane responded, "If I was, would it be OK?"

Elizabeth said, "Yes, I guess I would like it."

Hearing that Shane put his arms around her and kissed her softly on her lips. She increased the pressure of the kiss and told him I have been thinking about that all night.

Than both of them stepped back and smiled. Shane said, "That was the best good morning kiss that I have ever had."

Elizabeth replied, "It is not the kind of thing that happens to me I have always been too busy for that kind of thing."

Shane said, "I think we need to have breakfast and think about what we are doing and not move too fast because we have to be friends for a long time."

Elizabeth agreed.

They were soon back in the real world as they entered the laboratory. Clive, Tom and Bob were waiting for them.

Clive spoke first, "The Home Office has found out that two of the veterinarians on our list and their families are missing."

Shane asked, "What does that mean?"

Clive responded, "No one know for sure what that means, but the Home Office have people working on what has happened to them right now and they will contact us when they have more information."

Bob said, "It's hard to believe, but the FBI has found that one of the veterinarians on Dr. Price's list is also missing along with his family. Right now that's all they know."

Tom said, "We have some news from the CIA Operative in the Far East. He managed to have a conversation with the money carrier and learned that he had returned from Argentina. Somewhere near the border of Brazil. We have agents checking on everything in this general area, but it's a big area and it's going to take time. Our office in the Netherlands also found out that one of the people on Dr. Browning's list is missing and they are checking on his family."

Clive said, "Well it sounds like we have four veterinarians and their families kidnapped. I think I need to call the Home Office and let them know about these other missing scientists."

Shane agreed and Clive called the Home Office and advised them of the missing scientists and their families. They asked Clive to go to Iowa State University as soon as he could to work with Dr. Price and requested that his daughter Elizabeth work with the American's on identifying the missing UK scientists, since she knew them and could recognize them if she saw them.

Shane said, "I think we need to make arrangements to go back to America while other people are trying to get more information about the missing scientists and the location where the research maybe going on."

They all agreed.

Shane than asked, "If Elizabeth and Dr. Browning were OK with Elizabeth going with them?"

Dr. Browning spoke first, "I think that is up to Elizabeth."

Elizabeth replied, "I am willing to do whatever I can to help."

Shane said, "I guess that settle that. We need to get everyone packed up and get back to our plane in Manchester."

Tom said, "I will call Captain Martinez and have him get the plane ready and contact our driver Harold and have him arrange for another car and driver to take us back to the plane."

Clive said, "Elizabeth if you drive the Range Rover home. I will come home in my car and after we are packed we can drive my car back here to the laboratory and leave it here while we are gone."

In less than three hours later they were all in the Gulfstream and on their way to America.

CHAPTER THREE

Captain Martinez landed the Gulfstream at Andrews Air Force Base just outside Washington, DC in the late afternoon. They dropped Tom Parker and Bob Barker off and had the plane refueled for their trip onto Ames.

Tom and Bob were to get some rest at home and check in with their agencies in the morning to see what if any progress had been made concerning the missing scientists and their families. When they had additional information they would contact Shane and decide what they needed to do next.

After having time to refuel the plane and let everyone stretch their legs, make stops in the bathroom and say goodbye to Tom and Bob the Gulfstream was again airborne making its way to Ames.

Two hours latter Captain Martinez announced over the intercom that they were in final approach into the Ames Airport. They soon were taxing up to the fixed base operator's hanger. Captain Martinez advised Shane that he and Lieutenant Wheatley would be staying in Ames at the Holiday Inn.

Shane took time to call Dr. Price during their stop over at Andrews to let him know that Dr. Browning and his daughter, Elizabeth would be arriving in Ames with him around eight p.m. Shane requested Logan to make arrangements to have a couple of cars to pick them up when they arrived.

Just as Shane stepped off of the plane he could see Dr. Price being wheeled out on the tarmac in his wheelchair to meet them. Dr. Price shouted out to Shane, "Hello and welcome home!"

Shane ran over to Dr. Price and shook his hand and gave him a hug. About the same time Dr. Browning arrived at Dr. Price's wheelchair and said, "Well aren't you the lazy one having somebody pushing you around in a wheelchair."

Dr. Price replied, "Well if I was your weight no one around here could push me around we don't have anybody that strong."

Than the two men shook hands and told each other how wonderful it was to be together again.

Dr. Price than asked, "OK where is that daughter of yours you have been hiding for so long?"

Dr. Browning said, "She is just getting off the plane now."

Dr. Price replied, "That beautiful young woman is your daughter, obviously she got all of her looks from her mother. Clive if I was you I would be watching Shane around her he will be stealing her away from you."

Dr. Browning turned to Elizabeth and said, "Love, I want you to say hello to Dr. Logan Price one on my best friends. Logan this is my daughter Dr. Elizabeth Victoria Browning."

Dr. Price said, "I want to welcome you to the United States and to Ames, Iowa and to tell you how much of a pleasure it is to meet you Elizabeth."

Elizabeth leaned down to Dr. Price and gave him a hug and a kiss on his cheek and replied, "That was a very nice welcome. I have so been looking forward to meeting you. My father thinks so much of you. I feel like I already know you because I have heard so much about you."

Dr. Price said, "Now don't you believe everything that you've heard about me I am only half as bad as you father lets on."

Elizabeth laughed and Dr. Price said, "Let's get to the cars Molly is waiting for us with some food and drink. She might even let you take a shower before dinner if you like."

Elizabeth said, "That sounds like a wonderful idea."

Dr. Price asked his drivers to load the luggage into the cars and to drop Captain Martinez and Lieutenant Wheatley at the Holiday Inn and to take Shane home.

Dr. Price asked if the two pilots would like to come over to the house for dinner but they said no they thought that they would like time to get cleaned-up and go to bed.

Shane and the two pilots went in one car and the rest of the group went in Dr. Price's car. As soon as the pilots were dropped at the Holiday Inn the driver dropped Shane off at his home.

Shane opened the door to his house and thought that it seemed like it had been months since he had been there not just four or five days. Shane hit the shower, put on clean clothes and was soon on his way over to Dr. Price's house.

By the time he arrived everyone was gathered in the family room with a drink in their hand.

Molly said, "Shane, welcome home and by the way I am mad at you for not saying goodbye to me when you left the other day."

Than Molly said, "But since it you, I will forgive you if I get a kiss and a hug."

Shane complied by giving her a big hug and a kiss and all was forgiving.

Shane turned to say hello to the rest of the group and get a drink for himself when Molly said, "Shane bring your drink and Elizabeth to the dinning room because dinner is ready and a little past ready."

Shane took his drink in his left hand and Elizabeth in his right hand and started into the dinning room right behind Dr. Price's wheelchair that Dr. Browning was pushing.

Shane waited to seat Elizabeth until Molly had directed everyone to their place at the dinner table. Than Shane pulled out a chair for Elizabeth and helped her position it back under the table.

Molly said, "Logan, Clive do you see how wonderful Elizabeth and Shane look together."

The two men had to agree that they did look very good together.

With that Dr. Price proposed a toast, "Here's to Elizabeth and Shane two young people that the world will be depending on in the future. Well, I need to correct that toast, here to Elizabeth and Shane the world is depending on them right now and they will be successful in stopping this terrible plot to destroy America."

Dr. Browning said, "HERE HERE!"

Shane said, "Well Elizabeth, we don't have a choice now we have to stop the terrorist plot."

Dr. Price said, "I'll drink to that and let's have some of those good Iowa Steaks."

Shane said, "It's hard to think that we might not be able to have a good steak dinner because of some terrorist."

Logan said, "Well it's up to us to see that that never happens."

Clive replied, "Amen."

With that Molly said, "Let's eat before I start thinking about all that's going on around here and lose my appetite."

The meal was very quite with all of the folks gathered around the table thinking about what if the terrorist could succeed. The whole concept was unthinkable.

As soon as dinner was over Shane said, "That he felt like he needed to go home and get some rest because the way things had been going for the last few days who could tell what tomorrow might bring."

Soon after Shane had left to go home. Molly and Elizabeth were clearing the dishes from the table Molly asked Elizabeth what she thought of Shane.

Elizabeth said, "You know I only met him two days ago but I like him a lot."

Molly said, "You know that I am his Godmother so I am prejudice but Shane is really someone special. He was first in his class when he graduation from Iowa State and from his high school in Oklahoma. Did you know that his father is a veterinary too and that his dad has a very big cattle ranch in Oklahoma?"

Elizabeth didn't know that or almost anything else about Shane or his family.

Molly began telling Elizabeth more about Shane's family. Elizabeth I am going to tell you things that coming from England you would not know anything about. Shane's great-great-grandfather was one of the people in the opening of the Cherokee Strip back in 1893. People lined up near the Kansas-Oklahoma border and raced to claim land in Oklahoma. The land he claimed that day is still the home place of the Smith Ranch today.

During the dust bowl days of the 1930's thousand of people had to leave their farms and ranches because they couldn't earn enough money to feed their families and pay the taxes on their land. Shane's grandfather bought as much land as he could, paying as little as a dollar or even twenty- five cents an acre. He was the only person in the whole area that would or could buy land at that time. At the end of the dust bowl days he owned thirty-two section of land in Oklahoma, Kansas, Texas and New Mexico 20,480 acres.

Shane's father came to Iowa State to be a veterinary like his father had. Shane's father John Paul was my husband Logan's roommate. John Paul sent Shane to Iowa State to follow in his and his grandfather's footsteps. So far Shane has stayed here at the University to work on research with Clive. We know someday Shane will have to go back to Oklahoma to take over the family business since he is the only heir. Some of the farms Shane's grandfather bought turned out to be located in the Hugoton gas fields one of the largest natural gas fields every found.

Elizabeth, Shane is a very rich young man. I am sure that he has been very slow in finding someone to share his life with because I know that he wants to be sure that his wealth is not the reason that someone falls for him. Did you know that his mother was killed in a car wreck when he was ten? Elizabeth didn't know that either.

Molly continued to tell Elizabeth that she got to know Shane very well after he came to live with them when he started to the University. I am telling you all of this because I saw how he looked at you tonight and I can tell you he is really interested in you. I wouldn't want to see you break his heart. I am sorry if I sound like a mother, but I am very protected of him.

Elizabeth smiled and said, "I like Shane a lot even after knowing him for only a couple of days and maybe I could even fall in love with him. I promise that I won't break his heart and I hope he won't break mine."

Molly replied, "Thanks for your honesty. I think you would be good for Shane."

Than Molly said, "Elizabeth, you must be getting very tried after your long day why don't you take yourself up to bed and get some rest."

Elizabeth replied, "I think you are right I am getting awfully tried." Than Elizabeth said good night to Logan and her father and went upstairs to bed.

Logan and Clive visited a few minutes longer and Clive said that he needed to get to bed himself.

Molly and Logan sat and talked for awhile and Molly told Logan about her conversation with Elizabeth about Shane. Logan told Molly that he thought that Elizabeth came from good stock and if she and Shane did get together it would be good for both of them. They finished their ritual nighttime coffee and conversation. Logan said he thought that they needed to go to bed too since with the time change Clive and Elizabeth would be getting up early in the morning.

As tried as Elizabeth was she was having a hard time getting to sleep thinking about what Molly had told her about Shane. The part that surprised Elizabeth the most was how Molly had caught on to how Shane had been looking at her. Molly must be very perceptive. The more she thought about Shane the longer she stayed awake. Finally the body took over from the brain and she was sleeping.

Shane had gone home to get sleep and try to get some rest since these last few days had been taking a toll on him. Just as his head hit his pillow his mind went straight to Elizabeth as it had been doing every night since he meet her. Shane didn't know how she felt about him but he knew that the more he saw of her the more that he cared about her. He had never felt like this about any woman that he had ever knowing. Could he be in love with Elizabeth in such a short period of time? He tried to reason this in his mind but instead he fell asleep.

Early the next morning Shane was awaken by his telephone ringing it took him a few minutes to remember where he was and where the telephone was. Finally he rolled over to the right side of his bed and found the loudly ringing monster that woke him up.

Shane answered, "This is Shane Smith."

Shane heard a response, "Shane this is Tom Parker. I just got some news that our agents in the Netherlands found out from a neighbor of Dr. Arden Borland that he and his wife went on a trip to Rio de Janeiro. Some kind of a seminary. Dr. Borland was to be one of the speaker at the seminary. The neighbor said that Mrs. Borland was really excited about the trip because the sponsors of the seminary sent first class air tickets for her as well and was paying for the hotel.

Plus all of the food and ground transportation. She also said that Dr. Borland would be getting a speaking fee of $5,000 US Dollars."

Shane said, "Well I guess we know why Dr. Borland could not be found at home. Sounds like he got a pretty good offer to speak."

Tom replied, "It does sound all right except that the neighbor said that Dr. Borland and his wife were to have returned home two weeks ago and no one has heard from them since they left."

Shane said, "I guess that puts a different spin on things, but I guess they could be just taking an extra couple of weeks vacation."

Tom said, "You would think that's possible, but we need to wait to see what our friends in the United Kingdom have to say about their missing scientists. Shane, can you find out if there was some kind of international veterinary seminary scheduled to be held in Rio?"

Shane said, "I will try to check that out this morning. Tom what time is it in Washington?"

Tom replied, "It's a little after seven in the morning."

Shane said, "Now I know why I think its still early, it's only a little after six here in Ames."

Tom laughed and said, "Doc do you want to just sleep your life away. I thought you farmer types got up early."

Shane replied, "Not if we can help it."

Tom said, "OK Doc, I'll let you get some rest. Let me know if you find out anything on the Rio seminary."

Shane put the telephone down and decided that he might as well get up and get going. After getting ready for the day he called Molly to see if Dr. Price was up and about yet.

Molly told Shane that Logan and Clive had finished a whole pot of coffee and part of another one and just left to go to the University.

Molly suggested that he come by the house and have some breakfast and take Elizabeth with him if he was going to the University. Shane said that he would be on his way in a few minutes. He forgot to ask if Elizabeth was up but he was sure she must be by now.

Shane put the top down on the Thunderbird and backed out of the garage and drove to Molly's home. True to her word she had breakfast ready for him on his arrival. Molly had fixed two eggs; toast; orange juice; bacon and black coffee for him. Shane's favorite breakfast. Molly said that after putting his breakfast on the table in the breakfast room she would be working in the kitchen.

Just as Shane sit down to eat his breakfast Elizabeth came into the breakfast room. Shane got out of his chair and said to Elizabeth, "Good morning Dr. Elizabeth, how did you sleep? Better than I did I hope?"

Elizabeth replied, "Since I don't know how you slept I guess I can't say for sure, but I know when I finally fell asleep I did very well. Thank you!"

Shane said, "Are we a little testy this morning?"

Than Shane said, "You are the cause of me having trouble getting to sleep."

Elizabeth curtly replied, "I caused you not to be able to get to sleep?"

Shane said, "Yes, I was too busy thinking about you."

Elizabeth said, "That's funny I was having the same kind of problem. I was thinking about you."

Hearing that Shane put his arms around her and kissed her once than again. Than he said, "I think I am falling in love with you and the reason I don't know for sure is that I have never been in love before."

Elizabeth looked into his dark brown eyes and said, "I think I have the same problem that's why I couldn't get to sleep. I never let myself get into a position of falling in love with anyone. I always had too much work to do and too many things to accomplish."

Shane said, "I think we have a problem and right now we have this important task to accomplish but all I want to do is to be with you."

Elizabeth replied, "I know we have to help solve this problem, but all I really want to do is just go somewhere that we can be alone." Then Elizabeth turned her head up to kiss Shane again.

Just as their lips parted Molly came into the breakfast room and said, "Oh, excuse me."

Shane said, "It's all right Molly, Elizabeth and I were just saying good morning.

Molly said, "Oh, I see."

Elizabeth said, "I guess you did." As she smiled at Molly. Molly gave a knowing smile back to Elizabeth.

Shane said, "I guess we better have breakfast before it gets cold." Than Molly asked Elizabeth what she would like for breakfast. Elizabeth told her that some toast would do her very well, thanks.

Molly went back into the kitchen as Elizabeth and Shane sit down at the breakfast table. Soon Molly was back with Elizabeth's toast and asking if she was sure that she didn't want anything else to eat. Elizabeth assured her that the toast was quite enough.

After Shane and Elizabeth finished breakfast Shane told Molly that Elizabeth and he were going to the University. As they walked to the car Shane reached out his hand to hold Elizabeth's hand. Molly watched from the kitchen window as the two of them walked hand in hand. She thought to herself she was watching two people in love.

Shane opened the door of the Thunderbird for Elizabeth and as she was sitting down on the seat her skirt slid up to her thighs. Shane thought how beautiful her legs were. Elizabeth quickly pulled her skirt down and straighten it up. Shane fasten her seat belt as he told her I don't want you getting away from me. Elizabeth said that was the last thing on her mind.

Shane got in the car, fasten his seat belt and started the engine of the Thunderbird and pulled away from the curb. Elizabeth asked Shane what kind of a car is this? Shane explained that it was a Ford Thunderbird designed to be like the ones Ford made back in the nineteen fifties. Shane told Elizabeth that he really loved this car and had even given it a name. Elizabeth asked what name you gave it. Shane told her "Blackbird."

Elizabeth thought that made sense, the car was black and a bird. So "Blackbird" fit nicely. She told Shane she liked the Blackbird.

Shane told Elizabeth that he would take her by his house sometime while she was in Ames if she would like to see it. She assured him that she wanted to see it.

In a few minutes they arrived on the campus of Iowa State University. Elizabeth thought that the campus was very pretty. Shane agreed but said that most universities were very nice looking. Elizabeth said that yes that's true, but they didn't have Dr. Shane Smith that's what made Iowa State special. About the time Elizabeth said that they arrived at Dr. Price's office.

Shane and Elizabeth went inside the building and went straight into Dr. Price's office. There they found Logan and Clive deep in discussions on how they could develop a super strain of mad cow disease. Clive was at a chalkboard listing possible approaches that they could use to experiment with. Just about the time Shane was going to say something his worldwide cell phone ran.

Logan and Clive looked back at Shane and Elizabeth and said good morning as Shane took his phone out of its holster and answered, "This is Shane Smith."

Shane, "This is B.G. Murphy."

Shane said, "Who is this calling?"

The reply, "Billy Gene Murphy with the CIA in the UK."

Shane said, "Oh, Billy Gene, how are you?'

B.G. replied, "I am all right, but I just came from a meeting with the Home Office here in London and got a report on the two missing scientists and their families. It appears that they went to a seminary in Rio de Janeiro where they were to be speakers. The sponsors of the seminary were paying for the trips for them and their families. The only thing funny with that is they are both over two weeks late returning from their trip. The Home Office is continuing to investigate. Do you have anything new?"

Shane said, "I got a call this morning from Agent Tom Parker and he told me that the CIA in the Netherlands had the same story about Dr. Borland and his wife."

B.G. said, "It looks like the plot thickens. I would say that our missing scientists have been kidnapped during their trip or at the end of the seminary. What is your thought Shane?"

Shane said, "You have a lot more experience in these kind of things than I do but I think that you must be right. Have you communicated this to CIA Headquarters yet?"

B.G. said, "No, I was told to report directly to you about any thing that I found, but I will pass on the information to Headquarters right now. However, the Home Office may have been in communications with CIA Headquarters regarding their findings already."

Shane thanked B.G. for the information and than told the others what he had learned about the disappears of Dr. Anthony Hinson and Dr. David Allen and their families from the United Kingdom.

Logan said, "I tried to call Dr. Charles Van Meter with the University of Illinois to see if he would work with us on our project and was told that he was out of the country attending a seminar."

Shane said, "I will bet you that Dr. Van Meter was invited to this same seminary.

Saying that Shane put in a call to Bob Barker at the Headquarters of the FBI to see if he could find out anything about Dr. Van Meter. When Shane got Bob on the phone Bob told Shane that he had been trying to reach him to tell him that the FBI had found that a Dr. Van Meter from the University of Illinois had gone to a seminary in Rio and was two weeks late in returning home with his family.

Shane asked if he could use Dr. Price's computer to see if there was anything on the Internet regarding this conference that was scheduled to be held in Rio last month. Dr. Price handed his computer to Shane and Shane log on to the Internet and found nothing.

Next Shane asked Dr. Price's secretary to bring him the file on conferences or any brochures on seminars that they had received lately. A few minutes went by before Betty Johnson; Dr. Price's long time secretary brought Shane the file.

Shane begin the process of looking through a file folder almost two inches thick of announcements about conferences.

Shane said, "It looks like we could attend a conference every week some where in the world."

About that time Shane found a very professional brochure regarding a veterinary conference in Rio de Janeiro that was scheduled for last month. Bingo!

The sponsor of the conference was a drug company named Adeaq-La. Shane had never heard of such a company neither had anyone else in the room. Shane again went back to the Internet and used the search engine Google to check on the Drug Company Adeaq-La. No results.

Shane checked the brochure again and than tried the Internet address shown on the brochure. No results. He read over the brochure in great detail to see if he was missing something. The brochure had an address in Ciudad del Este, Paraguay and a telephone number. Shane took his worldwide telephone out and punched in the numbers. After several rings an operator in Spanish advised him that number had been disconnected.

Shane than put a call in to Tom Parker. After three rings the phone was answered, "Tom Parker here."

Shane said, "Tom, this is Shane Smith."

Tom replied, "Shane we were just speaking of you here at CIA Headquarters. What's up?" Shane said,

"I have some information on the seminary in Rio, but I need the CIA to follow up on some of the information. Dr. Price had a brochure on the seminary here in his office. Here is what I know about the seminary from the brochure. A company called Adeaq-La from Ciudad del Este, Paraguay sponsored it. I tried to check them out on the Internet but couldn't get a hit on them. Than I tried to call them on the phone using the number listed on the brochure and was told in Spanish that the number had been disconnected. My Spanish isn't to good so maybe I didn't get it right. I will fax you a copy of the brochure and ask if the CIA could see what they can find out about the company and the seminar."

Tom said, "Well it's a starting place anyway. I'll request our people in Brazil and Paraguay to see what they can find out down there. I think Bob and I had better come to Ames tomorrow unless you think we need to come tonight."

Shane said, "No, I don't think you need to come here tonight but I think you should come to Ames tomorrow. It looks like we are going to go to South America soon. What do you think Tom?"

Tom replied, "I think everything points in that direction and we need to go to Rio. Since that's was the destination of our four missing scientists and their families. It also the site of the where the seminar was suppose to be held."

Shane said, "That makes sense to me. Tom, how long do you think that it will take for the CIA to get answers for us on the Drug Company and the seminar?"

Tom replied, "I would think that it would take a couple of days maybe more."

Shane said, "I guess we should stay in Ames until we get some answers back from South America."

Tom said, "OK, Bob and I will be in Ames tomorrow afternoon or early evening if that's all right."

Shane said, "Sounds good to me. See you tomorrow."

After Shane hung up the phone he filled the others in on the conversation with Tom Parker. Everyone agreed that it sounded like Shane and Elizabeth would be leaving for South America soon.

Shane sent a copy of the brochure to Tom Parker.

Than Dr. Price asked Shane if he knew of anything else that he needed to do at the University or if he had any other pressing things on the investigation to do right now. Shane told him that he couldn't think of anything. Dr. Price suggested that Shane take Elizabeth around Ames and show her some of the local sights. Dr. Price said that Dr. Browning and him wanted to get back to work organizing the research on developing SSBSE. Shane said that Elizabeth and he would be going.

Shane and Elizabeth left the laboratory offices and drove to Shane's house. Shane said that his house had not been straightened up since he returned home last night. He said that it was kind of a mess. Elizabeth told he that would be all right she wouldn't check on his housekeeping just look at his house.

Shane pushed the button on the garage door opener and waited until the door was up and drove the Blackbird into the garage. Shane had a three-car garage with two of the garage spaces empty. Shane told Elizabeth that normally he had his guest come into the house via the double front doors but since she was special she would get to come in through the garage into the kitchen.

Shane showed Elizabeth through the rambling ranch style house: he had four bedrooms; four and half bathrooms; a large country kitchen with a fireplace; a theater room with a large plasma screen TV; a family room with a wet bar and another fireplace; a formal living room; and dinning room that could seat up to sixteen people with the whole house furnished with traditional English style furniture.

Shane saved his master bedroom and bath to show to her last. It was located away from the other three bedrooms and baths. They entered the bedroom through double doors and Elizabeth was intrigued by the size of the bedroom and Shane's king size bed. She asked him if he thought his house was big enough for him and if he had enough room in his bed.

She was really shocked by the size of the two walk in closets. One was filled with Shane's clothes and the largest of the two closets was totally empty. She asked him about the empty closest.

Shane said, "It's reserved for my future wife."

She didn't press that response.

When she went into the master bath she told Shane she felt like she must be in heaven. It was like the rest of the house, huge. It had all Italian Marble floors and cabinet tops, double sinks, an oversize walk in shower along with a corner sunken whirlpool bathtub large enough for at least two people. Shane's bathroom even had a bidet along with the toilet stool. Everything in the bathroom was trimmed in gold and all of the fixtures were gold.

Elizabeth said, "I might just stay in your bathroom the rest of her life."

Shane told her well she might get hungry sometime. Elizabeth told Shane I can't believe the size of your house the only thing she thought of was that Shane must be planning for a very big family or a lot of company.

Shane told her that when he got married he wanted to have al least two or three kids because he felt that he missed out being an only child. Elizabeth knew about that all too well.

Elizabeth told him if you had this house in London it would be worth at least four million pounds.

Shane said just lay down on the bed I want to show you something although she would normally be concerned with such an offer she laid down on the left side of the bed. Shane laid down on the right side of the bed and opened a control panel on his bedside table. He push a button and a door located in the walnut paneling across the room located directly across from the bed opened exposing another large plasma TV and a sound system. Shane explained that from his bed he could control almost all of the lights in the house and all of the door locks in the house. He also had close circuit TV security system throughout the area around the house and all of the doors coming into the house.

Shane told Elizabeth that he worked with a local architect to develop the plans for his house and to supervise having the house built. Elizabeth told him that she loved his house.

Shane told her that he was really glad that she liked the house. Than he rolled over and kissed her and just as quickly rolled back to the right side of the bed and got off of the bed. Shane told Elizabeth that they should go see more of the town and the countryside around Ames.

Elizabeth moved over to the edge of the bed and said, "OK we better go before I decide that I would rather stay in this bed all day."

Shane reached for Elizabeth's hands to help her to her feet. She put her hands in his and he pulled her up off of the bed. When she was standing on her feet, Shane leaned down to kiss her and hold her in his arms. Shane looked into her eyes as he was holding her and said, "Elizabeth, I love you."

Hearing this Elizabeth replied, "I know it doesn't make much sense for no longer than we have knowing each other, but some how it like some kind of magic. I love you too."

Kissing and hugging they fell onto the bed and spent the rest of the afternoon making love like two people that could not get enough of each other.

CHAPTER FOUR

Shane called Molly to tell her that Elizabeth and he had decided to drive to Des Moines for dinner and for him to show Elizabeth a little bit of our Capital city.

Shane asked, "Molly if she thought that Dr. Price and Dr. Browning would feel bad about them not being there for dinner?"

Molly said, "I don't think so, they will be too busy catching up on the past."

Shane and Elizabeth drove to Des Moines and had a wonderful dinner and then took a drive along the Des Moines River enroute back to Ames.

When they returned to Ames, Elizabeth said, "I want to stay with you tonight."

Shane asked, "What will your father think about that, will he be upset with you if you stay with me?"

Elizabeth told him that she thought that her father would understand if she had a few minutes to talk with him by herself.

Shane said, "OK, let's drive over to Dr. Price's house and get your things and you can talk to your father."

When they arrived at Logan and Molly's home Shane unlocked the door with his key that he still had from living with the Price's. They found Logan and Clive drinking coffee in the family room and catching up on the events of the past two years.

They greeted Elizabeth and Shane warmly and asked them if they would join them for coffee.

Elizabeth said, "No thank you but, I do need a few minutes to speak with my father."

Clive said, "Certainly I always have time for my daughter."

Clive asked, "If they could please be excused and if it would be all right to use the living room for their conversation."

Clive and Elizabeth left the family room and proceeded to the nearby living room.

Elizabeth said, "Father, I have decided to stay with Shane at his house if it is all right with you. Maybe you have already concluded that we have falling in love."

Clive said, "Love, anyone that had ever been blessed with being in love could tell that by being present with the two of you for five minutes. Why did you think Dr. Price suggested that Shane take you around to see the sights. As bad as Logan is these days he could see that you two were in love."

Elizabeth put her arms around her father's neck and told him that she loved him too.

Clive said, "Yes I know, but it's not the same. You go with Shane, I don't know anyone that is a better person than him. You get every minute that you can with him. Don't get cheated out of being happy the way your mother and I did by wasting our lives and our love. No, you go and be happy!"

Elizabeth said, "I will father. I promise that I won't let us waste our love by being apart. Oh father, I do love you so."

Clive said, "I think we had better go back in the other room and tell Molly that you are moving out of her guest room to stay with Shane."

They went back into the family room and joined Logan and Shane.

Clive asked, "Where's Molly?"

Logan told him that she had just gone into the bathroom and should be back in just a few minutes. Almost before Logan had finished telling Clive where Molly was, she came back into the room.

Clive said, “Molly my love, Elizabeth has decided that she would prefer to move out of your guest room and stay with Shane. So, what do you think about that?”

Molly smiled and said, “I guess I have to say that the way Shane and Elizabeth look at each other. I am not very surprised. Also, if you saw Shane’s house you would rather stay there instead of my guest room.”

Clive said, “I don’t think it’s the house that’s the” attraction.”

Clive, Molly and Logan all laughed out loud and Shane and Elizabeth blushed.

It didn’t take long for Elizabeth to repack her clothes and for Shane to load her things in the T-Bird.

Shane said, “No more room than I have in this trunk it a good thing you travel light.”

Elizabeth said, “You mean the boot.”

Shane replied, “Yeah, I forgot that I am hanging around with an English girl, I certainly meant to say boot, not trunk. But it’s OK because this car has a big bonnet.”

Elizabeth said, “Yes love, as you say you are hanging around with a proper English girl now, and don’t you forget it.”

Shane replied, “Don’t worry I won’t. You are the most proper English girl that I have ever met and I love you.”

A few minutes latter they arrived at Shane’s home. They parked the T-Bird in the garage, unloaded Elizabeth’s things and took them to the master bedroom. Shane told Elizabeth that she could put her things in the empty closest.

She said, “I thought that was reserved for your wife.”

Shane said, “Well who do you think you are?”

Elizabeth said, “I hope you mean that.”

Shane told her, “I don’t say things I don’t mean.”

Shane helped her unpack her clothes and hang them up on hangers and told her that the built in drawers in the closest were for her undies and sweaters.

Elizabeth said, “You mean for my bras and knickers.”

Shane told her no, your bras and panties. Elizabeth told him you know we may have a problem with the language, between real English and American.

They finished putting Elizabeth's clothes away and she selected a nightgown from her newly filled closest drawers. She went into the bathroom and begin taking off her clothes as she continued talking to Shane. She was telling him again how much she liked his house and what a wonderful day she had.

But she was interrupted by Shane who said, "Elizabeth I want you to tell me all about yourself. I mean everything. I want to know what you like, what you don't like and if you have ever been sick. What's your favorite color, do you like to wear dresses, skirts or pants."

Elizabeth finished putting on her gown and came back into the bedroom and sit down on the bed beside Shane and begin speaking.

"I like working, a trait I got from my father I guess. I like fast cars, travel. Boats and ships. The British in me. I like sunrises and sunsets. I like horseback riding with English saddles. But today I found out that I like making love with you better than anything else." Elizabeth replied.

"I don't like bad films, including science fiction or scary ones. I can't stand to see people going hunger or sick or being mistreated."

"I had all of the childhood diseases and you said you wanted to know everything about me. Well from the time that my periods started when I was a young girl. Every month I had lots of pain with my periods. My cramps were so bad that I was almost doubled over and in bed for the first day of my period every month. About four years ago I had some minor surgery and that helped with the problem. Now my Gynecologist has me on the new birth control pills that I only have periods once every three months. Overall, I have been very healthy and still am. I have been keeping up with my breast examines since my mother had cancer and I am OK. Also I never tried one cigarette or drugs. My mother smoked all of her life."

Shane said, "Neither have I."

Elizabeth continued, "My favorite color is blue, but your dark brown eyes may make me change my favorite color."

Shane laughed.

"I like wearing skirts and dresses because my mother always dressed me in them and she said that ladies shouldn't dress like men. I do have some pant outfits that I like to wear very much."

"My mother was the most important person in my life while I was growing up. She and all of her friends were academicians so my childhood was spent in universities, libraries and museums. My friends were all people my mother's age so I was expected to be an adult from the time I was seven. I was always the top student in my classes all through school and at the university. In America you have a slang word that fit me perfectly, a geek. I liked boys but didn't date I didn't have time for such things. My mother always told me, Elizabeth you will have time for such trivial things in the future. Than when she was dying and father came into our lives she told me that she was wrong, that I needed to make time to live while you can. Because you didn't know how much time you have to live."

"Now you know all of my deepest dark secrets and why I just threw myself at you after knowing you for just a few days."

Shane said, "Well I don't think you exactly threw yourself at me I believe that I had something to do with us being together here tonight."

Elizabeth said, "Yes you did with one little kiss in England. I never would have believed that I was so easy that one kiss would have me chasing after some man all the way to America."

Shane than took Elizabeth into his arms and said, "I think we have had enough talking for tonight. I think we need to go to bed and get some sleep as he pulled her gown up to her shoulders."

Sleep would come a little bit latter.

Shane heard his telephone ringing and he begin to try to wake up and when his eyes opened he saw the most beautify young woman in his bed. His mind than woke up and realized he was in his bed and the beautify woman was Elizabeth. Shane reach for his telephone and answered it by saying, "Shane Smith."

"Good morning Shane, this is Tom Parker."

Shane said, "Okay, it my morning wake up call is it."

Tom said, "Shane, are you still in bed again this morning? I guess I am going to become your morning alarm clock. Are you awake enough to talk?"

Shane replied, "Well I am now."

Tom said, "Good, I got some news. I gave the copy of the brochure that you faxed me yesterday to our analysts and this morning they said if you look at the name of the Drug Company, Adeaq-la and if you use the letters in the name in reverse they spell al-Qaeda."

Shane said, "Isn't that interesting and why didn't we see that?"

Tom said, "That's what we have analysts. To think about things like that. The other news is from Paraguay our agents there found out that some people rented offices at the address given on the brochure for the Adeaq-La Drug Company for six months. The same deal for the telephone service. In both cases they paid in cash and the receipts made out to the Company. Our agents interviewed other tenants in the building and no one knew anything about the people that worked in the office. The other tenants told our agents that these people kept to themselves and didn't even speak to them. They did think that the people might have been from the middle east or maybe from Brazil."

Tom continued, "I don't think we learned much from Paraguay. Except it confirms our thinking that this was just a front for the terrorist."

Shane asked, "Are you and Bob coming to Ames today?"

Tom said, "We will be leaving this afternoon and should see you tonight or in the morning."

Shane said, "OK, thanks for the up date. We will see you soon."

Elizabeth asked Shane, "Who was that on the phone?"

Shane told her it was Tom Parker with the CIA and than Shane told her of their conversation about al-Qaeda and Paraguay.

Elizabeth said, "I guess we better get out of bed and go over to the University as soon as we can."

Shane responded, "Yes dear!"

Then they reluctantly got up from the bed and got in the shower together. The water was wet and warm and soon they wanted to forget about those awful terrorist and just stay home making love. But this time their desires were put on hold to try to do something to help stop the terrorist plot.

On the way to the University Shane told Elizabeth that they were going to make a stop at the National Veterinary Services Laboratories located in Ames and speak with Dr. Janice Dawson. Janice was one of his classmates when he went to veterinary school at Iowa State University.

Shane parked the car in front of one of the large buildings at the National Veterinary Services Laboratories. He told Elizabeth to come in with him to speak to Janice. When they entered the reception area of the building the receptionist asked them if she could help them. Shane told her that they wanted to speak to Dr. Janice Dawson. The receptionist asked what their names were. Shane told her Dr. Shane Smith and Dr. Elizabeth Browning. Soon Dr. Dawson appeared coming from one of the labs.

Dr. Dawson saw Shane and said, "Hello classmate."

Shane replied, "How is Dr. Dawson?"

She replied, "Busy that how we are here at NVSL. Always busy."

Shane said, "I am sure you are."

As he held out his hand to greet Janice, Janice reached out to Shane and instead of shaking hands put her arms around him and gave him a kiss.

Shane said, "I want to introduce you to Dr. Elizabeth Browning from England, Elizabeth this is one of my classmate from university, Dr. Janice Dawson."

The women shook hands with each other and Janice turned to Shane and said. "I thought for a moment that you were going to tell me this was you wife or something not a colleague."

Shane said, "Well I might tell you that someday, but for now we are doing some work together for the British and America Governments and you might be able to help us out with it.

Janice said, "How can I help you. You know that I would do anything I can to help you. Elizabeth, I am sure that Shane hasn't told you but he almost single- handed got me through veterinary school. So I own him big time."

Elizabeth smiled and Shane said, "Janice we need you to give us anything you have on any new developments on cures or new test for mad cow disease that may not be public yet."

Janice said, "OK, let's go to my office and see what I can tell you that you don't already know."

The three of them went into Janice's office and she checked on her computer for anything new on mad cow disease.

Janice said, "Here are two big announcements that have not been confirmed or tested yet but they could be significant findings. First, a new test developed at the University of California at San Francisco. They claim that their test can be done on live cattle. If it works it would be the first successful test ever that could be used to test live cattle. The next thing is a potential vaccine developed by our colleagues at the University of Toronto to prevent mad cow disease. That would be wonderful news."

Shane said, "Those two developments could be wonderful if they work. I appreciate your help Janice. Elizabeth and I will see you latter we need to go because I have to get a report off to my supervisor today."

Janice said, "I didn't ask what you were working on, but I assumed that if you could tell me you would have already."

With that she told Elizabeth that it was good to meet her and than gave Elizabeth a hug and told her to take good care of our guy.

Elizabeth told her she would do her best to look after Shane.

When Shane and Elizabeth were back in the T-Bird driving to the University.

Elizabeth said, "I think Janice has a thing for you."

Shane said, "No, I don't think so. We are just good friends we were in almost all of the same classes while we were studying at Iowa State. We never dated or anything like that but we did spend several nights together cramming for test."

Elizabeth said, "As a woman I can tell you that's not all that she would have liked to have been doing, spending nights with you."

Shane laughed and said, "Well I guess I will never know now, will I."

Elizabeth said, "No, you certainly won't!"

Shane thought that it was perfect timing to arrive at Dr. Price's office to end this conversation. After arriving in Dr. Price's office Shane filled in Dr. Price and Dr. Browning in on his conversations with Tom Parker and Dr. Janice Dawson.

Than he said, "He needed to send his weekly written report to Secretary Ridge on the progress that they had made in the investigation."

Shane was surprised that no one said anything about him and Elizabeth spending the night together. In fact everyone acted as if it was the normal thing for them to do. Somehow Shane and Elizabeth thought it was.

Tom and Bob arrived in Ames around six pm and checked into the Holiday Inn and after they put their luggage in their rooms they called Shane. Tom told him that he received some news from CIA Headquarters during their trip from Washington. He felt they should meet right away. Shane told them that he would meet them in about fifteen minutes at the Country Kitchen Café that's was only a few blocks from the Holiday Inn.

When Shane and Elizabeth arrived at the Country Kitchen Tom and Bob had already been seated in a table near the rear of the restaurant. Tom saw Shane and Elizabeth when they arrived and motioned for them to come back to their table.

As soon as Shane and Elizabeth were seated Tom told them that he had some additional information from England. Tom told them that the Home Office had enlisted the help of MI-5 to look into the two missing scientists. MI-5 found a copy of the letter sent to Dr. David Allen at his home with details of the seminar in Rio. In addition they found a copy of the Allen's travel itinerary.

The itinerary indicated that they were scheduled to return on Varig Air Line to London over two weeks ago. MI-5 checked with Varig and was told that the Allen's never showed for the flight. Then MI-5 checked to see if Dr. Anthony Hinson and his family had reservations on the

same flight and were told by Varig that yes they did and they were also no shows.

Tom said, "It no doubt that at least these two scientists and their families disappeared before they tried to return to London. I think that they must have gone missing in Rio either during the seminar or at the end of the seminar. One thing that MI-5 didn't find on the itinerary was the name of the hotel that they planned to stay in while they were in Rio. My guess was that the sponsors were picking them up at the airport and taking them to their hotel and that all of the arrangements for the hotel rooms were being made by the sponsors."

Shane asked, "Tom have we heard anything from the CIA Agents in Brazil on where the seminar was suppose to being held yet or anything else about the seminar?"

"Not yet." Tom replied.

Shane said, "Than I think we should stay here in Ames until we get some additional information from Brazil."

Everyone agreed that this was the best approach. Shane told Tom and Bob that he and Elizabeth would be leaving to meet Dr. Price and Dr. Browning for dinner.

Tom said, "After Bob and I have dinner that they would be going back to the Holiday Inn and would contact Captain Martinez to let him know that the four of them would probably be leaving for Brazil tomorrow."

Shane and Elizabeth drove to Dr. Price's home and had dinner. Shane told Drs. Price and Browning about what they had learned from the investigation by MI-5 about the two English scientists. After dinner Shane and Elizabeth returned to Shane's house.

Shane said, "He needed to call his friend Jake Johnson to let him know that he would be leaving again tomorrow and ask him to look after the house."

After Shane finished his call to Jake. Shane and Elizabeth went to the master bedroom to get ready for bed.

Elizabeth said, "Shane, I have to tell you something that you need to know. Molly told me that you have been reluctant to fall in love with anyone because you were afraid that they might be more interested in your money than you."

Shane said, "I certainly am not concerned about that with you. I know you are just after my body!"

Elizabeth started laughing and said, "I didn't think you had figured that out already. But, that's not what I am trying to tell you."

Shane laughed and pulled her down on the bed and begin kissing her and Elizabeth said, "Shane, just wait a minute I want to tell you something important about me."

Shane let go of Elizabeth and they both sit up on the side of the bed and Shane told her OK, please go ahead with what you are trying to tell me.

Elizabeth said, "What I have been trying to tell you was that my mother was from very old English money. As her only heir I inherited her trust funds that pay me two hundred thousand pounds a year, that's about three hundred thousand dollars a year and my trust funds are growing by about another hundred thousand pounds a year. My mother's grandfathers were very rich, one of them was a member of Lloyds of London and the other one was a principal owner of the Hudson Bay Trading Company. I am sorry to tell you this. I guess I am what people call, a rich girl. Maybe that's why money never meant much to me. I know that people that don't have money say, if you got money, money doesn't mean much. I guess that's true with me."

Shane said, "Elizabeth, I will try not to hold that against you. Just come here so that I can make love with my rich girl. You didn't know it before that I was after you for your money did you?"

Elizabeth said, "No, I thought you just wanted to go to bed with a dark headed, brown eyed English girl. One that's in love with you."

That was the end of the conversations for the night. Conversation changed to removing of clothing and lovemaking. The last bit of verbal communications between Shane and Elizabeth that night was expressions of how much they loved each other.

Morning was announced the same way that it had been for the last several mornings. With Tom Parker's regular wake up call. Shane untangled himself from Elizabeth and answered the phone, "Good morning Tom."

Tom said, "Good morning Shane. I got the information from our agents in Brazil this morning on where our missing scientists were staying in Rio. The Sheraton Rio Hotel. Our agents also found out the seminar was to be held in the Rio Convention Center and a payment to reserve the Convention Center was paid but the seminar was canceled two days before it was to be held. How do you think the payment was made? Cash of course! Where do these people get so much damn money anyway? Well, boss it looks like we should get our gear together and get on our way to Rio de Janeiro."

Shane told Tom that he would make arrangements for him and Elizabeth to be at the Ames Airport in three hours and they would meet there.

Shane and Elizabeth had a good morning kiss and made themselves get out of bed and into the shower, dress and begin packing to go to Brazil. Elizabeth told Shane that she would much rather stay here in Shane's wonderful house and bed.

Shane said, "If you promise to be here with me, OK!"

Both of them knew that they had to do their duties for their countries so they finished packing and loaded their things in the T-Bird.

After leaving Shane's house they drove over to Dr. Price's home to tell Molly, Logan and Clive that they were leaving for Brazil. Before they left their loved ones tears begin appearing in everyone eyes. No one knew what kind of danger that Shane and Elizabeth might encounter on this trip. All that they could hope for was that they returned safely and that they could help find the missing scientists before they could develop a super strain of mad cow disease.

Arriving at the Ames Airport they found Tom and Bob talking with Captain Martinez about the flight plan to Rio de Janeiro. Lieutenant Wheatley had already stored luggage in the plane and was waiting for Shane and Elizabeth's gear before closing the luggage compartment of the Gulfstream.

As Lieutenant Wheatley loaded their luggage into the plane.

Tom said, "He needed to talk to Shane and Elizabeth about the approach the CIA and MI-5 thought they should take during their stay in Brazil."

The three of them went into a small conference room in the fixed base operator's flight center building.

Tom began by saying, "The CIA and MI-5 understands that you two are not regular agents. They want you to use a cover as the reason you are in Rio. I don't know if either of you have had any acting experience in the past. But their concept will require some acting on your part. OK, here is their idea! They want you two to pretend that you just got married and are on your honeymoon. I know that it's asking a lot but CIA and MI-5 folks think that you have a better chance of traveling around Brazil and getting information if you are seen as tourist. The big question will you both agree to do it?"

Shane looked at Elizabeth. Elizabeth looked at Shane neither said a word. They were about to give performances that would be worthy of Academy Awards.

Shane responded first, "Tom don't you think that it is asking a lot and I mean not just of me but of Elizabeth?"

Tom said, "Well I understand your feelings, but the Agencies think it will be safer for you if you aren't seen like CIA or MI-5 Agents."

Elizabeth said, "Tom, I don't want to just say no without knowing what they mean for us to be pretending to be newlyweds. What are they suggesting?"

Tom replied, "Well they have reserved the honeymoon suite at the Sheraton Rio for you and would make arrangements for wedding rings and things to give you on your arrival in Rio. You would need to stay in the suite together. I am sure there must be a couch or something that Shane could sleep on. They want you to take tours and do things that honeymoon couples would do. You know like having dinner in your room. Go dancing at the nightclub in the hotel. Well you know, act like you just got married and you're in love."

Shane said, "Tom, I don't think Elizabeth and I would be comfortable doing this. What do you think Elizabeth?"

Elizabeth replied, "I do think it's asking a lot, but if they think it's necessary for our safety and it helps find the missing scientists, than I guess we don't really have a choice do we."

Shane said, "No, I guess we don't."

Tom said, "Well I am sorry to put you two in this position, but it probably will allow you to get more information than the CIA and

MI-5 have been able to get about the missing scientists. Shane looked at Elizabeth again and it was all that they could do to keep from laughing out loud. What a performance they had given.

Tom got measurements of Elizabeth and Shane's ring fingers so that wedding rings could be ready for them when they arrived in Rio.

After they had finished their conversation they went out to the plane and got aboard and were off to Rio de Janeiro and whatever was waiting for them there. One thing that Shane and Elizabeth knew was waiting for them in Rio, each other. Shane thought to himself what a joke on the CIA and MI-5.

Tom told the others before they left for Rio about what had been planned for Shane and Elizabeth pretending to be on their honeymoon while they were in Brazil.

One thing Tom had not told Shane and Elizabeth until they were airborne was that their hotel reservations had been made in their real names. In the now way of doing things, they would not be registering as Dr. and Mrs. Shane Smith. They would be registering at the hotel as Dr. Shane Smith and Dr. Elizabeth Browning. Just in case the terrorist might be interested in acquiring two more world class research veterinarians.

"Thanks, Tom, I am sure you had just forgotten to mention that when you were talking to us earlier that you were sitting us up as targets for the al–Qaeda." Shane said.

Elizabeth said, "Is that true Tom?"

Tom said, "Well the CIA doesn't think so, but it could happen."

"Thanks." both Elizabeth and Shane said at the same time.

Tom said, "OK, I am glad we got that settled. This is how this is going to work when we arrive in Rio we will be met by local CIA Agents and they will give you your rings, commercial airline tickets and some other things that the CIA thinks newlyweds would bring with them. Our plane will be parked in a secluded hanger when we arrive. Than the two of you will be cleared by specially selected immigration and customs officers."

"After that you will be taken to the passenger terminal in a bus like you were the last ones off of the plane. You will be dropped off at the passenger terminal and than go through the normal immigration and custom routine like the rest of the incoming international passengers. You have your regular passports and nothing to declare at customs. Your bags will be coming on the regular baggage belt just as if you had come in on a flight from London."

"After you get your bags and clear customs take a taxi to the Sheraton Rio. I forgot to tell you that you will need to exchange several US Dollars for Brazilian Real for your trip. I would suggest that you exchange a couple of thousand dollars to take care of the cost of taxis, tips and sightseeing. The rates will be better at the airport than at the hotel and besides taxi drivers don't like to wait for their fare."

"When you arrive at the hotel I would suggest that you stay in your suite for the night and order room service. That's what anyone working at the hotel would expect a newlywed couple to do on the first night of their honeymoon. Order Champagne, act like you are celebrating your marriage. Be sure that you are wearing the bathrobes that the hotel will have in your room when you open the door for room service. We want you to look and act like honeymooners as best that you can."

"Bob and I will be staying at the Caesar Park Hotel Ipanema just a short distance from the Sheraton and tomorrow we will come to the Sheraton for a late lunch around two o'clock in the afternoon. We will start up a conversation with you in the lobby of the hotel, you know Americans talking to fellow Americans stuff like that. Bob and my cover will be international tour operators, which will give us cover if we need to go to other cities or locations in Brazil with you."

"When we find out you are on your honeymoon we will invite you to dinner some night during your stay. Of course you will agree to have dinner with us sometime latter in the week. This will establish a reason for us to call you. During our conversation you should talk a little loud about both of you being veterinarians that are involved in research. That's how you met Elizabeth traveling to England to do research during the terrible outbreak of mad cow disease there."

"We want people to know how you met and that you both were doing research on mad cow disease just in case al- Qaeda has someone working at the hotel. They don't have to know that you just recently met, it could have been several years ago when the disease first started in England. We want to use as much of your real lives as possible that way it's much harder for anyone to trip you up."

Shane and Elizabeth for the first time begin feeling very uncomfortable acting as CIA and MI-5 Agents. What had they gotten themselves into? But it was too late now they were committed to the plan.

The rest of the flight had little conversation going on. The four of them tried to sleep and Shane and Elizabeth tried not to think about what might happen and tried to concentrate on playing the part of honeymooners. Part of playing the role would come easy to them.

On their arrival in Rio everything went exactly as planned by the CIA. The Brazilian CIA Agent gave Shane a ring box from H. Stern. Shane took out a two carrot diamond engagement ring from the ring box and placed it on Elizabeth left ring finger, next he put on the diamond wedding band. Elizabeth took out a man's diamond wedding band from the ring box and slipped it onto Shane's left ring finger.

Shane said, "I guess that makes us on our honeymoon now."

Shane exchanged two thousand dollars for Brazilian Real. Next, Shane and Elizabeth followed the signs for Taxis.

Shane said "You know Elizabeth, no matter where you go in the world signs for taxis are at least understandable. Also, I think about everyone in the world understands OK. Well at least every where that I have been to."

Elizabeth replied, "You know I think your right. Come on and let's see if we can get a taxi. I want to get to the hotel."

Shane said, "Oh, the bride is anxious to get to the honeymoon suite is she?"

"Of course I am. I would be surprised if the groom wasn't a little anxious to get there too." Elizabeth replied.

They found a taxi and showed a brochure of the Sheraton Hotel Rio that had been given to them by the local CIA Agent and asked the taxi driver to please take them to the hotel. It turned out the taxi driver spoke a little English, which made things easier for them. Shane and Elizabeth's Portuguese was zero. Shane didn't think he could get far in Brazil with the little bit of Spanish that he knew.

After about an hour ride in the taxi they arrived at the Sheraton Hotel. The doorman opened the taxi door for Elizabeth and she exited the taxi in the meantime Shane was busy trying to make sense of the charge for the taxi and his Reals. The taxi driver helped Shane get the correct amount of Reals for the taxi ride and than Shane gave him a 15% tip above the fee.

While Shane was busy paying the taxi driver the doorman and a bellman had loaded Shane and Elizabeth's luggage onto a luggage cart. The bellman welcomed them to the Sheraton and directed them to the front desk.

Arriving at the front desk Shane told the desk clerk that they had reservations for the honeymoon suite. The desk clerk welcomed them and asked what name the reservations were under. Shane told him Dr. Shane Smith and Dr. Elizabeth Browning.

The desk clerk looked up the reservation on the hotel computer and said, "Yes sir Dr. Smith we have the honeymoon suite all ready for you and Dr. Browning. The desk clerk made two electronic passkeys for their suite and handed them to Shane. Than he asked if he wanted to keep the charges on the credit card that the reservations were made with. Shane told him yes that would be fine. The desk clerk said we will need to run your credit card and would need to see their passports.

Shane took out his billfold and gave the desk clerk his American Express Card that had been given to him by Secretary Ridge. Elizabeth had put both of their passports in her purse after they had cleared immigrations and Shane asked her to please give them to the desk clerk.

Elizabeth took their passports from her purse and handed them to the desk clerk. The desk clerk ran Shane's credit card through the credit card machine and returned the card back to Shane. After the desk clerk recorded information off of Shane and Elizabeth's passports he returned them back to Elizabeth.

The desk clerk again welcomed them to the Sheraton and told them if there was anything the staff could do to make their stay more enjoyable to please let them know. He also wished them a very happy honeymoon.

Than the desk clerk asked the bellman to show Shane and Elizabeth to the honeymoon suite. He said it loud enough for several people in the lobby to turn to look at them. Shane thought to himself I wonder what these people are thinking about the honeymooners. He had a good idea of what most of them would be thinking.

The bellman guided them to the elevators; punched the button for the 14th floor and when the elevator stopped at the 14th floor he pointed to the right as they were exiting the elevator. He followed them with the luggage cart until they reach the end of the hallway, than he pointed to the last door on the left. Shane used his hotel passkey to unlock the door of the suite. The lights in the suite were already turned on so Shane and Elizabeth could see the layout of the suite.

The suite had a large living room with a wet bar; an oversize TV set and a large couch with several matching chairs. Next was a dining room with seating for six people along with a buffet complete with sliver ware and a set of

dishes for six. The bedroom was equipped with two reclining chairs; another TV set, nightstands next to each side of the king size bed and one very large chest that matched the rest of the bedroom furniture. The hallway to the bathroom had closets on each side of it with sliding mirrored doors. The entire suite appeared to have just been refurbished. It was very nice.

The bellman placed the luggage on luggage stands in the bedroom and opened the drapes in the bedroom and in the dining room. Since they were in a corner room the dining room overlooked the Southern Atlantic Ocean and the bedroom overlooked the huge swimming pools where people were swimming and appeared to be having a lot of fun.

Shane tipped the bellman and the bellman left the room leaving Shane and Elizabeth in the suite by themselves. They stood there looking at each other for a few minutes without saying anything.

Elizabeth broke the silence by saying, "Shane, I am only sorry that we are not really on our honeymoon, just look at this place."

Shane replied, "Our associates did a fine job in making arrangements for this suite. You don't think they bugged this place do you?"

Elizabeth said, "I certainly hope not!"

Shane than moved closer to Elizabeth and whispered, "If they did than I think we should get started doing the things that people on their honeymoon would be doing."

Elizabeth whispered back, "What do you think honeymooners would be doing?"

Shane put his arms around her and softly kissed her lips and said, "They would probably start with something like this. Than they would close those drapes and start taking off their clothes."

As he said it Shane moved to the windows in the dining room and closed the drapes and than on into the bedroom with Elizabeth holding on to his hand as he closed the drapes in the bedroom. Next he unfastened her blouse and removed it than he undid her bra. His hands slid down to the back of her skirt and unzipped it and it fell to the floor. Elizabeth walked out of her skirt that was now on the floor around her feet.

Shane than lay her down on the bed and proceeded to remove her shoes and stockings. He pulled her back up off of the bed and slowly began pulling her panties down until they were around her ankles. Elizabeth stepped out of the panties.

Shane said, "Next you would help me get undressed so that we could take a nice long shower and than we could see what would come up next."

Almost before Shane finished saying it Elizabeth had unbuckled his belt and unfastened his pants and was pulling them down. She pushed him down on the bed and untied his shoes and removed them and his socks. Next, she pulled off his pants and than took off his white cotton briefs and finished undressing him by taking off his shirt.

Elizabeth said, "OK Shane, let's try out that long shower and see if anything comes up in there."

She pulled him up from the bed using both of her hands and led him to the bathroom and into the shower. Than she turned on the cold water and laughed as Shane started yelling, "My God you're freezing me to death!"

Elizabeth laughed and told him, "I think the cold water will slow down anything from coming up too fast."

With that Shane pulled Elizabeth into the shower with him. He readjusted the temperature of the water to warm and things did come up. They begin making love in the shower, than on the floor of the bathroom and finished making love on the bed. They were wrapped up in the Sheraton bathrobes as they lay resting on the bed.

As they continued lying on the bed in each other's arms.

Shane said, "Tom said we should answer the door in these bathrobes, but he didn't say anything about why or how we put them on."

Elizabeth said, "I love you and you were right when you said that I was only after you for your body. I feel like we just invented sex! You are wonderful! You make me feel like a real woman. I never felt like this before."

Shane said, "Elizabeth I love you so much. I can't describe how you make me feel. Wonderful, just doesn't seem descriptive enough. There must be a word, exquisite maybe! I don't think we really invented sex we just perfective it. I want to spend my life extolling your virtues. I want to marry you when we finish this assignment, will you. Will you marry me?"

Elizabeth softly replied, "Yes. Yes, a thousand times yes!"

Shane began kissing her and holding her body as close to his as he could get it.

"You made me the happiest man in the world with your answer and it was very nice that the CIA furnished us an engagement ring don't you think." Shane said.

Several minutes latter they sat up in bed and decided that they should order something for dinner. They would need to keep their energy up to be on a honeymoon. They looked over the in room dinning menu and decided on lobster tails, baked potato, a green salad and champagne to celebrate their engagement.

After they ordered their dinner and were waiting for it to be delivered to their suite they continued to explore every inch of each other's body. It was exciting to just touch and feel the other ones body.

Than a knock came at the door and they quickly extracted themselves off of the bed, straighten their robes and answered the door. They thought that they must look like two people in love and on their honeymoon. Because they were certainly in love and practicing for their honeymoon.

They toasted their love and engagement with their champagne, ate their lobster and went to bed. After they finished making love again they said they loved each other and fell asleep.

CHAPTER FIVE

The next morning Shane was awaken by the sound of the shower running. He sat up in bed and rubbed his eyes and looked around the bedroom. He saw Elizabeth's clothing and his still scattered around the bedroom floor and realized where he was.

Shane called out to Elizabeth, "Good morning love!"

With the shower running Elizabeth could not hear him so Shane got out of bed and went into the bathroom. He could see Elizabeth was busy washing her hair. He opened the shower door and reached in and touched Elizabeth on her back. She quickly turned around and reach for Shane and pulled him in the shower with her.

Elizabeth said, "Good morning love, I was missing you. I am glad you could join me in the shower."

Than she leaned her head up to kiss Shane good morning.

Shane pulled her closer to him and began kissing her lips ever so gently and than he said, "I missed you and I love you."

After they finished their showers and getting dressed for the day.

Shane said, "Well love, what do you think you would like to do for the day?" Elizabeth replied, "We should contact the travel and tour agency I saw located in the lobby of the hotel last night. They probably could make arrangements for a tour of the sights of Rio."

Shane agreed that was a good idea and after breakfast they would see what kind of tours that they had available.

Shane and Elizabeth left their honeymoon suite hand in hand and proceeded to the restaurant located just off of the lobby of the hotel. The restaurant was not very busy since it was pass the normal morning breakfast time. The waiter showed them to a booth with a wonderful view of the ocean. The waves of the ocean was pounded the beach this morning and off in the distances they saw several large ships waiting to off-load their cargo. Breakfast was a buffet style with lots of different types of food available. Shane was happy to find his favorites. Eggs, bacon and toast even though he had to toast the bread himself. Elizabeth chose a lot of different types of fruits, juices and breads.

After they finished their breakfast they went into the lobby of the hotel and found that on a lower level of the hotel were several shops. Shane bought Elizabeth a straw hat with a wide brim to protect her beautiful face from the sun. He found a baseball style cap with the name of the local football team on it and bought it.

Shane said, "Well it says football, but us Americans know that they are really talking about soccer."

Elizabeth corrected him by saying, "You Yanks don't know anything about real football."

They laughed about the cultural differences between America and the rest of the world, than went happily on their way hand in hand. They took an escalator up to the lobby level and found they were looking at the travel agency office directly across from were they came up on the escalator.

They went into the travel agency's office and inquired about different tours that were available around Rio. The lady working in the travel agency gave them a brochure with several tours that they could take. They decided to take a city tour that would let them get an overall look at Rio.

They also decided to book a tour of the Christ of the Andes and one that would take them to the top of Sugarloaf Mountain. Last they booked a night tour to take them to different nightclubs that featured Brazilian samba dancers with dinner at one of the clubs.

Shane paid for the tours with his American Express Card. The travel agent told them they looked like they were on their honeymoon and they told her, yes we are. She said that was nice and asked where they were from. Elizabeth explained that they were both veterinarians and that her husband was from the United States and she was from England. Than the travel agent asked since they were from countries so far away from each other how they met. Elizabeth said that they met while doing research on an important project.

The travel agent told them a few weeks ago she had worked with a group of veterinarians that were guests in the hotel and she made some travel arrangements for them and their families.

Shane and Elizabeth perked up their ears when she told them about the other veterinarians but didn't say anything to her about being interested in where they went. They thought that they should report this to Tom and Bob and see what they had to say.

Their city tour was scheduled to leave at three this afternoon. That should give them time to run into Tom and Bob. Shane and Elizabeth left the travel agent's office and started walking around the lobby when they noticed a H. Stern Jewelry Store located only a few feet from the hotel registration desk. They had not noticed it last night when they checked in since it was closed and dark. They smiled knowingly at each other and wondered if their rings had come from this store.

Then they went over to a group of several large chairs and couches arranged around a huge fireplace in the hotel lobby and sat down on one of the couches. They sat there holding hands and talking about how much fun they were having on their honeymoon when they saw Tom and Bob coming from the restaurant that they had breakfast in a short time ago.

As Tom and Bob were passing by them suddenly Tom stopped and said, "Hello, are you two Americans?"

Shane responded, "Well half of us are the other half is English."

Tom said, "Well I am Tom Parker and this is my business partner Bob Barker. We are in the tourist business in Washington, DC and we are working to put together tours of Brazil and several other South American Countries. So what brings you two to Rio?"

Shane was surprised as how well Tom portrayed a tourist agent.

Shane responded, "Elizabeth and I are on our honeymoon." Than he said, "Oh, I am sorry I am Shane Smith from Ames, Iowa and this is my wife, Dr. Elizabeth Browning from England."

Shane extended his hand to Tom. Tom shook hands with him. Than Bob shook hands with him as well.

Tom said, "Wonderful Mr. Smith, Bob and I would like to know how you two like this hotel since we are planning to put it in our tour package of Rio?"

Shane started telling them how Elizabeth and him liked the hotel and their honeymoon suite. Tom told them that the hotel manager had been showing them around the hotel and had shown them several of the different styles of rooms they had in the hotel. They had just finished having lunch with him before they met them.

Tom said, "Well it's awfully nice to meet you two. Maybe if you have some time while you are in Rio you would have dinner with us some night. We are scheduled to visit several restaurants as their guest and we would like to have your thoughts on one of them."

Shane said, "Well you know we are on our honeymoon and want to have most of the time to ourselves."

Tom said, "I certainly understand that, don't we Bob?"

Bob replied, "Well I certainly do, I don't know about an old bachelor like you understanding it."

Tom said, "Let me tell you something, if I had met a girl that looked like Elizabeth I would not be an old bachelor. Besides, even honeymooners have to eat sometime. I'll tell you what we will do. We will take you two to one of the best Brazilian Churrascaria Restaurants in Rio; they specialize in all kinds of meat dishes. They keep bringing you different meats until you take down your green flag and put up a red flag to surrender. You aren't vegetarians are you?"

Elizabeth said, "Oh no, we like meat we will go with you to dinner one night while we are in Rio."

Tom said, "Good that's settled we will give you a call. No, I mean for our English girl, we'll give you a ring to set up the night and a time."

Than Tom and Bob said goodbye and Shane and Elizabeth continued to stay and talk for awhile.

Shane said, "You didn't really want to go to dinner with those Americans did you?"

Elizabeth said, "Of course not, but you Americans are so pushy that was the only way to get rid of them."

Shane said, "Good. I'll find a way to tell them we can't go when they call. Smart thinking my good wife. You got rid of those two. I thought we might be stuck with them the rest of the day."

Elizabeth replied, "See I told you I was good for something."

Shane said, "Yes you are, and I could tell you something else you are good for, me!"

With that said Shane put his arms around her and pulled her close to him and kissed her. This caused everyone around the lobby and even Tom and Bob who were waiting for a taxi in front of the hotel to stare at them but neither Shane nor Elizabeth could have cared less.

Shane and Elizabeth met the tour guide at three in the hotel lobby. Two other couples from the Sheraton joined the tour group. One was a couple Shane guessed were in there sixties from Germany. The other two were men that were working on some type of computer systems for banks in Brazil. They worked out of Springfield, Missouri. Their

city tour took them past Ipanema Beach, they saw Tom and Bob's hotel just across the street from the beach. Neither of them said anything about the Caesar Park Hotel they just looked at it and nodded to each other like some kind of secret between them.

Next they past Copacabana Beach across the street from the beach was a beautiful new J.W. Marriott Hotel. The tour bus pulled into the J.W. Marriott Hotel and took on six more passengers. These people were tourists from Canada that had come to Rio together for some fun in the sun.

The tour than took them to the north part of the city near the airport that they had landed at last night. Was it only last night, a lot had happened since then. They passed Sugar Loaf Mountain on their way to the north part of the city. The guide told them that the city was about four hundred fifty-two square miles in area with a population of over seven million.

From the north part of the city they traveled over many small streets until they reached the center of the city. They saw several large churches along the way and now that they were in the city center were they saw numerous high raise office and apartment buildings.

They also had past a large lake that lay on the Westside of the central city. When they past the local football stadium Shane was glad he wore his new football cap because the tour guide made a comment about what a wonderful team they had and pointed out Shane's cap to the group.

After traveling around the various parts of the city for over three hours the tour begin making it's way back to the hotels. The first stop was to drop off the people at the J.W. Marriott than slowly made their way back to the Sheraton. Shane said that traffic in Rio was certainly a lot worse than in Ames or Des Moines. The two men from Springfield

laughed and said yes the traffic was sure worse here than it was in Springfield, Missouri. It took them almost forty- five minutes to get back to the Sheraton. By the time they returned everyone was really ready to get off of the bus.

The tour guide told them other tours offered by his company would be a lot different since you would be out of the bus doing things.

Elizabeth whispered to Shane, "I hope so because this was one of the worst tours that I have ever been on."

Shane and Elizabeth headed for their suite as soon as they got off the bus. When they arrived at their suite the first thing they saw was the message light flashing on their telephone. Shane checked the message. It was Tom asking them to please call him about dinner arrangements. Shane wrote down the number for the Caesar Park Hotel and Tom's room number.

Shane called the number and asked for Tom Parker in room 417. After two rings Tom answered the phone. He asked what night Shane and Elizabeth would be available to go to dinner with him and Bob. Shane told him whatever night they wanted to go except for Friday night because they had a tour of the nightclubs in Rio that night.

Tom asked, "If it would be all right if they went to dinner tonight?"

The way Tom said it Shane knew that something was up in just the way he said it. Shane told him that would be fine.

Tom said, "We'll pick you up in an hour.

Elizabeth said, "I want to change to my black dress for dinner if that's all right."

"Shane said, "Tom said they would pick us up in an hour."

Elizabeth began disrobing and putting her clothes on the bed.

She asked, "Shane if he would be a good husband and hang up her skirt and blouse."

Sure he would because he intended to be a very good husband to Elizabeth.

As Shane was hanging up her clothes Elizabeth was busy taking off her bra and panties.

She said, "I'll just take a quick shower before getting dressed."

Shane picked up her underwear and put them in one of the dirty clothes bag supplied by the hotel.

Than he begin taking off his clothes and hanging them up as he took out a black suit, white shirt and a red tie from the closet. He checked his black dress shoes to see if they needed to be shined and decided that they were OK. Next he made a run to the shower before Elizabeth turned it off. As Shane got into the shower Elizabeth was getting out.

Elizabeth proceeded to redo her makeup and brush her teeth before getting dressed. Shane was getting out of the shower and drying himself off as Elizabeth began to put on black pantyhose, black bra and black panties over the pantyhose. Shane stopped her from putting on her dress by pulling her close to him.

He said, "Wow. I like your black underwear and with your black hair you are so beautiful."

He put his arms around her and pulled her closer to him.

Shane said, "Yes I know we have to finish getting ready or we are going to be late. But the true is, I would rather stay here and make love with you."

Elizabeth said, "Yes, so would I, but duties calls."

Shane said, "Do you have to be so dedicated to the cause?"

Elizabeth replied, "Yes, and so are you or I couldn't love you like I do."

Shane said, "Well if you are going to be truthful like that we better get dressed."

They were soon finished dressing and Shane thought Elizabeth looked stunning and he told her so.

She said, "Well for an old Oklahoma Cowboy you look pretty good yourself, fancied up in that black suit with your red tie."

With that said Shane and Elizabeth left their suite and went down to the lobby to wait for Tom and Bob. They didn't have to wait long before Tom and Bob showed up.

Tom told them that they had a car and a driver waiting for them in front of the hotel. Tom told Elizabeth that she looked spectacular and told Shane that he cleaned up pretty good himself.

After they got into the car Tom introduced them to MI-5 Agent Robert Dalton that was assigned to Brazil.

Robert Dalton told Shane and Elizabeth that they needed to know what MI-5 had found out about the missing UK scientists. MI-5 got information on the name of their wife's and the names of their children and their ages.

He than give them the information on the missing scientist's family members: Dr. Anthony Hinson and his wife Betty. Their children; Tony 12 and Beverly 10.

Dr. David Allen and his wife Lou Ann. Their children; Lori 13; Wayne 11; Troy 9; and Joan 7.

Tom picked up the conversation from there. He said that between the CIA and the FBI they had information on the other two missing scientist's families.

He told them that Dr. Arden Borland from the Netherlands and his wife Dorothy were missing. They didn't have any children.

Dr. Charles Van Meter from the USA and his wife Lois were among the missing along with their three children. Tuesday 12, Charles 10 and Brenda 8 were missing along with their parents.

Tom said, "We know that you already knew the names and the countries of the missing scientists, but we didn't have the information on their family members until today."

Shane said, "Elizabeth and I do have some news ourselves. When we were booking our tours this morning the travel agent said that she had recently booked tickets for some visiting veterinarians and their families that were staying at the hotel. We didn't push her for information until we talked to you."

Tom said, "That maybe the break we need to try to find our missing scientists. Tomorrow we want you to go back into the travel agent and ask her if she can suggest someplace that you should go while you were in Brazil. Than ask her if your friends went to the same place. If so ask her to book you two tickets the same as she did for them. Even the same accommodations if they had any."

Shane said, "We'll go into the travel agent in the morning and see what we can find out."

Robert Dalton asked Elizabeth, "If she was doing OK? We were concerned about asking you to pretend to be newlyweds, but we thought that it would be a good cover and might keep you both alive in case the al-Qaeda kidnapped you."

He added, "I will have to say you two make a very believable newlywed couple."

Elizabeth said, "We are doing our best to play the part."

Bob said, "Well you've got Tom and mine's vote, you two certainly look like newlyweds. You've convinced us."

Dinner was fantastic and Tom was right they just keep coming with all types of meats until they all agreed to raise the red flag and give up eating. The waiter even asked them if they wanted desert. Some nerve!

Elizabeth made quite a stir everywhere she went dressed in her black sheath dress. The men eating in the restaurant couldn't keep their eyes off of her and the same reaction of the men in the hotel lobby. Shane could hardly wait to get her out of that dress.

When they returned to their suite Shane immediately began helping her to undress.

Elizabeth laughed and said, "I never had this much help taking my clothes off in my life. I never got this much help from my mother when I was a little girl."

Shane said, "I guess your life has changed, now you have help."

Elizabeth replied, "Yes, but I think you are more interested in what's in the dress than helping me out of it."

Shane than started removing her panties and pantyhose and last her sexy lace black bra.

Shane said, "I think you should always were black undies they go so well with your raven black hair."

Than he quickly removed his own clothes with a little help from Elizabeth.

They were soon on the bed making love.

Shane said, "I love you and I was jealous sharing you at dinner with Tom, Bob and Robert and the way the men in the restaurant looked at you. I thought they were going to devour you with their eyes."

Elizabeth said, "Shut up and make love to me. You know I only love you for your body and how you make love to me."

Shane said, "And you know, I only love you for your money."

Most of the rest of the night was spent making love.

The next morning Shane woke up and saw that Elizabeth was still sleeping. He looked at the beautiful young woman lying next to him and thought how lucky he was to have someone that beautiful and so smart in love with him. He didn't know why or how come she loved him he only knew how much he loved her.

He took hold of the bottom hem of her nightgown and gently began rubbing his fingers around the hem. Elizabeth immediately woke up and said, "Good morning my love."

Shane said, "Good morning to you too my love. I am sorry if I woke you up."

Elizabeth said, "No, you didn't wake me I was just waiting to see if you were going to wake up before I got up. Besides I was thinking about when my mother sent me to boarding school for two years in Switzerland. You didn't know I was in boarding school when I was thirteen and fourteen did you?"

Shane said, "No, I didn't know that, why were you thinking about that now?"

Elizabeth replied, "Well I was thinking about all of the talk about boys and sex and how little us girls, knew about love and sex."

Shane said, "Do you know a lot more now?"

"Actually I was thinking about a joke the girls had about nightgowns. It went like this; do you know the difference between a nightgown and pajamas? Elizabeth asked.

"No my love, what is the difference between a nightgown and pajamas?" Shane asked.

Elizabeth replied, "About ten seconds?"

Shane laughed in spite of the fact that he thought it was a pretty lame joke. Than he rolled over on top of Elizabeth holding his upper body weight off of her by using his arms to hold him up.

Than Shane said, "What else did you learn at the boarding school besides sex and jokes?"

Elizabeth said, "Well I don't think I learned many jokes or much about sex but I did learn to speak French fluently."

Than she began speaking in French, about a hundred words, a minute.

Shane said, "I don't know what you are saying, but it certainly sounds sexy."

Elizabeth told him, "I will never tell you what I said, but I will tell you this it was really dirty."

Than Shane leaned down and kissed her softly of her lips. Than pressed his lips against hers much harder. Elizabeth lifted her head to meet his kisses.

Than Shane rolled off of the bed and told Elizabeth, "Duty calls we have to get up and get dressed to talk to our travel agent about our missing scientists. Get up my little French wench!"

Elizabeth replied, "Oh yeah, you love me up all night and than just leave me in bed will you."

Than she jumped out of the bed and raced Shane to the shower throwing off her gown as she ran.

They both arrived at the shower door at the same time and Shane took hold of the shower door handle and opened the door and said, "After you my lady."

Elizabeth entered the shower triumphantly with her head held high as she had just won the Wimbledon Cup.

Shane said as he joined her in the shower, "Pretty proud of your self are you for beating me to the shower."

"Of course not my good man just soap up my back please." Elizabeth replied.

Shane said, "Yes, your majesty."

As he begin rubbing her back with the soap and a little bit lower than her back.

Elizabeth told him, "Remember, duty calls, we don't have time for personal pleasures my good man."

After they finished bathing and dressing they left their suite hand in hand and it was easy for anyone that saw them to see two people very much in love.

After they finished their breakfast they went into the travel agent's office. The lady that worked in the travel agency remembered them from yesterday and said "Good morning, may I please help you."

Shane said, "We wanted to see if there was someplace that we should see before we leave Brazil. We want to go to someplace really spectacular in Brazil before we go home."

The travel agent told them, "Than you must go to the Cataratas Do Iguacu."

Than she said, "Your friends, the veterinarians that were staying in the hotel a few weeks ago they booked trips there."

Shane and Elizabeth looked at each other and smiled because they had just learned where their missing scientists went when they left Rio and the information was given to them voluntarily. They didn't even have to ask.

Shane said, "What are the Cataratas Do Iguacu?"

The travel agent said, "Oh, you know they are water falls, like America's Niagara Falls, only bigger."

Shane said, "Please make airline reservations for us to go there on Saturday if you can. Is there some place to stay when we visit the falls?"

She replied, "There is only one place you should stay and that is in the hotel in the National Park of Iguacu. The name of the hotel is, Hotel Das Cataratas Brasil."

Elizabeth said, "Please get us a room there if you can please."

Shane asked, "How many days should we stay there to see everything there is to see?"

The travel agent said, "You should stay for at least four days. That's how many days your friends were booked at the hotel."

Now Shane and Elizabeth knew where their scientists had booked rooms for their stay at the falls.

The travel agent said, "It would take me sometime to make the reservations for you. If you go on Saturday and stay for four nights than you would need a flight coming back to Rio on Thursday. OK?"

Shane said, "That should be all right because we will be leaving for home on Friday night."

The travel agent said, "I will need your credit card for the airline tickets and the hotel."

Shane took out his billfold and handed her his American Express Card.

The travel agent said, "I am sorry, but the hotel will not take this card, do you have a Visa or MasterCard?"

Shane than took out his MasterCard out of his billfold and gave it to her.

The travel agent said, "I am sorry, but it is the way the hotel does business or in cash. Your friends had a sponsor or some kind of a salesman with a drug company with them that paid for their trips. He paid in cash. I don't get many people that pay with that much cash."

Shane said, "We'll come back latter and get our tickets and reservations for the flights and the hotel after we return from tour of the Christ of the Andes."

Shane and Elizabeth left the travel agent's office and went back to their suite to wait until it was time for their tour to pick them up.

Once inside the suite Shane said, "We need to call Tom and thank him for taking us to dinner last night. In fact I think you should call him Elizabeth he likes you better than he does me."

Than Shane whispered to Elizabeth, "We've got to let Tom know what we found out from the travel agent."

Elizabeth said, "OK, if you have Tom's number I will call him to thank him and Bob for taking us to dinner last night."

Elizabeth dialed the number for Tom Parker as Shane read it to her. When the hotel operator answered she told him that she wanted to speak with Tom Parker in room 417.

After two rings Tom answered the phone.

Elizabeth said, "Hello Tom, this is Elizabeth Browning and on behalf of Shane and myself I wanted to thank you for taking us to dinner last night. It was really something special."

Tom said, "It was certainly Bob's and my pleasure to have yours and Shane's company. We hope you didn't think it was too much of an imposition asking you to dinner while you were on your honeymoon."

Elizabeth responded, "No, we enjoyed it very much."

Tom said, "Well in that case maybe we can get together again for dinner before you return home."

Elizabeth said, "That would be lovely, but Shane and I are going to leave on Saturday to visit the Cataratas Do Iguaçu's."

Tom said, "Is that right, Bob and I are going there on Friday. Where do you plan to stay while you are there?"

Elizabeth said, "At the Hotel Das Cataratas Brasil."

Tom replied, "That's funny, Bob and I are checking out that hotel, we wanted to see if we should include it on our tours next year. When did you say you were arriving?"

"Saturday is when we plan to arrive at the Hotel Das Cataratas." Elizabeth replied.

Tom said, "Oh, that's too bad, because Bob and I are leaving on Saturday to go to check on hotels in Sao Paulo. Well maybe we can see you and Shane sometime back in the USA."

Elizabeth said, "It too bad you're leaving when we arrive, maybe we will see you at the airport there. If not maybe we can see you sometime in Washington."

Tom replied, "We hope we do get to see you in Washington sometime. Bob and I want to wish you a wonderful honeymoon and a happy married life. Take care of your self and Shane. Goodbye for now."

Elizabeth hung up the phone.

Shane said, "You were terrific with that call you got Tom every bit of the information. Darling you are as smart as you are beautiful. I love you."

Elizabeth replied, "Sure you say nice things now, but I think you just want to get into my knickers."

Shane said, "You do have great idea's my dear! However, as my lovely wife says, duty calls, we got to go on that tour of the Christ of the Andes. Come on love, let's go down and meet the tour bus."

Elizabeth put her hand in Shane's and said, "Are you sure we have to go as she began kissing him."

Shane said, "I think we have to go otherwise it might look suspicious and we don't know who is watching us or even if there is someone watching us. So, reluctantly I guess we have to go, but can we save getting into your knickers until latter."

Elizabeth replied, "OK, if that's what we have to do. You know Shane until I met you I never understood what the fuss was about sex. Right now that's about all I can think about. Love, you have had a very bad influence on me and I am afraid I will never return back to my old self and I don't want to.

Shane led her to the door of the suite and opened the door so that they could go down to the lobby to want for the tour bus.

When they were in the elevator going down.

Shane said, "I hate to tell you this, but what you said in our room about sex was the same thing I was thinking about you. You have changed everything about what I thought about sex and love. I can hardly think about anything except making love with you."

Just as Shane finished saying that, the door of the elevator opened at the lobby level. Hand in hand they left the elevator and sat down on a couch in the lobby to wait for their tour guide.

Only a few minutes past until the same tour guide that they had gone with yesterday came directly up to them and said, "You are going with us on the tour of the Christ of the Andes, yes?"

Shane said, "Yes we are."

The tour guide said, "We are to have two more couples joining us today, but I don't think they are as prompt as you two. If you like you may go out and board the bus now if you like or you can wait here, it is your choice."

Shane said, "What would you prefer my love, do you want to wait here or get on the bus?"

Elizabeth said, "After yesterday bus ride, let's just wait here until we are ready to go, OK."

Shane said, "That's fine with me."

The tour guide said, "He would try to call the rooms for the two couples that were not here yet."

After about ten minutes the tour guide can back and told them that he had not been able to contact one of the couples and the other couple was on there way down and should be here in a few minutes.

Only a few minutes past before a young couple came out of one of the elevators and went straight out to the bus. The tour guide shrugged his shoulders and motioned for Shane and Elizabeth to come onto the bus.

The tour guide said, "We can't wait any longer for our lost couple. In order to make it to the funicular railroad and have time to see everything at the statue of the Christ of the Andes we must be leaving now. Please remember that the latest time the funicular railroad cars leave the top of the mountain is five o'clock. We would hate to have you spend all night stuck on top of the mountain. It can get pretty cold and windy up there over night."

Than he told the bus driver in Portuguese to get going, since they still had to pick up passengers at the J.W. Marriott before going on to their destination. The tour guide was not a happy camper losing so much time and never finding his lost couple. Shane could see that this would be a happy tour and than something impossible to happen, did.

The young woman that was half of the couple that got onto the bus that they had to wait for suddenly said, "Elizabeth, Elizabeth Browning is that you?"

Elizabeth turned to look at the woman that had just said her name and replied, "Janie Williams. What in the world are you doing here?"

The young woman answered, "It's not Williams anymore its Jane Johnson and I'm on my honeymoon and this is my husband Richard Johnson. So what are you doing here?"

"Well you are never going to believe this, but I am on my honeymoon. This is my husband Dr. Shane Smith." Replied Elizabeth.

Jane said, "Your right I can't believe it. You, on your honeymoon! The girl that was never going to get married. The girl who never went on dates and thought that boys were yuck."

Elizabeth said, "Well, I found one that wasn't yucky. How about you? Tell me about your wedding and how long have you been in Rio?

Elizabeth knew that Jane liked to talk so she thought that Jane would be so busy telling all about her new husband and her wedding that she would never bother to ask about her wedding.

Jane started telling her about her husband. He was a stock broker in London and since he was her second husband, her father told her she could do with a simple church wedding with no more than two hundred guests. She told Elizabeth that father said that her first wedding lasted longer than her marriage. So he would not put out that kind of money again for another large wedding. She told Elizabeth that she left her first husband two days after she married him.

She said, "I found out that I didn't like him."

Than she asked Elizabeth, "Tell me all about your new husband and your wedding?"

Elizabeth was taken back for a few minutes and than began telling Jane all about Shane and her wedding.

Elizabeth said, "Shane is a research veterinary like I am and we met while doing a project together. Shane is in research at Iowa State University in Ames, Iowa. We got married in Oklahoma on his father's ranch. It was a very small wedding. We just had a few of Shane's family and friends and my father there. I think you know that my mother died last year from cancer and I am sure you know that I never knew that my father was alive until my mother became ill."

Jane said, "I did know about you losing your mother and everyone in London was talking about your father and mother getting remarried. I am sorry about you losing your mother. I am sure it was very hard for you, you two were so close."

Elizabeth said, "It was very hard for me and it was a real blessing that my mother told me about my father and that he came into my life. He has been so much help for me. Than to meet and marry Shane has really changed my life."

Jane said, "I am sure you have had a huge change in your life after you met Shane. You were so anti boys some of us girls wondered if you were a lesbian."

Richard said, "Jane, what a terrible thing to say!"

Jane said, Oh, I am sorry. You know that sometimes my tongue is not attached to my brain."

Everyone laughed at that and Elizabeth laughed the loudest.

Elizabeth said, "It's all right Richard, I have known Janie since we when to boarding school together in Switzerland when we were thirteen. She hasn't changed a bit. You never knew what she was going to say next."

The tour bus pulled into the J.W. Marriott and took on six more passengers. After about another forty-five minutes the tour bus arrived at the lower station of the funicular railroad. The tour guide told everyone to please stay on the bus until he bought the tickets for the trip to the top of Corcovado Mountain.

The guide returned to the bus with the tickets for the entire group and began handing them to each passenger as they exited the tour bus. He reminded each of them that the last train was at five o'clock so be on that train. He also told them that the official name of the statue was Christ the Redeemer so if you hear people calling the statue that, it is the same statue as Christ of the Andes. Last he said please take your cameras with you because if the weather is clear you can get some very good pictures of the City of Rio from the top of the mountain.

Shane and Elizabeth took their tickets for the train and Jane and Richard were right behind them as they boarded the train. All of them quickly took seats after boarding the train. A few minutes latter a conductor closed the doors on all of the train cars and the little train began to climb almost straight up and continued to climb until about the middle of the trip they met another train descending the mountain. The trains seemed to stop when they were straight across from each other than they began moving up the mountain until the train came to a stop at the top of the mountain.

The conductor opened the doors of the cars and everyone exited the train. Shane, Elizabeth, Jane and Richard began walking up to the huge statue. When they arrived at the statue.

Jane said to Elizabeth, "We must take pictures of you and Shane in front of the statue so I can take it home to London to show all of our friends that we meet you on your honeymoon while we were on our honeymoon. Our friends are never going to believe that you went to America and got married, I want prove to them that its true by showing them pictures of the two of you."

Elizabeth said, "Of course, than we can take yours and Richard's picture in front of the statue."

Shane and Elizabeth dutiful posed in front of the statue for their picture. When Jane finished taking the picture she handed the camera to Shane for him to take hers and Richard's picture.

As Shane was getting into position to take the picture of Jane and Richard so that he could get as much of the statue of Christ in the picture.

Elizabeth said to Shane, "I guess you know that you have to marry me now! Jane is the busiest gossip in England. Before I get back to England everyone in the country will know about me getting married in Oklahoma."

Shane whispered to Elizabeth, "Got you now! You can't back out from marrying me because you would be too embarrassed to go back to England and face all of your friends."

Elizabeth said, "It works both ways you know. You could never go home if I told everybody how you took advantage of me while we had to pretend to be married. So I guess you are stuck with me."

Shane said, "Isn't that too bad."

Jane said, "What are you two talking about? Do Richard and I look funny or something?"

Elizabeth said, "No, I was just giving Shane problems about taking your picture. I wasn't sure he knew how to use your camera, but he did."

Than Elizabeth asked, "How much longer will you two be in Rio?"

Jane told them that Richard and she were returning to London in the morning.

Elizabeth thought that's good, because Shane and I didn't need any more distractions than we already had, falling in love and trying to stop a terrorist plot. Plus, they were working at perfecting sex for the rest of the world.

The four of them went into the small gift shop and looked around for a few minutes. Next they stopped at the snack shop and Shane bought cokes for the four of them. They sat down at a small table and continued talking about the statue of Christ.

They couldn't decide how tall the statue was and if it was taller than the Eiffel Tower in Paris. Shane and Elizabeth were certain that the statue wasn't as tall and Jane and Richard were just as certain that it was taller. One thing they agreed upon was that being on top of the mountain gave them a wonderful view of Rio.

Jane took several pictures of the City of Rio de Janeiro down below them, including several pictures of Shane and Elizabeth looking down on the City. She said she would show them to Elizabeth's friends in London. Elizabeth told her that was very nice of her since she didn't know when Shane and she would be back in London.

It was now getting close to five o'clock so the four of them made their way back to the train. They found seats across from each other and talked about getting together for dinner this evening. They agreed to have dinner at eight o'clock at the restaurant on the top floor of the Sheraton.

Shane said, "I will make reservations for dinner for us when we return to the hotel."

They decided it would be best to just meet at the restaurant at eight instead of trying to meet somewhere else in the hotel.

The trip down the mountain and back to the hotel was uneventful; just slow do to the rush hour traffic of folks trying to get home after a hard days work. When they arrived back at the hotel Shane gave a tip to the tour guide as they exited the tour bus. Than each couple went to their rooms to get dressed for dinner. When Shane and Elizabeth arrived at their room Shane made dinner reservations for the four of them.

Elizabeth spoke first about their encounter with Jane and Richard she said, "Now you know what kind of friends I have."

Shane said, "I liked Jane, and Richard seemed all right. He's just not allow to do any talking when Jane around. She can do the talking for both of them."

Elizabeth said, "I believe you totally understand Jane now. I went to school with her in Switzerland for two years and she never shut up for the two full years. I think that's why her parents sent her away to school to rest their ears."

Shane laughed and said, "You are probably right my love. They had a good reason to send her away to school. They needed to rest their ears. That's a good one and you are probably right."

Elizabeth said, "Shane, I guess what I told you on the top of the mountain is right. You have to marry me now I couldn't ever show my face in London again after Jane gets home with the news of our marriage."

Shane said, "That's the least of your worries. I plan on marrying you as soon as we finish our assignment. You can plan on getting married on my daddy's ranch in Oklahoma when we get back to America."

Elizabeth began holding and kissing Shane and said, "I love you my Oklahoma cowboy."

"I know you do and I love you," Shane replied.

They began getting undressed and making their way to the shower. They couldn't believe how dirty they felt after being on the tour. The shower was refreshing and they had plenty of time to get dressed and ready for dinner with the Johnson's.

Promptly at eight o'clock Shane and Elizabeth arrived at the top of the hotel for dinner. Jane and Richard had not arrived yet so they advised the waiter that they were the Smith's and were waiting for their guests. Ten minutes went by before the elevator door opened and Jane and Richard popped out of the elevator.

Richard said, "I am sorry we are late. I have been pushing Jane to hurry up as fast as I could."

Jane said, "Elizabeth you know how slow I am getting ready."

Shane said, "It's not a problem. We have not been here too long and the restaurant is not very busy."

The waiter showed them to their table.

Shane said, "Elizabeth and I would like to treat you to dinner to honor our marriages and to renewing old friendships."

Richard replied, "Please let us, meeting you two has certainly been a pleasure and we were so happy to spend the afternoon with both of you."

Jane said, "Richard, it's all right for them to buy dinner for us. Elizabeth's got more money than the Queen."

Richard said, "Jane, you got to control your tongue! I think what you said this afternoon may be right. Your tongue is not connected to your brain."

Elizabeth said, "Richard it's all right. I know Jane doesn't mean anything bad when she says strange things. She has been my friend for a lot of years. Besides, she right I do have more money than the Queen!"

Shane, Richard and Jane began laughing hardly. Elizabeth saved the evening. After that Jane held her tongue and Richard even had the chance to do some talking. Shane found Richard to be a very likable fellow. The four of them laughed and enjoyed a wonderful dinner together and when it was time to say goodbye there were now four friends.

They agreed that as soon as Elizabeth and Shane got to London, Richard would host a dinner for them. The four of them got on the elevator together and when they got to Shane and Elizabeth's floor they said goodnight and goodbye for now.

Jane and Elizabeth hugged and kissed each other and Richard and Shane had a hardy handshake. Before Shane got off of the elevator, Jane gave him a kiss and told him that he got a wonderful wife.

Shane said, "Yes, I do, I am really lucky and I think you are a very good friend." Shane and Elizabeth were soon in each others arms and enjoying trying to perfect sex for the world. Shane told Elizabeth it feels good to make love with someone that's richer than the Queen of England. Elizabeth just laughed.

CHAPTER SIX

Thursday morning after Shane and Elizabeth finished their breakfast they went directly to the travel agent's office to pick up their tickets to go see the Cataratas Do Iguacu. The travel agent was ready and waiting for them. She explained that she had gotten them two first class tickets for the price of coach due to them being on their honeymoon. She said it took her some time to get the airline to let her have the upgrades, but she said she just kept talking until they gave her the upgrades.

She returned Shane's two credit cards and assured him that she had kept them in her safe overnight for security. She told them that she was able to get them a suite at the Hotel Cataratas Brasil for the price of a regular room. She told them she wanted them to enjoy their honeymoon, because she thought they were such a nice young couple. So she said she pulled in a lot of favors from the hotel and the airline.

The travel agent told them their flight would leave on Saturday at two forty-five in the afternoon and would arrive at the Aeroporto Internacional Foz Do Iguacu at four forty- five. A car from the hotel would be there to pick them up and take them to the hotel.

Shane and Elizabeth thanked her profusely for her help. She said it was such a pleasure to work with two people that she could tell were so much in love, it made her feel good just to be around them. They thanked her again and left her office after she had given each of them a hug and a kiss on each cheek.

Shane stopped at the concierge's desk and requested that he make arrangement for a large bouquet of flowers to be sent today to the travel agent from Shane and Elizabeth. He asked the concierge if they could please be charged to his room. The concierge told him that would not be a problem. Shane gave the concierge a small tip for his help with the flowers. Shane asked if the concierge knew the travel agents name. The concierge told him that her name was Marie Barras. Shane thanked him for his help and to be sure that the flowers were sent with a card to Ms. Marie Barras from Dr. Shane Smith and Dr. Elizabeth Browning.

Shane and Elizabeth had a few minutes to go to their room before leaving on the tour of Sugar Loaf Mountain. When they got to their room.

Elizabeth said, "Shane, you are so thoughtful and so nice to think about sending flowers to that nice lady in the travel agency.

Shane said, "It's not too often that someone is as nice as she was to us. I think she will like the gesture of flowers from us."

Elizabeth said, "I am sure she will appreciate the flowers."

Shane asked Elizabeth, "What would you like to do tomorrow since we don't have any tours until tomorrow night?"

Elizabeth responded, "I would like to just lay by the pool and relax tomorrow if that's all right with you."

Shane said, "That sounds good to me. Just having the opportunity to spend time alone with you sounds real good to me."

Just as they were thinking about lying down of the bed to rest for a few minutes before going back down to the lobby to wait for their tour the telephone rang.

Shane picked up the phone and said, "Hello."

Shane heard a voice on the other end of the line say "Is this Dr. Shane Smith from America?"

Shane replied, "Yes it is. How may I help you and who is this please?"

The person on the phone said, "Dr. Smith my name is Dr. Abu al-Sadr. I am a veterinary like you. I understand you are on your honeymoon and I am sorry to bother you, but I think you might be able to help me with a problem with some very sick and dying cattle."

Shane said, "Why do you think I might be able to help you?"

Dr. al-Sadr said, "I have done some research on the internet on doctors that have been involved in research on mad cow disease and your name and Dr. Price's name was mentioned several times as being the leading experts on the disease in the United States. I called Dr. Price at Iowa State University and he told me you were in Brasil on your honeymoon."

"That's very good work with your research on folks that are involved with mad cow disease research, but how can I help you?" Shane asked.

Shane thought to himself that the CIA made sure that Elizabeth and his story about being on their honeymoon were told to everyone in the USA that might be called to find out about them. Good thinking Bob or whoever contacted Dr. Price about Shane and Elizabeth's cover story.

Dr. al-Sadr said, "We have some very sick cattle in my country and I would like you to have a look at them to see what you think is wrong with them. I don't want to alarm my government if it is something else wrong with them besides mad cow disease. I have kept the cattle in insolated and have not told anyone but the owner of what I fear is wrong with them. These cattle were imported from Northern England a few years ago before the disease became a problem there."

Shane said, "Dr. al-Sadr, I don't think I can help you. My wife and I will only be here for a few more days and than we will be returning to the United States."

Dr. al-Sadr said, "I understand that, but it would mean so much to me and my country if you could just spend a few hours examining the brains of some of the dead cattle to confirm my fears or to relieve my fears. I am just not sure of myself in making this diagnosis and we don't have anyone in my country that has any experience with the disease. I am sorry to insist, but my back is against the wall on this problem. Please help us."

Shane said, "I just don't see how that would be possible since my wife and I are leaving Rio on Saturday to go to the Cataratas Do Iguacu."

Dr. al-Sadr said, "I can't believe my luck because I am only a few kilometers away from Foz Do Iguacu in Paraguay. I could pick you up from where you are staying and only take a few hours of your time. I am located near Cidade Del Este which is only a little ways across the border from Brasil. It would not take more than maybe four hours of your time and it would mean so much. Please help us."

Shane said, "All right doctor, my wife and I will make Sunday available to look at you dead cattle's brains to let you know if you have a problem with mad cow disease."

Dr. al-Sadr said, "Thank you that will be wonderful. Where are you staying?"

Shane replied, "At the Hotel Das Cataratas Brasil."

Dr. al-Sadr said, "I will make arrangements to pick up you and your wife on Sunday around ten o'clock in the morning if that is all right with you."

Shane said, "Yes, that will be fine."

Dr. al-Sadr said, "Wonderful, than I will see you on Sunday. Goodbye."

Shane said, "OK, we will see you Sunday morning."

Shane said to Elizabeth, "I don't know if I have just been speaking to someone with al-Qaeda or just a poor veterinary with a problem he doesn't know how to handle."

Elizabeth replied, "Listening to only one side of the conversation I would have to guess that he was with al- Qaeda as persistent as he was on getting your help."

Shane said, "I am afraid you are right and maybe we are the next two scientists to disappear on a trip to the falls. At least we have the CIA, the FBI and MI-5 looking out for us. I have to be sure to wear my lapel pin all of the time so the military knows where we are at. I am only sorry that the CIA took all of my other equipment that was issued to me when we arrived in Brazil. We might be really happy to have the pistol they took when we arrived in Rio."

Elizabeth said, "Do you think we should get in touch with Tom and Bob to let them know about the telephone call you just had?"

Shane said, "Well if we were smart, I think we should, and we are smart so let's get Tom on the line before we have to go on this other tour. Damn, I am getting tried of going on tours aren't you?"

Elizabeth said, "Here is the phone and we have to go on the tour so it doesn't arouse any suspicion that we have any idea that we might be heading into a trap by the al-Qaeda."

Shane said as he placed the call, "I know that you are right, but don't honeymooners ever get to just stay in their room and enjoy each other?"

Elizabeth smiled and said, "We can do that on our next honeymoon."

Tom Parker answered the phone in his room after one ring.

Shane said, "Is this Tom Parker?"

Tom said, "Yes this is he. Who is this calling?"

Shane replied, "Hi Tom, this is Shane Smith. How are you and Bob doing?"

Tom said, "We are doing fine thank you. We are leaving tomorrow to go to the Cataratas Do Iguacu. I am sure Elizabeth told you."

Shane said, "Yes. She did tell me that and I am sorry that you and Bob will be leaving the same day that we arrive. I just wanted to thank you again for taking us to dinner. It was very nice of you."

Tom said, "I am sorry that we will not be able to get together again, before we leave on Friday."

Shane replied, "Yes, Elizabeth and I are sorry that we can't get together, maybe we can have dinner again if we are ever in Washington. We are looking forward to seeing the falls we understand they are spectacular. You will never believe this but I got a call awhile ago from a veterinary from Paraguay that wants me to look at a bunch of sick cattle on Sunday. I tried to tell him I was on my honeymoon but he kept insisting until I finally told him OK, I would take the three or four hours to go with him on Sunday. Have you ever heard of anything like that before, tracking a fellow down while he was on his honeymoon to look at some sick cows?"

Tom said, "Well doctor it sounds like you are too well known in your field to get away on a honeymoon for a few days."

Shane replied, "I don't know about that. The doctor told me he found me on the internet, due to my work on mad cow disease."

Tom said, "Well doctor, I am sorry that someone is trying to interrupt your honeymoon. Maybe it will not be too much time taken away from your honeymoon."

Shane responded, "Probably not, Dr. Abu al-Sadr said that it would only take about four hours for me to see these cows near some city with a name like Cidade Del Este in Paraguay. Anyway I guess Elizabeth and I will get to go to another country while we are in South America."

Tom said, "Maybe it won't be too bad. Just think of it as an adventure."

Shane said, "I am sure you are right. I just didn't want to have to think about mad cow disease while I was on my honeymoon. Anyway, Elizabeth and I wanted you to know how much we enjoyed meeting you and say thanks again. Goodbye and have a good trip back to Washington."

Tom replied, "Thanks for the call and we will look forward to seeing you in Washington one of these days. Bye for now."

Shane hung up the phone and turned to Elizabeth and said, "At least Tom knows about what is going on now."

Elizabeth said, "That's good. Do you think he got all of the information that you gave him on the phone?"

Shane said, "You can be sure that as smart as Tom is that he got all of the information that I just gave him."

Elizabeth said, "We need to go downstairs to meet our tour guide. Come on Shane let's go!"

"OK, if we have to." Shane replied.

The tour turned out to be a very good one. They enjoyed riding in the large cable cars that took them to the top of Sugar Loaf Mountain the cars had very large windows all around them so they had a wonderful view of the City and the ocean below them. Each of the cable cars held twenty to thirty people. Shane discovered that they were made in Switzerland and were designed for ski slopes. One thing Shane didn't like was the drop the cable cars made when they past the towers used to hold the cables that moved the cars up and down the mountain. Shane thought they must be dropping close to a hundred feet each time they past one of those towers. Elizabeth on the other hand had no problem with the drops. She thought they were fun. Shane thought to himself there is no accounting for what some people thought was fun.

They took numerous pictures using a throwaway camera they bought from the gift shop at the cable car's lower terminal. They took pictures of the ocean below them; the homes along the beach and one of the Christ of the Andes.

Plus lot's of pictures of each other and they got another tourist to take a couple of pictures of them together.

After the tour they had dinner in their suite and talked about what they planned to do about their future when they returned to America. They had a lot of questions about how to handle coming from two different worlds and how to make them work together. They decided that their love would find a way no matter what.

The next day they spend their time lying by the pool and just relaxing in their suite and making love all afternoon.

The night tour of Rio was exciting and they had a great time watching the samba dancers. The samba dancers moved parts of their body that Shane wasn't sure he even had. Shane told Elizabeth not to expect him to become a proficient samba dancer, it was only that he had two left feet or was it two right feet. He couldn't remember which it was, but whichever ones they were, didn't work like they were suppose too.

Elizabeth told him it's all right because you know I only love you for your body and how you make love to me.

Shane told her yeah, and I only love you for your money.

CHAPTER SEVEN

The next morning Shane and Elizabeth were up early packing and getting ready for their trip to see the falls and what ever else the trip might bring.

Shane had made arrangements for a car and driver to take them to the airport the night before with the hotel concierge. After breakfast Shane and Elizabeth stopped at the front desk and checked out of their suite and told the desk clerk how much they had enjoyed their stay.

They went to their suite and finished packing the last few pieces of clothes and toiletries articles. Shane and Elizabeth than sat down for a few minutes just to take a last look around their suite.

Elizabeth said, "I am going to miss our honeymoon suite. I will never forget the wonderful time we spent here and our trip to Rio. I love you so much I couldn't think of my life without you."

Shane got down on his knees with his hands on Elizabeth's hands and said, "Elizabeth Victoria Browning will you do the honor of marrying me. I love you so much."

"Shane William Smith, I will marry you at the first opportunity that we get." Elizabeth replied.

Elizabeth bent down and kissed Shane and took her hands out from under his hands and placed them on his cheeks as she continued kissing him.

Shane said, "I guess we need to call a bellman to have him pick up our luggage and take it to the car. It's getting close to the time we need to go to the airport."

Their luggage was loaded in the car and the driver closed the door for Elizabeth. Shane got into the car and before he could reach to close the door the driver proceeded to close it for him.

Traffic was not too bad on a late Saturday morning so it only took about an hour for them to reach the airport. The driver asked them if they were going on an international flight or a domestic flight. Shane told him they were flying on a Varig domestic flight.

The driver stopped at the domestic terminal and beginning getting their luggage out of the trunk of the car as Shane looked for a luggage cart. Instead he found a porter to help them with their luggage. The porter loaded their luggage onto his two wheeled car.

Shane gave the driver a tip and Elizabeth and Shane began following the porter through a very crowded terminal.

Shane said to Elizabeth, "It's a good thing we are early with all of these people trying to get checked in for their flights we may just make ours."

The porter took their luggage to the front of one of the first class check in counters and began unloading their luggage on the floor in front of the counter. Shane gave him a tip and found that in this line they were next to check in for their flight.

Elizabeth said, "I guess we won't have to wait too long after all. You did a great job getting us a porter that knew his way around the terminal."

Shane said, "See I told you I was good for something even if it's only for getting a porter."

Elizabeth replied, "I can think of something else you are good at."

Shane started to ask her what else she thought he was good for when the folks in front of them finished checking in for their flight and left the counter. The woman behind the counter began asking for their tickets in Portuguese and although they didn't understand Portuguese, Shane handed her their tickets. Next she asked to see identification in Portuguese.

Shane said, "I am sorry but we don't speak Portuguese."

The airline clerk said, "Sorry, may I please have some picture identification.

Elizabeth took their passports out of her purse and handed them to the airline clerk.

Next the clerk asked them for twenty Reals for airport tax. Shane looked through his billfold and found a twenty Real note and gave it to the airline clerk.

The clerk asked them how many bags they wanted to check and Shane began putting their luggage on the scale under the counter for the clerk to tag each piece. They had a total of six bags.

The clerk placed tags on each piece of luggage and attached copies of each bag check numbers and flight numbers onto their ticket jacket.

She told them they would need to go through security check on their right and than go to gate fourteen to wait for their flight to be called for their flight to Foz Do Iguacu.

Shane thanked the airline clerk for her help and Shane and Elizabeth cleared the security check and found their way to gate fourteen and took seats in the waiting area.

It was not long before their flight was called and they were soon on their way to an uncertain destiny. Each one had an uneasy feeling of what lay ahead when they reached Foz Do Iguacu.

As they waited for their luggage to come off the conveyor belt a porter asked if he could help them with their luggage. Shane told him could help them. The porter asked if they needed ground transportation, Shane told him that they had a car from the Hotel Do Cataratas picking them up. The porter told Shane that he had seen the hotel car outside of the terminal.

Their bags were the last ones to come off of the conveyor belt the porter loaded the bags on his cart and directed Shane and Elizabeth to the hotel car. The driver was sleeping in the front seat, but the porter woke him up by banging on the trunk of the car. The driver got out of the car and unlocked the trunk and helped the porter load the luggage. Shane gave the porter a nice tip and they were on their way to the hotel.

The driver told them that it would take them about an hour to reach the hotel. Shane and Elizabeth spent the time looking at the landscape and roads to try to establish some road marks in case they needed them latter.

After almost an hour their car reached the entrance to the National Park. Their car was stopped and the driver told them they would have to pay an entrance fee to get into the park. Shane was surprised but, gave the driver the twenty Reals he had requested. The guard at the gate gave the driver a receipt for the fee and they were on their way to the hotel.

Another fifteen or twenty minutes past before the driver began approaching the hotel. As Shane and Elizabeth got out of the car they could hear the falls making a mighty roar. Once inside the lobby of the hotel the driver pointed them to the front desk to check in.

The desk clerk welcomed them to the hotel and asked for confirmation of their reservations. Shane found the document in his briefcase and handed it to the clerk. The clerk looked over the paper and returned it to Shane. The desk clerk told them that their room had already been charged to their credit card but if they wanted to make charges to their room he would need to make a copy of their credit card. Shane gave him his MasterCard and the clerk made an imprint of the card and returned it to Shane.

The clerk than said he would need to see their passports. Elizabeth dutiful took the passports out of her purse and gave them to the clerk. The clerk wrote down some information from the passports and returned them to Elizabeth. The clerk than gave them two keys for their room. Shane and Elizabeth looked at each other and smiled at the keys. It had been a long time since either one of them had seen keys to a hotel room. Now days all of the hotels that they had stayed in had electronic keycards of some type.

The driver had unloaded their luggage and was waiting to show them to their room. He took them to room 124 and asked for a key to open the door Shane handed him one of the hotel keys and he unlocked the door and motioned them to go inside. The room was a small suite, clean but sparely furnished. The room was certainly not the honeymoon suite at the Sheraton Rio.

After they were alone Shane said, "The suite does have a bed and it has a bath with a shower at least. I would guess the room hasn't been remodeled since sometime in the nineteen fifties maybe the sixties, what your guess Elizabeth?"

Elizabeth replied, "The fifties for sure. I don't think people come here to stay in their rooms so let's go see the falls before it gets dark."

Shane said, "You are right, it's the fifties. Can you believe how quick it gets dark here in Brazil?"

Elizabeth said, "No, so lets go."

Shane and Elizabeth started to ask which way it was to the falls but when they went outside of the hotel all they had to do was to follow the sound of the falling water. The closer they got to the falls the louder the noise. In a few minutes they got their first look at the falls from an overlook only a few feet from the hotel parking lot.

Shane spoke first, "My God the falls have chocolate milk coming over them instead of water!"

Elizabeth said, "It does look like chocolate. I love these falls because I am a chocolateholic."

Shane said, "No, not you too. I am a chocolateholic! You know my favorite candy bars is Cadbury's Caramel bar. The chocolate is wonderful and the caramel is to die for and you can't buy them in America. Anytime I was in England I would buy all of the Caramel bars they had in the store and swear I was taking some back home but I ate them all before I got off of the plane. It didn't matter how many of them I bought I swear I ate them all before I got home."

"Shane, no wonder I love you. That's my favorite chocolate bar in the whole world. I once sat and ate eight of those candy bars one right after the other as fast as I could eat them." Elizabeth said.

"I guess we were meant for each other." Shane replied.

Shane took several pictures of the falls and many of Elizabeth looking at the falls or looking at Shane or whatever she was doing. Shane knew the camera loved her she was so beautiful.

They went back to the hotel room had dinner in the dinning room and went to bed very early. They thought they needed time to make love since they had no idea of what tomorrow would bring them.

After breakfast the next morning Shane and Elizabeth went back to the room to wait for Dr. al-Sadr to call them. Elizabeth was dressed in the safari outfit that she was wearing when Shane saw her for the very first time back in England. He thought she looked great than, now he thought she looked fantastic.

Shane said, "I wonder where Tom and Bob our guiding angels are? I hope they are close by and didn't leave for Sao Paulo like they told us they were on the phone a couple of days ago. What do you think Elizabeth?"

"I am sure they are not too far away right now, at least I hope there not." Elizabeth replied.

Just as Elizabeth finish making her statement the telephone rang Shane slowly lifted up the phone and said hello. The voice on the other end of the line said, "Is this Dr. Shane Smith?"

Shane replied, "Yes, this is Shane Smith."

The voice said, "Dr. Smith this is Dr. Abu al-Sadr are you and you wife ready to go with me to check on the cattle I spoke with you about when I talked to you a few days ago?"

Shane said, "Yes Dr. al-Sadr, we have been waiting for your call."

Dr. al-Sadr said, "Good, I am waiting for you in the lobby, near the front door."

Shane said, "We will be right there."

Shane hung up the phone and said, "Elizabeth my love our fate awaits. Come and give me a kiss and a big hug before we go meet Dr. al-Sadr."

Elizabeth came over to where Shane was standing and gave him a hug and a kiss. She picked up her purse and hand in hand they left the room and started walking to meet Dr. al-Sadr.

Arriving at the hotel lobby they saw a man looking as if he was waiting for someone at the very front of the hotel.

Shane said, "My God if that's Dr. al-Sadr he looks just like Omar Sharif."

Elizabeth said, "Are you sure that's not Omar Sharif?"

Shane replied, "I don't think so this man is younger looking than Omar. This man looks like Omar did when he made Lawrence of Arabia. He certainly looks very well dressed."

Elizabeth said, "He is a very handsome man."

Shane said, "I knew that I didn't want to meet this guy, now I know why. He is way too good looking for me to be introducing my new wife to."

Elizabeth laughed and said, "Oh, I think you don't have anything to worry about. Tall dark and handsome is just not my type.

Shane said, "It's a good thing I love you for your money."

Elizabeth laughed and squeezed Shane's hand harder. Shane and Elizabeth were now almost to the front of the hotel lobby when the man at the front of the hotel spoke and said, "You must be Dr. Shane Smith and this must be your lovely bride. I am Dr. Abu al-Sadr."

Shane extended his right hand out to shake hands with Dr. al-Sadr and said, "Yes, I am Shane Smith and this is my wife Dr. Elizabeth Browning. How do you do."

Dr. al-Sadr right hand went out to meet Shane's hand and gave his hand a hearty shake.

Dr. al-Sadr said, "It is a pleasure to meet you and your wife Dr. Smith."

Dr. al-Sadr than turned to Elizabeth and said, "Dr. Browning it is a pleasure to meet you as well. I must say that I am sorry to interrupt your honeymoon. Also, I must tell you what a beautiful woman you are and your husband is a lucky man to have you as his wife."

Elizabeth said, "Thank you Dr. al-Sadr. I think I am pretty luck to have Shane for my husband."

Dr. al-Sadr said, "I am sure you are right, he seems like a very nice chap from talking to him on the phone and that he is willing to take time to help me with my problem. I hope you don't mind, but I have taking the liberty to order some orange juice and coffee for us before we leave if that's OK with you."

Shane said, "That's very kind of you. Thank you."

Dr. al-Sadr said, "I am not sure it was kindness, it was do to me leaving home early this morning and not having any breakfast, but thank you for thinking it's was my kindness."

Shane and Elizabeth laughed along with Dr. al-Sadr.

Shane thought to himself, this guy is smooth as silk. He should be an actor.

As the waiter began serving orange juice to Elizabeth his hand slipped off of the silver serving tray and spilled the other two glasses of orange juice on Shane. The wet sticky juice was all over his shirt and jacket. The waiter was so upset and Shane told him it was all right he would just go back to his room and change.

The hotel manager came over to Shane and told him how sorry he was and that he wished to make it up to them by giving them dinner in the hotel dinning room as his guest. Shane thanked him and said it was very nice of him and that he would just go back to his room and change his shirt and jacket.

Shane excused himself and went back to his room to change clothes. When he opened the door to his room he was surprised to see Tom and Bob waiting for him.

Shane smiled and said, "Elizabeth and I were wondering where you two were just before we got the call that Dr. al- Sadr was waiting for us in the hotel lobby. The spilled orange juice was no accident was it?"

Tom said, "No, it was no accident. We thought you two would be looking for us and we wanted to talk with you before you left with Dr. al-Sadr. We are here as you can see and we will be looking out for you."

Bob said, "Do you have any idea of who Dr. al-Sadr is? No, I am sure you don't. I'll tell you who he is. He is one of the most wanted terrorist in the world. He is a doctor all right, but not a veterinary; he's a medical doctor from Egypt. He has been involved in all types of successful terrorist plots in countries around the world."

"He was trained to be a doctor in the United Kingdom and in the USA. His parents are very wealth and why he turned to terrorisms no one knows. No one has had any idea where he has been, he hasn't been seen for almost seven years. He is one guy we really want to get."

Shane said, "Why don't you grab him right now?"

Tom answered, "We would love to, but if we did we would never find our missing scientists and we wouldn't find out if they had been successful in developing the super strain of mad cow disease. No, as bad as we want him, we can't take the chance that the plot has moved past the development stage. No, we have to play the hand out that we have been dealt. Sorry."

Shane said, "That means that Elizabeth and I are still the bait, right?"

Bob responded, "Sorry, but you are still our best chance of stopping this terrorist plot. You are going to have to go with him and see where he leads us. I didn't tell you his code name in the al-Qaeda, it's Dr. Death. That should give you a warm fuzzy feeling."

Shane said, "I better get my shirt and jacket changed and get back with Elizabeth now. If it's any consolation, I am glad you guys are here looking out for us."

Shane changed his shirt and picked up another suit jacket that kind of matched his pants and bid Tom and Bob goodbye. Armed with this news Shane hurried back to the lobby and to rejoin Elizabeth and Dr. al-Sadr.

Dr. al-Sadr said, "I am so sorry about the waiter spilling the orange juice on you. May I please have another glass brought to you?"

Shane said, "No, that won't be necessary I think one bath in orange juice is enough for the day."

Dr. al-Sadr and Elizabeth laughed.

Shane said, "I am ready to go when ever you are Dr. al-Sadr. How about you Elizabeth are you ready to go or do you need to go back to the room before we leave?"

Elizabeth said, "No, I'm fine I am ready to leave when ever Dr. al-Sadr is ready."

Dr. al-Sadr said, "I am sorry to cause you to be leaving latter than we planned by have orange juice and coffee ordered. I am sure you want to get back to the hotel as soon as you can.

Shane said, "It's not a problem leaving a little bit latter than we planned. But, we would like to get back as soon as we get finished helping you."

Dr. al-Sadr said, "Fine, let's get started."

They got up from the chairs and went out to the front of the hotel. Just as soon as they were out of the hotel a black Chevrolet conversion van pulled up in front of the hotel.

Dr. al-Sadr said, "This is my car and driver. Please Dr. Smith and Dr. Browning, sit in the back seats if that's all right and I will sit up front with the driver."

After he finished saying that the right rear door slid open and Shane helped Elizabeth up into the van and she took the seat just behind the driver. Shane got into the van sitting in the seat that would be directly behind Dr. al-Sadr seat.

As soon as they were all seated in the van the driver pulled away from the front of the hotel and began driving on the road out of the National Park back toward the city.

After traveling a few minutes Elizabeth said, "Shane you don't have your lapel pin on your jacket, did you lose it?"

Shane said, "No, it was on the jacket that took an orange juice bath. It's OK, I am sure it will be all right in our hotel room."

Dr. al-Sadr said, "Is there a problem?

Shane replied, "No, I just forgot to take a lapel pin off of the jacket that I was wearing before the orange juice problem. It's not a big deal."

Both Shane and Elizabeth knew it could be a real big deal.

Dr. al-Sadr asked, "Did you bring your passports with you?"

Elizabeth replied, "Yes, I have them in my purse."

Dr. al-Sadr said, "Good, we will need them when we cross the border. You can give them to me and the driver will take care of the procedures when we get to the border."

Elizabeth took the passports out of her purse and handed them to Dr. al-Sadr.

They continued driving and past the entrance to the airport that they had arrived at yesterday. A few miles past the airport entrance the driver turned onto a different highway and soon came to a border guard station. The border guards just waved them through without stopping. Next they crossed a bridge over the Rio Iguacu. A few minutes latter they came to another border crossing station the driver stopped and handed the border guard their four passports. The driver looked at each of the passports and looked at the four people in the vehicle. He spoke to the driver and asked him in Spanish how long they plan to stay in Argentina. The driver replied that only for the day. The guard handed the passports back to the driver and motioned him to drive on.

Shane said, "Dr. al-Sadr I thought you lived in Paraguay and that's where we were going to look at your cattle problem. Was I mistaking?"

Dr. al-Sadr said, "Yes I do live in Paraguay, but my cattle problem is on a large ranch in Argentina. I am sorry if I didn't make that clear in our telephone conversation. I hope that's not a problem for you."

Shane said, "No, of course it's not a problem I just assumed that when you said you and your country needed my help that you were speaking of Paraguay."

Dr. al-Sadr said, "I am a citizen of Argentina, but have my home and office in Paraguay. My veterinary practice covers a large area in Brazil, Paraguay and Argentina. We don't have very many veterinaries in this part of the world so my practice takes me to three different countries. Some days I think I need an airplane to cover all of this area. My poor driver has to put it some very long hours driving while I sleep, but when I am working he sleeps, so maybe it comes out even.

Dr. al-Sadr gave a hearty laughed and than explained to his driver in Spanish what he had just said in English.

Dr. al-Sadr said to Elizabeth, "Dr. Browning I didn't realize that you were also a veterinary? Do you have a private practice in the United States?"

Elizabeth said, "No, I am in research like my husband, that's how we met. We were both studying mad cow disease and he came to the United Kingdom when we were having so many problems with the disease. The rest is the old story, boy meets girl, and boy and girl fall in love and get married. However, it took us awhile to get married since one was working in England and one in America. We still haven't resolved where we are going to be living and working yet."

Dr. al-Sadr said, "Marriage, always problems when you get married, that's why I never got married."

Elizabeth said, "You mean you never been in love?"

Dr. al-Sadr replied, "Of course I fall in love with every beautiful woman I meet."

Elizabeth said, "Doctor, I not sure that's love, maybe lust!"

Dr. al-Sadr said, "Oh, perhaps you are right."

Dr. al-Sadr, Shane and Elizabeth laughed at his admission.

Another hour past before the driver turned off of the highway onto a dirt road. About fifteen more minutes past before he turned off of the dirt road into a gated entrance to a ranch. He pulled up next to a security call box and pushed a button to speak to someone to open the large iron gates. Shane noticed that these gates and the fence around the area must have been at least twenty feet high with razor wire on top of the fence. In addition Shane saw closed circuit TV cameras were aimed at the driveway and others that continued to move and monitor the fence.

Shane started to make a comment about the security when the gates began slowly opening allowing the driver to enter the ranch. The driver drove the van inside the gates and began traveling down the ranch road. After the van entered the ranch the iron gates began closing and out of nowhere a jeep with two guards appeared. Shane could see they were carrying weapons of some type and portable radios.

Shane said, "Your rancher certainly has a lot of security doesn't he."

Dr. al-Sadr replied, "Well it's pretty dangerous around here. We are a long ways from any police station, so the owner of the ranches in this area has to provide their own security."

Shane said, "I see. What is the biggest danger here?"

Dr. al-Sadr replied, "There are several bandits operating in the area and cattle thieves, I think in America you call them rustlers. It's pretty easy to steal cattle in one country and sell them in another one. You would be surprised how easy it is to get from one country to another. You can bribe border guards for a little amount of money. The border guards don't see any problem taking the money since they are paid so little."

Shane said, "How big is this ranch we are on? It seems really big."

Dr. al-Sadr said, "I don't know for sure, but it is one of the largest ranches in this part of Argentina. Maybe in American measurement terms it's about a hundred thousand acres, perhaps a little more."

Shane said, "That's a big ranch. How many head of cattle do they have?"

Dr. al-Sadr replied, "Only about five thousand head at this time. They are trying to change from a mixed herd to Black Angus. That's why they brought cattle from the United Kingdom."

The van was now approaching the ranch house with it's surrounding out buildings including four very large barns. Shane could see that several of the buildings sitting away from the main ranch house were residence for families and three appeared to be bunk houses that you might have seen on his families Oklahoma ranch.

The main ranch house Shane saw as they got closer to it was a very large two or three story home. The design was a cross between an English Tudor and French Country mansion. It had an eight foot fence around it with a garden full of flowers and trees. It looked completely out of place after seeing the other houses and yards in the area.

Shane said, "Who owns this ranch?"

Dr. al-Sadr said, "It is owned by a Saudi Prince. I don't know his name. I only work for his ranch manager and this foreman."

Shane said, "That explains the style of home I guess. It seems so out of place here."

Dr. al-Sadr replied, "I understand the Prince only comes here maybe two or three times a year and brings a lot of friends. I guess they have lavish parties when the Prince is here."

Shane noticed among the buildings was an airplane hanger with a Gulfstream IV plane sitting outside of the hanger. He could even see a paved runway that from here looked like it was built to accommodate a large jet.

Shane said, "I see the ranch even has a small airport over there."

Dr. al-Sadr replied, "Yes, the Prince can fly here in his personal 747 Boeing Jet, I am told. Some people have too much money and never do anything to earn it or to help anyone."

The driver parked the van near one of the large barns and Dr. al-Sadr asked them to get out. The driver pushed the switches that opened the rear doors of the van and Shane and Elizabeth got out.

Dr. al-Sadr asked them to follow him and he led them into the barn, which turned out to have a rather extensive lab on one side of the barn. Here Dr. al-Sadr went into a large walk in refrigerator and brought out a large pan with a cow's brain in it. He sat the pan down on a lab bench and asked Shane to see if he could tell if this cow died of mad cow disease.

Shane and Elizabeth both examined the cow brain under a microscope and Shane ran an immunohistochemical test of some of the brain tissue this test had been developed at the National Veterinary Services Lab in Ames. said, "No, this brain indicates no damage from mad cow disease."

Dr. al-Sadr asked, "Dr. Browning is that your opinion too?"

Elizabeth said, "There is no doubt in my mind this cow didn't die from mad cow disease."

Dr. al-Sadr went back inside the refrigerator and brought back another pan with a cow brain. He asked Shane and Elizabeth to examine this brain.

Shane said, "They ran the same test of this brain and stated it's not mad cow disease."

Again Dr. al-Sadr went back into the walk in cooler and brought out another pan with another cow's brain in it.

Shane and Elizabeth examined this brain and Shane ran the immunohistochemical test on it and both he and Elizabeth said this cow died of mad cow disease.

Dr. al-Sadr said, "OK let's me take you out to where we have some cows isolated to see if you think they have mad cow disease."

Shane said, "That's a very complete lab to be located on a ranch. I have never seen a ranch that had a lab so well equipped as this one."

Dr. al-Sadr replied, "The ranch manager wanted to have everything we might need to conduct a study of mad cow disease if these cows had it. The Prince doesn't care how much money is spent here. He is only interested in building the finest cattle ranch in South America. The ranch manager authorized me to contact suppliers of lab equipment and have them supply every piece of equipment that might be needed to do research on diseases of cattle."

Shane said, "That's very impressive."

The three of them got into one of the many ranch jeeps that were parked near the barn. Dr. al-Sadr took the wheel and began driving away from the ranch buildings. They continued driving until they came upon a corral build away from the ranch house complex. In side the corral were about twenty or twenty-five cows. Dr. al-Sadr stopped the jeep and the three of them got out and approached the corral.

When they got near the corral the cattle came directly to were they were standing expecting they were about to get feed. Shane climbed over the corral fence and began looking over the herd one cow at a time. After moving one of the cows away from the herd he gave the cow a hard slap on its hip. The cow jump forward and began staggering and

having a hard time walking. Shane did the same thing with another one of the cows with the same results.

Shane climbed back over the corral fence and said, "I am sorry to say but I am pretty sure these cows are infected with mad cow disease. The only way to know for sure would be to kill one of the cows and examine the brain. We might be able to do it with one of the new test that can be used on live cattle. These test called conformation-dependent immunoassay or CDI detect prion proteins. The only problem is it has not been released or approved to be sold yet. The trial of this new test has proven to be prefect, but it's not going to do us any good right now."

Dr. al-Sadr said, "That's too bad, I am sorry that we can't use this new test. Let's go over to another herd of cattle that we have in a corral in another location."

The three of them got back into the jeep and after traveling for a few minutes they came to another corral with about the same number of cows in it as the first corral that they visited.

Shane did the same type of examination on several cows in this corral and found that none of these cows had problems walking when Shane gave them a slap on the rump.

Shane said, "I would be pretty sure that these cows are all right and don't have any symptom of mad cow disease."

Dr. al-Sadr said, "Good, let's go back to the ranch house."

They drove back to the ranch house and on their arrival they found that the jeep with the security guards that had met them at the front gate was parked in front of the main ranch house. The two security guards were talking to an older man and he was pointing to something in the area of one of the long bunk houses.

Dr. al-Sadr said, "Good I want you to meet the ranch manager I see him talking to those security guards."

Dr. al-Sadr drove the jeep up next to the security guards jeep and he got out of the jeep and walked over to talk to the ranch manager. They were far enough away that Shane and Elizabeth could not overhear their conversation.

Dr. al-Sadr and the ranch manager came over to where Shane and Elizabeth were waiting in the jeep. Shane and Elizabeth got out of the jeep when the two men approached them.

Dr. al-Sadr said, "Dr. Shane Smith and Dr. Elizabeth Browning I would like to present to you Fahad al-Saud the manager of the El Arriba Ranch. Fahad, this is Dr. Shane Smith and his lovely wife Dr. Elizabeth Browning."

The three of them shook hands and expressed that they were glad to meet one another. When suddenly another jeep drove up very fast and parked just next to where they were standing. The jeep had three men in it. The driver was dressed in khakis and was carrying a pistol in a holster on his belt. The other two men with him had automatic weapons of some type. The driver got out of the jeep and came up to where the four of them were.

Fahd al-Saud said, "Dr. Smith and Dr. Browning, I would like to introduce you to my ranch foreman, this is Ahmed Bin Aziz. Ahmed, this is Dr. Shane Smith and his wife Dr. Elizabeth Browning. They have been here today helping Dr. al-Sadr check on the cattle for mad cow disease."

Shane and Elizabeth shook hands with Ahmed.

Ahmed said, "Well doctors what do you think, do we have a problem with mad cow disease or not?"

Shane said, "I believe you do with the cows we saw in the first corral that Dr. al-Sadr took us to, but I think in the second corral those cattle are all right."

Dr. al-Sadr said, "Dr. Smith, I am afraid that you and Dr. Browning are going to have to stay with us and help us with a project that we are working on."

Shane said, "I am sorry Dr. al-Sadr, but Elizabeth and I have to go back to the United States in a few days to be back to work on our own project. I am sure we would like to help you but we need to return to our own work. Sorry."

Dr. al-Sadr said, "I don't think you understand. We are not asking you to stay we are telling you that you are staying. The choice of how you stay is up to you. You can either be our guest or you can be our prisoners."

Shane said, "I don't understand. You could hire a lot of research veterinarians to help you work on finding a cure for mad cow disease with the lab you have and unlimited funds."

Dr. al-Sadr said, "No, you don't understand. We don't want to find a cure for mad cow disease we want to find a way to make it develop faster in cattle and in humans."

Shane said, "Why in the world would you want to do that for?"

Dr. al-Sadr replied, "Because we want to kill as many infidels as possible and destroy their way of life, that's why."

Shane said, "You must be crazy that will never work. You could never infect that many cattle in America."

Dr. al-Sadr said, "We already have in place the way to do that we just need you to develop a faster acting disease."

Shane said, "There is no way I am going to be a party to such a plan. I would rather die right now."

Dr. al-Sadr said, "Of course that could be arranged, but it would not be quite that easy. First, you could watch my men rape and torture your beautiful young wife for days on end until she begs them to kill her. I have seen that happen before and I don't think you would get much pleasure from watching. No, Dr. Smith, you will join our little group of scientists and help them do what they have so far failed to do. If you ask really nice we will let Dr. Browning work with you in the lab or she can stay with the other women and children and you can see her once a week like the other men get to see their families."

"What do you think now doctor, do you still want to die or do you want to help?"

Shane said, "I don't want to help, but I guess I don't have any choice do I?"

Dr. al-Sadr replied, "No, not really. I gave you your choices earlier. Are you our guests or are you prisoners?"

Shane said, "Of course we are your guests."

Dr. al-Sadr said, "Good choice. Ahmed, please show our guests to their quarters."

Ahmed took Elizabeth by her arm and led her to his jeep and helped her get in. He told Shane he would be back for him in a few minutes. But before Ahmed could get in the jeep.

Shane said, "I thought we were going to be you guests. So where are you taking my wife?"

Dr. al-Sadr said, "Ahmed, Dr. Smith is right. Since she will be working with the others she and Dr. Smith can stay in the small house next to the men's bunk house."

Ahmed said, "All right. Dr. Smith get in the jeep with us."

Ahmed told one of the security guards to get out of the jeep so there was room for Shane to sit.

Ahmed drove Shane and Elizabeth to a small house located next to one of the long bunk houses and told them to get out of the jeep and go into the house and stay there. He told them they were not allowed to leave the house without him or one of his men with them. He also told them as you can see as he pointed to the security cameras located to observe the front and back doors of the house we have someone watching you every minute of the day and night.

Ahmed said, "Dinner will be brought to you about seven pm. You are not to speak to the servants that brings your meals. Your meals will be served everyday at the same time, breakfast at seven-thirty; lunch one-thirty and dinner at seven. You will be in your house at these times. No excuses, otherwise no meals for two days. Do you understand?"

Shane and Elizabeth nodded their heads yes, they understood.

Shane opened the door and Elizabeth went inside followed by Shane. The small house was furnished very nicely. It had a sitting room, dinning area combination, a small bedroom with a double bed and a bathroom off of the bedroom. The house didn't have a kitchen, but in the dinning area it had a refrigerator and a small microwave oven.

Elizabeth spoke first, "Well I think we found our missing scientists and I hope that Tom and Bob can find us."

CHAPTER EIGHT

Tom and Bob left the hotel after getting a radio message that Dr. al-Sadr car had left the hotel parking lot. They took care not to be seen as they went to their car. After they got into the car they waited to start the car's engine until they received a call that Dr. al-Sadr's car was approaching the entrance to the National Park.

Tom and Bob had spent hours working with their team of CIA and MI-5 Agents assigned to help with the surveillance and tracking of Shane and Elizabeth after they were to be picked up by Dr. al-Sadr. They had gone over all of the possible routes up to crossing the bridge into Paraguay. They had agents at the entrance to the airport and at the interchange of Estrada Das Cataratas and highway BR277 watching for Dr. al-Sadr's car to pass. At each check point the agents were to report back to Tom when Dr. al- Sadr car passed them.

After Dr. al-Sadr's car passed immigrations and customs in Paraguay they had several cars waiting to follow Dr. al- Sadr's car. Tom had assigned other agents in cars waiting along several different routes that lead into Cidade Del Este. Tom didn't know were Dr. al-Sadr might be taking Shane and Elizabeth, but he and Bob had spent many hours checking on potential routes that might be used leaving Cidade Del Este.

Tom received a radio signal from his agent at the entrance to the airport that Dr. al-Sadr's car had just past him. So far so good, Tom was concerned that his agent at the intersection of Estrada Das Cataratas and BR 277 didn't have a good parking place that let him observe the intersection. However, the next agent waiting in Paraguay, just passed the immigrations and customs station would not have a problem spotting Dr. al-Sadr's car since he was parked just outside of the station with a clear view of all vehicles that stop at the station.

Just in case Dr. al-Sadr didn't go to Paraguay, but stayed in Brazil Tom had agents assigned on the highways leading to Itaipu and the road to Curitiba.

Tom and Bob had past the Park entrance and were now approaching the entrance to the airport when his agent at the intersection of Estrada Das Cataratas and BR 277 called Tom on the radio. The agent told Tom that there had just been an accident at the intersection and traffic was beginning to back up in all four directions. Tom said that they would watch for the traffic and try not to get to close to Dr. al-Sadr's car.

Tom asked, the agent if Dr. al-Sadr's car had past through the intersection before the accident. The agent told Tom that he had not seen Dr. al-Sadr's car pass by. The agent than told Tom that it looked like a large truck hit a bus and that several people seemed to be injured. He also told Tom that the police had just arrived. Next report from the agent told Tom that the police were trying to get traffic moving again around the accident, but now ambulances were arriving at the scene of the accident.

The agent called again and told Tom that the police had slowly began moving vehicles around the accident. What a mess the traffic was in. The drivers had no patience and were blowing their horns and screaming at the police. Now the police beginning screaming back at the drivers.

Tom said, "Bob, I think somehow we got transported to Italy, maybe Rome. I have only seen this kind of thing at an accident once before and that was in Rome. A taxi hit two young people on a motor scooter and their dead bodies were lying on the street and the people just wanted to drive around them and I think some of the drivers were willing to drive over their dead bodies, so they could get where ever they were going. It was disgusting watching the drivers and the police yelling at each other and these two poor young people lying there dead in the middle of the intersection. You know Bob sometimes people just hack me off."

Bob replied, "I think that would do it for me."

The agent from the intersection radioed Tom again and said that it looks like the people in the bus were not hurt as bad as everyone one thought and the police had cleared the intersection and were moving the traffic smoothly now. The agent said there was still no sign of Dr. al-Sadr's car.

Tom and Bob's car cleared the intersection and Tom radioed the agent at the immigration and custom station in Paraguay and asked him if he had made visual contact with Dr. al-Sadr's car. The agent replied that he had not seen the car yet. A few more minutes passed and Tom and Bob's car was approaching the immigration and custom station. A few minutes more and they cleared the station. They stopped the car and spoke with the agents at the station. They said that there was no way that Dr. al-Sadr's car could have passed them without them seeing the car.

Tom got on the radio an advised all of the agents to stay in their current positions. Next, he contacted the agents that were watching the roads to Itaipu and Curitiba. They both responded that Dr. al-Sadr's car had not passed them. Tom again contacted all agents to remain in their positions and keep watching for Dr. al-Sadr's vehicle. Tom told the agents that Bob and he would backtrack to see were Dr. al-Sadr's

car might have turned off while they were waiting for the accident to clear. Tom told Bob since these people know this area maybe they thought they could go around the accident and when the traffic got moving again, they couldn't get back on the road to Paraguay.

Tom was getting worried that somehow one of the agents missed seeing the car or they switched cars somewhere and we didn't see them make the switch. Tom told Bob I just can't believe that we lost them or that somehow they had time to switch cars where we couldn't see them.

Tom said, "Bob, something has gone terribly wrong! We've lost them and it's going to be hell to pay if we can't find them."

Bob said, "We'll find them. I am sure they couldn't have gotten very far since we watch them leave the hotel."

Tom said, "I think we better contacted the military and asked them to track Shane's personal ID."

Bob said, "I am sorry that we have to do that, but I think we better do it sooner than later."

Tom called CIA Headquarters in Langley and requested that they contact military tracking and get a fix on Dr. Shane Smith's location from his personal ID. They would call him back with the information in a few minutes. Tom told them we may need them to continue providing us updates on his location on a real time basis until we can pinpoint his exact location.

Minutes past and Tom received a call from Langley they were getting a direct feed on Dr. Smith's personal ID. It was stationary at a GPS location, that Tom had Bob write down so they could check the GPS concordances to know exactly where Shane was. They checked the concordances and found that he was at the Hotel Das Cataratas Brasil.

Something must have caused them to return to the hotel. Maybe Elizabeth or Shane had become ill and they had to return to their hotel room. Tom drove as fast as he could back to the hotel. They looked around and found a side door that they could get into the hotel without going through the main lobby and to Shane's room.

Tom knocked on the door. No answer. Tom took a pass key from his coat pocket and opened the door. No one was there. Tom and Bob looked around the room and Bob said, "Shane's suite coat is here that the orange juice was spilled on this morning. You don't think his lapel ID is still on that jacket do you."

As he picked up the coat and found that it was!

Tom said, "Oh my God, we're screwed. We thought we were being so clever having the orange juice spilled on Shane to get him back to his room and now he doesn't have his personal ID that we need to find him. Not only have we not been able to keep track of Dr. al-Sadr's car, we've lost Shane and Elizabeth's tracking device."

Bob replied, "Langley, we've got a problem!"

Tom said, "No, we've got the problem. The question is how do we solve the problem? The first thing we need to do is to bring all of the agents in here to the hotel except we will leave one car at the border of

Paraguay to make sure that in the next few hours Dr. al-Sadr doesn't show up at the immigration and customs station.

Tom radioed all of the agents to return to the hotel except the prime agent that was assigned to the border.

Tom made arrangements for a meeting room in the hotel so that he could address all of the agents at one time and see if anyone could come up with any ideas that might be helpful in locating Shane and Elizabeth. Tom figured if they could locate them they would also find their other missing scientists.

It took over an hour to assemble all of the agents in the small conference room. Before they began the meeting Tom had the room swept for any electronic bugging devices. Next he posted guards at the two doors that you could enter into the conference room and told these two agents that they were not to allow anyone in the room during the meeting. Also, they were told that their partners would fill them in on the meeting after it had concluded.

Tom began the meeting by saying, "Fellow agents, we have a major problem. We not only didn't spotted Dr. al- Sadr's car after it passed the airport check point we caused Dr. Shane Smith to not have his personal ID tracking device on his person. We caused this by having orange juice spilled on his sports jacket this morning so he would return to his room so we could tell him who Dr. al-Sadr was and to let him know that we were here looking after him and Dr. Elizabeth Browning."

"Tonight if he knows had badly we have blown looking out for them, he should be shaking in his cowboy boots. We have got to find them and we have got to find them fast. I hate to have to tell Langley and White Hall that we set a trap for al-Qaeda and they took the bait; hook, line and sinker and vanished in thin air. Let's go through what we know and try to find out where we went wrong."

"We know that Dr. al-Sadr was in this hotel this morning and picked up Drs. Smith and Browning. We know the make and model of the car they were in and we know the vehicle's license plate number. We know they left the National Park and they past by our check point at the airport, than they never made it to the next check point at Estrada Das Cataratas and highway BR277. Somewhere between these two points our vehicle and our people disappeared. So where did they go? Does anyone have any idea I know some of you agents are familiar with this area, what's your guess?"

"Mr. Parker I am MI-5 Agent, Walter Rodgers. I think our people turned and went to Argentina and crossed over from Brazil at the Ponte Internacional Tancredo Neves, that's the only thing that makes sense. It's pretty easy to cross into Argentina without a visa by telling the border guards that you are going over the border for a day. They don't keep track of anybody that does that."

Tom said, "Why didn't we have someone at the intersection leading off of Estrada Das Cataratas toward that border crossing?"

Bob Barker replied, "We were concentrating on all of the roads going to Paraguay, because that's were Dr. al-Sadr said they were going and the vehicle they were driving had license plates from Paraguay."

Tom said, "Folks we have been taken in by what an al-Qaeda operator told our people and the sad part is we believed what we were told and we screwed up badly. Now what do we do to find our people in Argentina?"

Walter Rodgers said, "I think we need to contact some of the local people in the area and see what we can find out about anything strange that has been going on in the area or if they have seen a number of foreigners in the area. We know that there are a number of large ranches in the area and it makes sense that our people must be on one of them. If you are going to have cows, you're going to need some kind of a farm or ranch to keep them in."

Tom said, "Walter, I think you are right. The first thing in the morning we will all go to the area of Cidade Puerto Iguazu and begin canvassing the area and see what we can find out. Folks let's hope and pray that we can find our people really fast. Bob and I will put together a schedule tonight and get a copy made for each of you so we don't miss any areas or another road like we did today. Walter Rodgers would you please meet with Bob and I after the meeting to help us put together the schedule. Good hunting tomorrow, we got to find our good doctors soon."

Just as the meeting was finishing Tom got a call on the radio from the agents at the border in Paraguay who told Tom that the car they had been looking for just past through the border crossing, but there were only two people in the car. He said he tried to follow the car but lost them before they got into Cidade Del Este. He couldn't decide if they turn off of the road or what happened to them after the road made a turn and when he got around the curve the car was gone. He backtracked, but couldn't find them in the dark.

Tom thanked him for the information. They now knew for sure that Dr. al-Sadr didn't take Shane and Elizabeth to Paraguay. They must be either in Argentina or still somewhere in Brazil.

After talking over the report from the agents at the border of Paraguay and Brazil with Bob, Tom decided to get them back on the radio and tell them to set up twenty-four hour surveillance at the immigration's station. They had to find Dr. al-Sadr's car to be able to follow it and be able to find Shane and Elizabeth.

Tom than contacted two other teams of agents and assigned one team at the intersection of Estrada Das Cataratas and Highway BR277. The second team was assigned to the immigration station in Argentina. Both teams were to be on surveillance twenty-four hours a day watching for Dr. al-Sadr's vehicle.

Next, Tom and Bob decided to establish a command center in the Hotel Das Cataratas Brasil. All agents were advised of the command center now being in operation twenty-four hours a day. Tom assigned Walter Rodgers to work in the command center with him and Bob.

Tom knew that Dr. al-Sadr or his car had to show up again in order for them to find Shane and Elizabeth.

Shane and Elizabeth woke up early on Monday morning and tried to visualize just what had happened to them. Here they were captives when their job was to find the missing scientists and stop the terrorist plot to introduce mad cow disease into America. They wondered if Tom and Bob would be able to find them and if the other missing scientists were in the same place that they were.

About an hour after their breakfast was delivered someone knocked on the door of their small house. Shane opened the door and Ahmed Bin Aziz was standing there.

He said, "Good morning Dr. Smith are you and Dr. Browning ready to go to work?"

Shane replied, "I guess we are."

Ahmed said, "Good we will go over to the lab now and I will introduce you to your associates."

Shane and Elizabeth followed Ahmed as he walked over to the large barn they were in yesterday. As they entered the lab three men looked up as they came into the lab.

Ahmed said, "Gentlemen, I would like to introduce you to your new colleagues. This in Dr. Shane Smith from Iowa State University; and his wife Dr. Elizabeth Browning of Browning Laboratories from the United Kingdom."

Ahmed continued, "Here we have Dr. Anthony Hinson from the United Kingdom; this is Dr. David Allen, United Kingdom and Dr. Charles Van Meter with the University of Illinois. Drs. Smith and Browning are here to help expedite the research on a fast acting mad cow disease. As you know the sooner you get this job done the sooner you can go home."

The three scientists left their work stations and shook hands with Shane and Elizabeth. Shane knew Dr. Van Meter and Elizabeth had met both Dr. Hinson and Dr. Allen.

Ahmed said, "I will leave you to your work and we hope you begin to make some progress. Your work so far has been less than satisfactory."

Shane said, "We have been told what you are working on by Dr. al-Sadr. What kind of progress have you made on the project?"

Dr. David Allen replied, "None, we don't think what they are asking us to do can be done. At least not in the short time frame they want us to do it in."

Shane asked, "How did you come to be here to working on this project?"

Dr. Anthony Hinson answered, "We got suckered in by being invited to speak at a conference in Rio. When we arrived in Rio we were told the conference had been cancelled. However, since we were the guests of the sponsors we were invited to spend a few days in Rio and than were invited to visit the laboratories of Adeaq-la in Cidade Del Este in Paraguay, but enroute we would be stopping off to see the Cataratas Do Iguacu. We were having a wonderful time until we left the falls to go to Paraguay. The next thing we knew we were being told to get off of our bus and we were here."

Shane asked, "Just the three of you?"

Dr. Charles Van Meter replied, "No Shane, we have our wives and children with us."

Dr. Allen added, "There was another veterinary from the Netherlands, Dr. Arden Borland was with us, but him and his wife were killed the first day we arrived here."

Shane asked, "How did that happen?"

Dr. Allen replied, "Dr. Borland told Dr. al-Sadr that he would not work on a project that could kill thousands of people. Dr. al-Sadr said what if I told you that if you don't work on the project than I will shoot your wife. Dr. Borland told him no, not even if you threaten to shoot my wife. Dr. al-Sadr just as cool and calm as someone buying an ice cream cone took out a pistol walked over to where Mrs. Borland was standing put the gun to her head and pulled the trigger. Dr. Borland ran over to her and when he leaned over to hold his wife, Dr. al-Sadr shot him in the back of the head."

Dr. Hinson said, "It was horrible. This happened the first hour we were here. Dr. al-Sadr shot and killed both of them in front of our wife's and children. Our kids are still having nightmares and our wives are not much better."

Dr. Allen said, "After he shot them he turned to the rest of us and politely asked if there was anyone else that felt like they couldn't work on the project."

Dr. Van Meter asked, "Shane, how did you and Dr. Browning get here?"

Shane said, "Elizabeth and I were on our honeymoon in Rio when I got a telephone call from Dr. al-Sadr asking me if I could look at some cattle that he though might have mad cow disease. First, I told him no because we were leaving in a couple of days to visit the waterfalls before we went back to America. When I told him that he said that his office was near the falls and that it would mean a great deal to him and his country if I could confirm if these cows had the disease. Next thing Elizabeth and I knew, we were here."

Shane than said, "The real question is how, do we get out of here?

Dr. Hinson said, "That's not very likely with the way they have this place guarded and all the close circuit television cameras watching everything and everybody."

Dr. Van Meter said, "We've tried to find some way that we could escape, but we got a lot of people to try to get out of here. Now with the two of you we have seventeen people to get out, that's not going to be easy!"

Shane asked, "If you haven't made any progress in developing a fast acting version of mad cow disease, where did the cattle come from that's infected with the disease?"

Dr. Allen replied, "Somehow they smuggled them out of England and into Argentina."

Elizabeth said, "I can't image where they found any cattle in the UK that were still living that had mad cow disease. As far as I know all of the infected cattle had been destroyed along with any cows that might have the disease. I guess that's not important right now. Where they got them and how doesn't matter much. Somehow they did, and by using them they have the means to infect a lot more cattle."

Shane said, "Tell us what you have tried to do to so far to develop a fast acting mad cow disease?

Dr. Allen replied, "We have not accomplished much of anything. All of our past research experience on mad cow disease has concentrated on finding ways to cure the disease or prevent it. None of us have any idea on how to accelerate the effect of the disease to kill cattle faster and infect all of the cuts of meat that people eat. Do you have any ideas on what we might do to do such a thing?"

Shane replied, "No, I don't have a clue on how to make the disease progress faster in cattle. I think the bigger question is how long do you think Dr. al-Sadr will let us work on this project before he starts killing us or members of your family?

Dr. Van Meter said, "I don't think he has a lot of patience and he won't hesitate to kill. He has already shown us that he has no problem killing people."

Shane asked, "Do you know if he stays here all of the time?"

Dr. Hinson replied, "No, we've seen him leave when we were being taken back to our quarters and sometimes he has been gone for a day or two at a time. At least if he was here he never came into the lab."

Shane than asked, "Do you think the other guards and the ranch manager Fahad al-Saud or the foreman Ahmed Bin Aziz would be as quick to kill as Dr. al-Sadr?"

Dr. Allen answered, "No, I don't think they would, but I would sure hate to guarantee it. I'm not sure that I would want to chance my life and the lives of my wife and kids on it."

Dr. Hinson said, "Me either. I don't think they are as likely to just shoot people like Dr. al-Sadr did, but if we were trying to escape I think they would shoot us just as I am sure that all of the guards would."

"How about you Dr. Van Meter, what do you think?" Shane asked.

"I agree with the others." Dr. Van Meter replied.

Shane said, "If that's everyone's opinion than I guess we better try to figure out something we can do to look like we are trying to do something. What if we tried mixing Arsenic trioxide in with prion PrPsc taken from the diseased cattle? Even if it didn't accelerate BSE, if we increased the Arsenic trioxide to a high enough level we could certainly cause some of the test cows to die and maybe we can stall our friends until we can find a way to escape or that somebody finds us."

Elizabeth said, "Well it's at least an idea, which is better than no idea at all. What do the rest of you think?"

The three other scientists agreed and they would request Ahmed to get them one hundred pounds of Arsenic trioxide. This should at least buy them sometime.

Shane said, "I glad everyone agrees with that idea, but Dr. al-Sadr is no dummy. I think we need to add several other drugs to our list of products that we need to try to accelerate BSE. Let's see what other drugs could we ask for? How about atropine; chloral hydrate; paraldehyde; sulfonamides; chlordane and corticosteroids, we'll ask for twenty-five pounds of each one of them. These are all liquids, but I want to ask for them in pounds to make it harder for them to find. I think knowing where we are will make it hard for them to find these chemicals right away and give us sometime to work on escaping.

Dr. Allen said, "That's a great idea. This way it will at least look like we are trying to do something to make an accelerant for BSE. Great idea, the only problem I have is I don't see that anyone will be looking for us and I can't see anyway we can escape.

Shane responded, "Let's take care of one problem at a time. First, we got to look like we are working on experiments to make a super fast acting mad cow disease. Next, I think someone will be trying to find Elizabeth and me when we don't return from our honeymoon next week. People knew that we were going to Foz Do Iguacu before coming home and last, but not least we have to try to find someway to escape.

Just as Shane finished speaking Fahd al-Saud came into the lab and said, "Well Dr. Smith I see you and Dr. Browning have met your new colleagues. How are you getting along on the project?"

Shane replied, "We have been discussing the approach we need to try to accelerate mad cow disease and have come up with some chemicals we need to experiment with to see if we can make the disease work faster. Everyone knows what causes the disease. We need to find a way to make it work faster, as I understand from what Dr. al-Sadr told us yesterday."

Fahd al-Saud said, "That sounds like we are finally beginning to get someone to pay attention to what we have been telling the other doctors since they got here. Give me the list of supplies that you want and I will make arrangements for them."

Elizabeth said, "I will write down a list of the chemicals that we want to try and have it for you this afternoon. We think we have an idea of some of them, but we should spend a little more time developing our list."

Fahd said, "Fine, I will be back late this afternoon to get your list."

After Fahd left the lab Elizabeth said, "I think we should add Cystoxic; Tetracycline; Meprobamate and Solu Medro.

Shane and the others agreed that they should add these to their list of products they wanted to have to test to see if they could accelerate the on-set of mad cow disease.

Dr. Allen said, "It is time for us to go to lunch and when we return we can write the list of products that we need."

Shane asked, "Why don't we write up the list now and go to lunch a little bit latter."

Dr. Van Meter replied, "No, we have to go now or otherwise we risk not get food for us and our families for two days."

Shane said, "You mean Ahmed was serious about being in our house for our lunch at one thirty or they would not feed us for two days?"

Dr. Allen said, "You can believe whatever they tell you, they are serious. We can't afford to let our families go without food for a couple of days."

Shane said, "OK, I understand."

After lunch Shane and Elizabeth were the first ones back in the lab and Elizabeth began writing the list of supplies they wanted. She listed them:

1. Atropine 25 lbs
2. Chloral Hydrate 25lbs
3. Paraldehyde 25lbs
4. Sulfonamides 25lbs
5. Chlordane 25lbs
6. Corticosteroids 25lbs
7. Cystoxic 25lbs
8. Tetracycline 25lbs
9. Meprobamate 25lbs
10. Solu Medro 25lbs
11. Arsenic Trioxide 100lbs

Just as Elizabeth finished her list of items the three other veterinaries came back into the lab. They spent the rest of the afternoon discussing how they might blend the various chemicals into food pellets and how much of each of the chemicals they should use.

Shane asked, "Where are you families?"

Dr. Van Meter said, "They are housed in one large barracks on the other side of the airstrip. It is about a mile from here. We get to see our families on Sundays at a soccer field next to the airstrip."

Shane asked, "How long do you get to see them?"

Dr. Van Meter replied, "Not long enough. Probably about a couple of hours that's all."

Shane said, "How many guards are watching over you during those two hours?"

Dr. Van Meter replied, "Not more than two. The rest of them are still recovering from Saturday night in town."

Shane said, "You mean that most of them go into town on Saturday night. That should be our time to escape."

Dr. Van Meter replied, "You would think that, but they have at least a few of them watching the barracks using the TV monitors."

Shane said, "That doesn't sound like a good chance for us to escape after all. Maybe Sunday would be better. Do the kids have a soccer ball?"

Dr. Van Meter replied, "Yes, the guards gave them a soccer ball when we got here."

"Do we have a chance of overpowering the two guards and making our way to the airstrip before other guards could reach us?" Shane asked.

"It might be possible. They don't have TV monitors watching the soccer field, but what do we do after we get to the airstrip?" Dr. Van Meter replied.

"I guess that depends on if that airplane that I saw sitting out in front of the hanger is there all of the time?" Shane responded.

Dr. Hinson said, "The only time that I ever saw that plane gone was about two weeks ago when Dr. al-Sadr flew it somewhere. I don't know if he was actually the pilot or not, but I know he took the plane and was gone for two days."

Shane said, "What I am thinking is that we all have a soccer game and work the ball near the guards if they are both close together. We grab them and tie them up using our belts if we can't come up with rope or something else and gag them with something and get to the airplane. You counted seventeen of us, how many are children?"

Dr. Allen said, "Nine total."

Shane said, "How old is the oldest ones?"

Dr. Allen answered, "Twelve, I have a son that's twelve and Dr. Van Meter has a daughter that's twelve."

Shane explained, "Good, than we should be able to get everyone in that plane and I can fly it. The plane is a Gulfstream IV and my family has one that I learn to fly and I have the rating to fly it."

Dr. Allen said, "Now I know what we can do if we can make it to the plane, but what if the plane doesn't have the keys in it?"

Shane replied, "Than we got a big problem, but with the plane parked on a private airstrip I doubt that they take the keys out of it."

They began talking about how they could kick the soccer ball to the guards and than rush to get the ball and grab the guards. They began to have hope that they might have a plan to get them out of here.

Fahd opened the lab door and came inside. He asked if they had completed the list of materials that they wanted. Elizabeth handed him the list they had prepared. Fahd told them that it might take a few days to find everything on their list but he would get started on it tonight.

Elizabeth said, "Shane and I need our clothes that's in the hotel in Brazil and I need my medicine from our room as well."

Fahd said, "I will see if we can make arrangements to get your things from your hotel room. Do you have the key for the room?"

Elizabeth replied, "Yes, I have one in my purse."

She opened her purse that was sitting on the lab bench and handed Fahd her room key.

CHAPTER NINE

Tom Parker's two way radio broke the silence in the command center it was the agents from the Paraguay border, check point one calling. The agent said, "Tom, Dr. al-Sadr vehicle has just passed through the custom and immigration check point heading to Brazil."

Tom asked, "How many people are in the car?"

His agent replied, "The driver and Dr. al-Sadr. He was stopped close enough to us for me to be able to identify him from the pictures we have of him."

Tom said, "Whew, that's great news."

Tom than called the agents at the intersection of Estrada Das Cataratas and BR277, check point two and asked them if they heard the radio transmission from check point one."

The agent at check point two confirmed that they were ready to follow Dr. al-Sadr's vehicle if his vehicle continued on Highway BR277 into Brazil.

Tom asked Bob to contact a couple of agents to get to the intersection of Estrada Das Cataratas and Ponte Internacional Tancredo Neves. Bob assured Tom that two agents were enroute to that location.

Bob said, "We will make that check point three and check point four will be the intersection of Estrada Das Cataratas and the airport and check point five will be the border of Argentina and Brazil."

The next radio call to Tom was from check point two they confirmed that Dr. al-Sadr's vehicle turned right on Estrada Das Cataratas.

Tom said to Bob, "I hope our agents get to check point three in time."

Bob said, "Call them and see where they are at."

Tom transmitted on the radio, "Check point three where are you?"

Check point three replied, "We are in position and Dr. al-Sadr vehicle just passed the intersection and was continuing on Estrada Das Cataratas toward the airport."

Tom asked, "Check point four have you see Dr. al- Sadr's vehicle yet."

Check point four replied, "He just passed the airport intersection and is continuing on Estrada Das Cataratas heading toward the National Park."

Tom replied, "Roger your transmission check point four. All agents remain in your positions."

Tom said, "What do you think is going on that Dr. al- Sadr is coming back to the hotel?"

Bob said, "I don't know, I guess we will have to wait and find out what he is up to."

Tom replied, "We don't have much of a choice do we. I will say one thing for him he doesn't think he is in much danger around here coming back to this hotel does he?"

Bob replied, "No, I don't think he has any concern at all."

Tom and Bob left Walter Rodgers in charge of the command center and went to the lobby to have coffee and watch to see if Dr. al-Sadr came into the hotel. They took seats near the back of the lobby and ordered coffee and began watching for the good doctor.

They didn't have to wait long as Dr. al-Sadr boldly walked into the hotel lobby and asked a bellman to go with him to pick up some luggage for his friends from their room.

Tom and Bob watched as Dr. al-Sadr handed the bellman a room key and followed him to Shane and Elizabeth's room. The bellman unlocked the door and the two men entered the room. The bellman left the door opened.

Tom asked Bob, "Take a walk back to their room and pretend to pick up some papers or something to see what they were doing in the room and ask Walter Rodgers to try to get a tracking device on the doctor's vehicle if possible."

Bob walked past the room and he could see that the bellman was packing up all of Shane and Elizabeth's things. He saw the bellman pack the jacket that had Shane's personal ID lapel pin on it. Bob went back to the couch where Tom was setting having his coffee and told him what he saw.

Tom said, "I can't believe how brazen that son of a bitch is can you? He's one of the most wanted terrorist in the world and walks into this hotel like he owns the place. Maybe that's what it takes to get away with all of the things he has done over the past twenty years or so."

About twenty minutes past and several cups of coffee downed before Dr. al-Sadr and the bellman came with a two wheel cart loaded with Shane and Elizabeth's things.

The bellman went out to the front of the hotel and Dr. al-Sadr's driver pulled the vehicle up and got out and began loading the luggage into the back of the vehicle. As they were loading the luggage into the back of the vehicle. Walter Rodgers past the front of the vehicle and placed a tracking device between the slots of the grill onto the radiator.

In the meantime Dr. al-Sadr stopped at the front desk and returned the room key and checked Shane and Elizabeth out of the hotel. He asked if there was any outstanding charges and was told that they had a few meals but the desk clerk would just charge them to their credit card.

Dr. al-Sadr walked to the front of the hotel just as the driver and bellman finished loading the luggage in the vehicle. Dr. al-Sadr gave the bellman a large tip got into his vehicle and the driver started the engine and drove off.

Tom and Bob immediately left the lobby and went back to their command center and alerted their field agents that the doctor was in his vehicle and on the move. Walter Rodgers returned to the command center and reported that he got the tracking device attached to the radiator of the doctor's vehicle. Tom than notified all of the agents via the radio that a tracking device had been placed on the doctor's vehicle and it only had about a two mile range.

Tom said, "Good work that should help us keep track of our elusive doctor. Too bad it only has a range of a couple of miles."

A few minutes past and check point four reported that the vehicle passed their position. Next check point three said that the doctor's vehicle had turned left and was headed toward check point five in Argentina.

Check point five said that there was a big line up of vehicles crossing into Argentina at this time and it might be a while before the doctor's vehicle made it to their position.

Tom told them to proceed to Highway NAC 12 and wait for them and try to follow the doctor's vehicle from a safe distant. Don't lose them, but don't let them know you are following them try to use the tracking device to help follow them.

Check point five replied, "We will do our best to keep them in sight without them knowing that we are following them."

Tom said, "Do your best and if you do you'll know that angels can do no more."

Bob said, "Tom I didn't know you were a philosopher."

Tom replied, "Just one of my many hidden talents."

Bob said, "I hope one of those talents is getting back our bait when we reel in the big fish."

Tom responded, "So do I. I would hate to have to go back to Iowa State and tell Dr. Price and Dr. Browning we lost Shane and Elizabeth because we used them as bait to find the missing scientists. That my friend would not be a good day! Never mind what Secretary Ridge would say and what he would put in our personnel files."

Bob replied, "No, let's not think about that."

Just as Bob finished his statement the radio in the command center barked, "This is check point five and the doctor's vehicle has just past us. We are now pursuing the vehicle. They are traveling at a fairly high rate of speed, but we have them in sight. We have them on our tracking device receiver as well."

Tom replied, "Don't get to close the doctor has not avoided capture for twenty years because he's careless or stupid."

"Roger, we are backing off and using the tracking device to follow them." Responded check point five agents.

After almost an hour past when they heard. "Tom this is check point five. The doctor's vehicle has just turned right off of NAC 12."

Tom asked, "Check point five what kind of road is it?"

"It's a dirt road, seems to be a well used road, it's in pretty good condition." Check point five answered.

After another fifteen minutes had past they heard, "Tom the doctor's vehicle has stopped, it just made a right turn off of the dirt road. Now it's moving again." Check point five reported.

Tom said, "Check point five, proceed with caution, but try to get a visual on that vehicle."

"Roger that." Check point five responded.

Check point five called again, "We can't see the vehicle, but we can see why it was stopped when they turned off of the road. They have turned into an entrance to a ranch and it has a very tall security gate at the entrance. We are just driving past it now and the doctor's vehicle has now stopped traveling. We will drive on by and continue down this road for awhile."

"Good job check point five. Get pictures of the ranch entrance when you come back by it." Tom said.

Check point five agents called again after about thirty minutes and said, "Tom this fence along the road and at the entrance to the ranch must be almost twenty feet high and has razor wire on the top of it along with TV security cameras along the whole length of the fence. We got the pictures and a GPS reading on the ranch entrance. We also got a picture of a jeep with a couple of heavily armed guards patrolling the fence line. From the looks of the tracks along the fence line it looks like the fence is heavily patrolled all of the time."

Tom replied, "Try to find someplace that you can park that you can watch the ranch entrance without being seen and we will have someone come pick up the pictures."

Check point five agents said, "No need to have someone do that, we will send them to you using our computer's wireless internet connection and along with the GPS concordance so you can find out who owns this ranch."

Tom replied, "Sorry, guess I am not up on all of our new equipment. What we will do, is send you some back up agents and something to eat and drink. You can work out with your back ups how you want to man the position."

Bob said, "I will send a couple of agents along with food and drink. We are going to have to decide if we need to keep the other agents in their current positions. What do you want to do about them Tom?"

Tom replied, "I think we can have them all come back to our headquarters here in the hotel as long as we know where the doctor is and we have a tracking device on his vehicle."

Walter Rogers said, "You might want to move your command center over to the Hotel Internacioal Iguazu in Argentina to be closer to the ranch."

"Good idea Walt. Do you mind if we call you Walt?" Tom asked.

Walter replied, "I wished you would I feel more comfortable as Walt, my dad was Walter."

Tom said, "OK Walt. I need to see what we can find out who owns the ranch that our doctor is operating at. I'm going to contact Langley to see what they can do to get that information for us."

Tom placed a call to CIA Headquarters in Langley, Virginia. He requested that they find out who owns the ranch at the GPS concordance provided to them by the agents from check point five. Tom also advised Headquarters that he was moving his command center to the Hotel Internacional Iguazu in Argentina.

Less than thirty minutes latter Tom was told that the ranch was owned by a Saudi Prince named Prince Abdullah Bin Turki. The ranch was a hundred thousand acres more or less and had its own airport with a runway long enough to accommodate a Boeing 747. Which by the way Prince Bin Turki owns a 747. The CIA's dossier on Prince Bin Turki indicated that he had never been considered a suspect for any type of terrorist activities unless you considered partying and chasing women. In these two activities he was a terror.

Tom requested that the CIA get photos of every square inch of the ranch using satellites and get copies to him ASAP.

Tom told Bob and Walt one of the hardest jobs we have in our line of work is waiting.

Dr. al-Sadr opened the door and came into the lab. He said, "Good Morning doctors. Dr. Browning I want you to know that even as we speak your clothing and things are being placed into your quarters just as you requested."

Elizabeth replied, "Thank you. I needed to get my medicine and I appreciate having a change of clothes."

Dr. al-Sadr said, "You are welcome doctor. I understand from Fahd that you have requested several different chemicals and medicines. Please explain what you plan to do with them Dr. Smith? Since you seem to be the new team leader for this research project."

Shane replied, "As I understand the project is to make a faster acting mad cow disease. Since the disease is not a bacteria or a virus we have to find something that could accelerate the disease and since we have no idea of what or if anything might cause such acceleration, we will try to use various chemicals to do it."

Dr. al-Sadr said, "I guess that makes sense, but for your sake I hope you can find something that works. The other question I have is how will you know if it works?"

Shane replied, "We will need to save all of the parts of the cattle that have mad cow disease to use to make feed pellets, that's the brains, spinal cords and the spleens."

"Next, we will require I would say about twenty cows per pen to be separated away from the rest of the herd and have at least twelve of these pens constructed so we have one pen for each of the chemicals that we requested to try to use as an accelerant. We have requested eleven different chemicals and we would use the cattle in the twelfth pen to observe how normal cattle function during the same time period.

"We will need to track all of the variations of the chemically tainted parts taking from cattle that have confirmed mad cow disease that we make into feed pellets."

"Unless you have a feed mill located here on the ranch we will need to obtain the equipment and construct a plant to make the food pellets we plan to feed to the cattle in each pen."

"Doctors do you agree with my approach and did I miss anything?"

The other researchers all shook their heads in agreement.

Dr. al-Sadr said, "Well it seems that we have a consensus on how we should proceed. I would say Dr. Smith although you and Dr. Browning appear to be the youngest of our scientists you know how to go about organizing a research project. If everyone agrees than we should make plans to build the test pens and locate the equipment needed to make a food pellet plant. Do you all agree with Dr. Smith's concept because you will all succeed together or all hang together? That's a little twist on a famous saying of America's Benjamin Franklin's saying from the American Revolutionary War.

There were no smiles hearing, what Dr. al-Sadr said. The five captives hung their heads in silence.

Dr. al-Sadr said, "I will begin organizing arrangements for the purchase and installation of the feed mill and Dr. Smith you are now officially in charge of this project. I expect you to work with Fahd and Ahmed on getting the pens built, you tell them how you want them to be built and select the cattle for each of the pens. Is there anything else you want or need?"

Shane said, "Although the lab is very well equipped we will need at least two computers to help us track our experiments and the amount of the chemicals we infuse into the food pellets. Access to the worldwide web would be very helpful if you could arrange that for us. That way we could tap into some of the various research centers libraries."

Dr. al-Sadr replied, "The computers OK, the web I don't think so. Perhaps you would prefer I have an American 777 land at the ranch's airport to take you back to Iowa."

Shane replied, "That would be nice, but if we can't have the web access I am sure the 777 is out of the question."

Dr. al-Sadr said, "I am happy that you have not lost your sense of humor Dr. Smith. You are a very funny guy. No wonder you got such a beautiful wife. They say women like men with a good sense of humor. Maybe that's why I never found anyone, no sense of humor. You should be sure to remember that in the future."

On that note Dr. al-Sadr turned around to go, but before he left he said, "I will not see you for a few days since it's going to take a lot of my time putting together acquiring the equipment for the feed mill and the chemicals you requested. By the way I did think it was cute asking for all of the chemicals in pounds. See I do have a little bit of humor after all."

Dr. al-Sadr left the lab and the five scientists breathed a sigh of relief.

Dr. Allen said, "I will not be sorry that we are not going to see his face around here for a few days and if possible forever would be even better."

Dr. Hinson added, "He is a scary bloke. I think he would shoot all of us given half a chance."

Dr. Van Meter said, "We certainly know he doesn't need much provocation to kill. One thing, he is certainly knowledge about American History, quoting and twisting a famous Benjamin Franklin saying from the American Revolutionary War."

Elizabeth said, "I am sure he has been educated in America. His English is too Americanized to have learned it in the Middle East. His accent is very American."

Shane responded, "Yes, we probably educated him in America. He probably took the place of some poor American that didn't have a good enough ACT score to get into one of our universities.

Elizabeth said, "Shane, you sound resentful helping to educate poor foreigners that want to come to America for an education."

Shane answered, "I do if they turn out like Dr. al-Sadr."

Shane said, "I hope you don't think that I feel like I am in charge of our small group as Dr. al-Sadr suggested."

Dr. Allen replied, "Frankly, he might not be right about anything else in his life, but personally I think you need to be our leader. You have a grasp of organization and we are going to need that if we ever expect to save our lives and get our families out of here. Giving us something to do will help pass the time until you can work the plan to fly us out of here Sunday."

Dr. Van Meter and Dr. Hinson both said that they agreed that we need a leader and you are the obvious choice. You came up with a plan to get us out of here and a scheme to fool our kidnappers into thinking that we would really try to develop some method of accelerating mad cow disease. You are our certainly our choice than they asked Elizabeth what she thought.

Elizabeth said, "I already made my choice by having Shane as my husband. He's my leader."

Dr. Hinson said, "Spoken like a faithful wife. Right now I not sure my wife would say the same thing about me and the longer we are here the more I will be blamed for us being kidnapped."

Dr. Allen said, "I don't think your wife can blame you for us being kidnapped, after all we are all in the same boat."

Dr. Hinson replied, "You don't know my wife!"

Everyone laughed at Dr. Hinson's remark. It felt good to laugh about something instead of feeling so much in despair all of the time.

Shane said, "OK, I will try to be your leader and if I get too far out of line let me know and we can revisit the issue. Let's get started; Dr. Allen would you work with Ahmed to construct the holding pens; Dr. Van Meter select the cattle to be moved into the pens and Dr. Hinson supervise the collection of the brains, spleens and spinal cords from the cattle that die from mad cow disease. Elizabeth and I will work on developing the computer programs for tracking data from the twelve pens and the formulas for the feed mill pellets so all of us can review them."

Shane continued, "We need to give the appearance of working on the project, just as we would be doing if we actually did a project."

When Shane returned to the house for lunch he searched through his clothes that Dr. al-Sadr had brought to them and found his sport coat that had been wearing when it got the orange juice dumped on it. Shane removed his personal ID lapel pin and put it on his shirt. Shane told Elizabeth that now Tom had a chance to find them using his personal ID tag.

Shane said, "We really should thank Dr. al-Sadr for bringing us our clothes, really thank him. Elizabeth you know he did us a big favor by bringing our clothes to us, how big a favor he will never know. Now to get my personal ID tag pined on. Find us Tom!"

CHAPTER TEN

Tom, Bob and Walt Rodgers received copies of the detailed maps of the area surrounding the ranch; a close up map of all of the buildings on the ranch and the ranch airport from military satellites.

As they studied the maps they began making plans on how and when to extract the scientists and their families from the ranch and capture Dr. al-Sadr and his cronies. They decided that they could be ready by Sunday if they could get enough intelligences and the required amount of military personnel and equipment in place.

The other problem they had was how to alert the Government of Argentina of this raid without having someone in the Government leak the information to an al- Qaeda operative. The decision was made at Langley to inform the Argentina Government when the raid actually began.

They decided that they needed real time observation of the ranch buildings and the entire ranch to determine how many men were on the ranch and the number and type of vehicles they had. They also needed to know which building their scientists and their families were being held in. They sent a request to Langley asking for equipment needed to use the satellites for that purpose. Tom advised Langley that as soon as they could determine the number of men and vehicles they would need they would request the number of Special Forces and equipment that would be required to rescue the missing scientists and their families along with Drs. Smith and Browning.

Langley advised Tom they would send three expert operators and the spying equipment necessary to keep tabs on everything going on at the ranch. They would be with them in the morning since they were coming from CIA Headquarters. Langley further advised that they would be sending a number of Special Forces troops and equipment to an undisclosed Brazilian Air Force Base arriving tomorrow.

Tom thanked them for their support and asked if Langley had given a code name for these operations yet? The reply was "Dangerous Food" and as of now the operations were under way.

The next morning the three operation specialists for observing the ranch using the satellites arrived and their equipment. Less than an hour latter the satellite equipment was set up and operating.

The satellite team leader, Charlie Thomas asked Tom Parker exactly what he wanted them to do. Tom explained that they needed to get a count on how many guards or people were working on the ranch and the number and type of vehicles were there. They also needed to know which buildings the scientists and their families were being held in.

Charlie introduced his two other team members to Tom, Bob and Walt. They were Roy Gene Rogers and Leonard Nix. Charlie told Tom that one of them would be monitoring the ranch twenty-four hours a day and when the "Dangerous Food" mission begins all three of them would be working to observe the entire ranch area.

Tom said, "I hate to ask this, but Roy how did you get the name Roy Gene?"

Roy Gene replied, "My dad was a big Roy Rogers fan and my mother was as big of fan of Gene Autry, so when I was born they comprised and named me Roy Gene."

Tom said, "Well I had to ask."

Everyone in the command center broke out laughing including Roy Gene.

Roy Gene said, "My friends just call me RG."

Tom said, "OK, RG let's get to work and save our scientists.

RG said, "OK, boss we will get you the number of people you have on that ranch and the number and type of vehicles, do you want the license plate numbers too?"

Tom said, "No just the number and type will do."

Charlie Thomas said, "RG was only kidding you we couldn't really get all of their license plate numbers anyway."

As the morning past Tom, Bob and Walt continued studying the layout of the ranch trying to decided where they could get a rescue team in without being spotted. Most of the security guards and security cameras were at the perimeter of the ranch. Except there were security cameras located around all of the ranch buildings.

Tom said, "With a ranch that covers almost a hundred thousand acres you would think it wouldn't be too big of a problem to find a good insertion point for our troops. I think we are going to have to go in at night to give our Special Forces a big advantage. We need the commander of the Special Forces assigned for this mission to be here with us to help coordinate "Dangerous Food."

Tom called Langley and requested they contact the Special Forces Commander to come to the command center as soon as possible. Langley advised him that Colonel Jack Hayes was enroute to them already. CIA Headquarters told Tom that Colonel Hayes should arrive at the Hotel Internacional Iguazu around noon.

Tom told Bob and Walt I know Colonel Hayes, he was under my command when he was a young Second Lieutenant in Nam. Jack's a good man and punctual he should be knocking on our door any minute.

A knock on the door was heard at straight up noon.

Tom said, "That will be Jack. Get the door somebody."

Bob opened the door and there stood a bird colonel in combat fatigues. He was lean and trim and looked hard as nails all six foot five of him. He had a rugged face with a slight scar above his left eye and tanned as he spent his time in the sun. Bob thought yeah this dude looks like what a Commander of a Special Force Team should look like.

Bob said, "Colonel Jack Hayes. I am Bob Barker with the FBI, come in. This is Walter Rodgers with MI-5 and I think you know the boss of the operation already, Tom Parker with the CIA."

Colonel Hayes came into the room and looked around and saw Tom looking at the ranch layout.

Colonel Hayes said, "Colonel Parker, I haven't seen you since you pulled me out of that fire fight in Nam and you loaded my ass in that chopper and sent me stateside to recover from my wounds. How in the hell are you?"

Tom said, "Well I am better than the last time I saw you when you left me surrounded by a few hundred VC's."

Colonel Hayes said, "Man I thought they killed you. I passed out as soon as I was in that chopper and didn't know much until I was back in Hawaii. It took a long time to recover from those wounds, so I lost track of everybody in our unit.

Tom said, "Well they sure as a hell tried to kill me, but I got lucky. It got dark and I got out of there, but we lost almost everybody else in the team. It was not a good day, poor information about what we were up against. I try not to think about it. I guess you know you were the last one to get a ride out of there. It was a long walk home."

Colonel Hayes said, "We lost a lot of good men. You had the best team in Nam."

The two men shook hands than they embraced. They were comrades as only people that had been through the horrors of combat together could be. No one else could understand how their very lives depended on their comrades. These men knew.

Colonel Hayes said, "I never got the chance to say thank you for saving me that day in Nam. Thanks Colonel. Now I want to know what the hell are we doing invading Argentina anyway?"

Tom said, "Well, we are only going to invade a little bit of it, just enough to get our people out of there and hope we can do it without starting a war with our friends in Argentina."

Colonel Hayes said, "What is the deal really Colonel Parker?

Tom said, "Just call me Tom, please. They kicked me out of the Army you know. Ended up in the CIA and here's the deal. We have six scientists and their families kidnapped by al-Qaeda and being held on this big ranch a few miles away from this hotel. There's a total of nineteen people we got to extract from the ranch and we want to capture one of the most wanted terrorist in the world. A man by the name of

Dr. al-Sadr and he may have other key terrorists with him on that ranch we don't know who is with him."

Colonel Hayes said, "How many people are against us and what kind of defenses do they have?"

Tom replied, "We got the specialists from CIA Headquarters working in the room next door on that right now. They will also tell us how many and what type of vehicles they have. I am sure they can give us some idea of what type of weapons they are carrying as well as which buildings the scientists are being held in."

Colonel Hayes asked, "What kind of plan, have you come up with so far to extract these folks?"

Tom replied, "I think we will have a better chance of success if we use our advantage by using a nighttime operation. We got to be sure we do our best not to get any of our hostages killed, nine of them are children, ages range from eight to twelve years old."

"Any down side to doing this operation at night?" Colonel Hayes asked.

Tom said, "One big one. Dr. al-Sadr normally doesn't stay on the ranch at night, but I think it's more important to save our people than to catch him even as bad as we want him."

Colonel Hayes said, "Tom who in the CIA comes up with the names for these operations anyway, "Dangerous Food"? What's that all about?"

Tom replied, "Sorry Jack. That's classified. Trust me it has a real meaning and one day when the operation is declassified I'll be happy to tell you."

Colonel Hayes said, "OK, CIA operations always have crazy names anyway."

Charlie Thomas entered the room and Tom introduced him to Colonel Hayes.

Charlie Thomas said "Gentleman, I believe we have already gotten the number of vehicles they have on the ranch. We can count a total of twenty-five vehicles. Twenty of them are some type of Jeep and we found four trucks. Three of them are flat bed ton and half trucks and one is an eighteen wheeler. They also have a limo. What would they need a limo for on a ranch?"

Tom replied, "This ranch is owned by a Saudi Prince, so I guess they must use it for him when he is at home on the range."

Colonel Hayes said, "Still making jokes are you Tom."

Tom said, "In our line of work you need all of the humor you can get."

Colonel Hayes responded, "Good point. We don't get many chances for laughs do we?"

Tom said, "Not enough."

Charlie Thomas said, "If you want something to laugh about we figure the bad guys have AK47's as their major weapons. So far haven't detected anything bigger than that. These guys must think they are pretty secure and aren't very worried about being challenged by anybody, at least not with much firepower."

Tom replied, "It's our thought that most of the people on the ranch don't have a clue as to who these people are. They think they are guarding the ranch from cattle rustlers. We have information from some of the locals that cattle's rustling is a big problem around here. They steal cows in Argentina and move them across the borders into Brazil or Paraguay. Sell them and make a little money. We are sure that's what most of the guards think they are doing protecting the cows."

Tom continued, "It's hard to believe, but we don't think the Saudi Prince that owns this ranch has the slights idea of what's going on at his ranch. The CIA can't find any ties between him or his family with al-Qaeda. We understand he only comes here maybe four times a year. The location of the ranch is ideal for al-Qaeda sitting up here in the corner of Argentina right next to Brazil and Paraguay. They can move between these borders really easy. They can just claim to be going across the border for the day and nobody checks to see if they stay longer. Sweet deal for them."

Colonel Hayes asked Charlie, "How long do you think it will be before you can tell which buildings the hostages are being held in?"

Charlie replied, "That depends on how much the hostages move around today. If they are in and out of the buildings much today we can tell pretty quickly. We know which buildings that Dr. Smith is in at night and which one he goes to during the day."

Charlie had a map with the ranch buildings located on it to show Tom and Colonel Hayes.

Charlie said, "At night Dr. Smith is in this small house right here." Charlie pointed to the house on the map. During the day he is in the building that looks like a big barn, which is what it is we are sure."

Tom said, "They probably have a lab located in that barn."

Colonel Hayes asked, "How did you pinpoint his location?"

"Easy," Charlie replied. "He has a personal ID Tag that he is wearing that let's us know where he is anywhere in the world."

Colonel Hayes said, "You mean he's CIA?"

Tom answered, "Not exactly, but right now he is a special agent for Homeland Security. He and Dr. Elizabeth Browning were bait and Dr. al-Sadr took the bait and he got it hook line and sinker. For a while we thought that our line broke and we had permanently lost our bait. We had orange juice dumped on Dr. Smith's jacket to have him come back to the room where we could talk to him and his ID tag was left on his coat. Fortunately for us Dr. al-Sadr took the coat to him and he got back his ID tag so we could find him. Trust me it a long story and you would only laugh at us if you heard it all."

Colonel Hayes said, "OK, I will take you word for it."

Charlie Thomas returned to the room and asked, "Tom, I know that you are aware that the ranch has a runway but did you know that the runway is long enough to land or take off a really big jet. It could handle a 747 without any problem. Also, they have a Gulfstream IV sitting in front of the hanger."

Tom said, "I knew that the runway could handle a 747 apparently the Prince has one that he uses to come here in. I didn't know anything about the Gulfstream. Right now I don't know if they have any runway lights on at night or not. I guess if they did we could use it to get our troops into the ranch."

Colonel Hayes said, "Yes we could, but I think we better use our Blackhawk's to get our troops in and our Cobras to provide air support for them after they are on the ground. We can use the air strip to fly the hostages out with our C-5's after we secure the ranch."

"Sounds good to me Jack. Now we just need to get the rest of the data on the number of guards on the ranch and where the other scientists and their families are housed." Tom replied.

Tom said, "Jack I have been studying the entire area around here and I think you could bring in your choppers in over Lago De Itaipu and follow the Rio Parana right down to the ranch, the north part of the ranch borders the river. Take a look at this map and you can see what I am talking about."

After Tom showed him the route that he had proposed to get the troops into the ranch.

Jack Hayes said, "That looks good to me. We can come in low right on top of the river and be on these guys before they know what hit them."

Tom, Jack, Bob and Walt sat down to have a cup of coffee and wait for the last part of the information before they could finalize their plans to extract their scientists from the al-Qaeda.

Than Tom said, "I guess we are back to my favorite part of the job, waiting. Good God I hate waiting!"

Shane and Elizabeth finished breakfast and talked a few minutes about how they thought they could try to escape from the ranch on Sunday. Shane was sure that if they could make it to the Gulfstream than he could fly them out of here. Shane didn't know what kind of plans Tom and Bob might be making to rescue them, but he thought that they should continue to make plans to get the scientists and their families out as quickly as possible.

Shane said, "I will ask Dr. Allen to try to steal some of the wire that they are using to build the cattle pens with to tie up the two guards. We will need something to gag the guards with do you have any idea of something we could use Elizabeth?"

Elizabeth said, "Sure we can use a pair of my pantyhose they don't weight much and we could cut them in two which will make them easy to conceal."

Shane said, "That's a good idea they are really strong and should be easy to stuff into the guard's mouths."

Elizabeth said, "I am concerned about what will happen to the children if we fail. Have you thought of that Shane?"

"Sure I have thought about it, but what do you think is going to happen to those kids if we failed or even if we succeed in making a fast acting mad cow disease? Don't you think they plan to kill all of us? The al-Qaeda is not going to leave any of us alive." Shane replied.

Elizabeth said, "Thanks a lot. I guess I never thought about it in that context."

Shane said, "Elizabeth you might survive judging by the way Dr. al-Sadr looks at you."

"Thanks a lot." Elizabeth responded.

Shane said, "Seriously we got to get out of here as soon as we can. Today we need to have Dr. Allen get busy working on the cattle pens with Ahmed and Dr. Van Meter sorting out groups of cattle for our twelve pens. We need to keep

everyone busy so we don't have to spend too much time thinking about our circumstances until Sunday comes or until Tom comes riding in with the Calvary."

Shane and Elizabeth saw that it was time for them to go over to the lab and as they went out the door of their little house they began walking hand in hand.

Shane said, "This detour has certainly cramped our honeymoon and our lovemaking, you know I am developing a serious dislike for these al-Qaeda guys."

Elizabeth smiled and said, "They are ruining our efforts in perfecting sex and just as I was really getting to enjoy the research project. I just decided, I am not thrilled with these guys either."

Shane and Elizabeth continued holding hands as they opened the door of the lab and saw that everyone else was already at their work stations. They greeted their colleagues "Good Morning."

Shane said, "This morning I would like to get started getting the test pens built and Dr. Allen I want you to steal some of the wire they are using to build the pens with so we can use it to tie up the guards on Sunday. I don't know how you can do it, just do it. Dr. Van Meter I would like for you to start working to round up the cattle for the test pens. If they don't have someplace they can hold them until the pens are ready maybe they can make rope corrals until the pens are ready. Dr. Hinson, Elizabeth and I will be working of the various forms and computer programs that we will need to track the various experiments that we will be running using the different chemicals and drugs to accelerate mad cow disease."

As Shane was finishing giving instructions for the days work Fahd and Ahmed came into the lab.

Fahd said, "Good morning doctors. How is everyone this morning? I understand everyone is ready to go to work on their job assignments this morning from listening to Dr. Smith as I was coming into the lab. Ahmed will take Dr. Allen to help design the holding pens for the twelve different test pens and I will take Dr. Van Meter with me to have him pick the cattle that he wants to use for the experiments."

Fahd continued, "I will leave you other doctors to work on whatever you are doing here in the lab. Ahmed, are you ready?"

Ahmed said, "Let's get going I think this is going to take a while to build these cattle pens that you want for your experiments.

Fahd said, "Yes, I am sure it will and it's going to take us sometime to round up the cattle that Dr. Van Meter picks out for the test."

After Drs. Allen and Van Meter left with Fahd and Ahmed.

Shane said, "Dr. Hinson if you could work at designing the forms for tracking the various types and amounts of the formulas that we will give to the different pens of cattle that would get us started on the tracking forms. Elizabeth without having the computers yet can you work at designing the programs or at least the protocol for the programs we will need to track the feed mill operations?"

Shane continued, "I am going to work on the combinations of various formulations for the eleven chemicals to be added to the feed pellets that we are going to make."

Ahmed and Dr. Allen got into a waiting jeep and the driver started the engine and pulled away from the barn, behind the jeep a flat bed truck with four men followed them. Dr. Allen could see a lot of rolls of barbed wire and steel posts on the bed of the truck as the jeep turned down a small lane.

Ahmed said, "Well Dr. Allen, how do you like this location for your holding pens? We tried to find a location that couldn't be seen from the air strip or from the main house we don't want too many people asking what we are doing with these new pens. We also didn't want them too far from the lab."

Dr. Allen replied, "It looks like a good location, but I would have preferred them to be right next to the lab for us to observe the cattle better."

Ahmed said, "Well doctor this is the closest that we could get you and accomplish what we needed to do."

Dr. Allen said, "What else can I say. If it's the closest we can get to the lab all right."

Ahmed replied, "Yes, this is the closest that we can get. Maybe we can get a small trailer brought here for you to work out of."

Dr. Allen said, "That would be good, since we will need to spend a lot of time observing the cattle to see how they react by feeding them the different chemicals."

Ahmed replied, "I will speak to Fahd to see what we can do about that. Please tell me how large each of the pens should be."

Dr. Allen said, "We plan to have twenty cattle in each of the pens. So I would say that we need each of them to be twenty meters wide by thirty meters deep. We will need a gate three meters wide in the front of the pen. Each pen will need a watering trough and a feed trough. We will also need a sign on each of the pens numbered from one to twelve. These signs should be about one meter square we don't want anyone to get mixed up on which food will go to which pen."

Ahmed asked, "How far do you want each pen apart?"

Dr. Allen replied, "Ten meters."

Ahmed told the workers from the flat bed truck to start unloading wire and post and to begin laying out the post for pen number one.

He explained to them in Spanish how large he wanted each of the twelve pens to be and where to set post for a three meter gate."

The workers laid out post for the barbed wire fence as Dr. Allen watched as they began digging post holes to set the post in concrete. He was trying to decide how he was going to get wire to use to tie up the guards on Sunday when they made their escape. He decided that maybe he could get some of the wire into his briefcase when the men began stringing the wire onto the post, but he was sure that would not happen today since they had not even started pouring concrete for the post. In fact he didn't know how long it would take them to get all of the post holes dug for the first pen. The work was not going very fast.

Dr. Allen asked, "Ahmed don't you have a tractor with a post hole digger on it? The way this is going it will take a month to get these pens built."

Ahmed replied, "What's your hurry doc, you don't have anyplace to go."

Dr. Allen said, "I don't think Dr. al-Sadr would agree with that he wants us to get started on these experiments as soon as possible."

Ahmed said, "I will see if we can bring one of the tractors with a post hole digger or a backhoe on it to speed up this process when we go in at lunchtime. I would not want Dr. al-Sadr thinking I was holding up your work."

Dr. Allen said, "I am sure you wouldn't want that would you?"

Ahmed didn't reply he just turned away to go over to where the crew was working on digging post holes. It was soon getting close to lunchtime so Ahmed told the men to load back onto the flat bed truck and he returned to the jeep along with his driver and told Dr. Allen to get into the jeep. They had soon returned to the lab and arrived just as the other veterinaries were leaving for lunch. The only one missing was Dr. Van Meter and Dr. Allen was told by Dr. Hinson that Dr. Van Meter and Fahd had not made it back to the lab yet.

Only a few more minutes past and Fahd and Dr. Van Meter arrived at the lab and Fahd told Dr. Van Meter that he would meet him after lunch back at the lab at two-thirty and they would continue picking out cattle for the experiments.

After lunch all of the scientists were back in the lab waiting for Ahmed and Fahd to return to go back out to build pens and pick out cattle. Drs. Smith, Browning and Hinson were already back working on their part of the project when Dr. al-Sadr came into the lab and asked what was being done today.

Shane explained to Dr. al-Sadr that Dr. Allen was working with Ahmed building the holding pens and Dr. Van Meter was working with Fahd selecting cattle to be used in the experiments. Further, he showed Dr. al-Sadr what he was doing designing formulas for the various chemicals compounds to add to the feed pellets. Elizabeth showed him what she was working on and Dr. Hinson did the same.

Dr. al-Sadr was pleased at the progress they were making. He told them that he had planned to be away from the ranch for several days, but changed his mind and decided to stay closer to the project. He was moving into the main ranch house until the project reached its conclusion. He wanted to be involved in the project every step of the way. This project had now become the most important project for his associates.

When Fahd and Ahmed came into the lab they were surprised to see that Dr. al-Sadr had returned to the ranch.

Fahd said, "Dr. al-Sadr I understood that you would not be here for a few days is there something wrong?"

Dr. al-Sadr replied, "No nothing is wrong, it's just that our project has become al-Qaeda most important project for attacking America. They want us to move as quickly as possible to develop a quick acting mad cow disease. For that reason I have decided to move into the main house here on the ranch, is that a problem?"

Fahd replied, "It's no problem unless the Prince decides to come for one of his visits."

"Good, so let's everyone get back to work while I get moved into the main house and get busy acquiring the items our scientists need for the project." Dr. al-Sadr said.

When Shane and Elizabeth were back in their house for the night Shane said, "This could present a problem for us getting out of here on Sunday. Since the al-Qaeda is pushing Dr. al-Sadr he may push us to work on Sunday and our chances of jumping the two guards and getting to the Gulfstream from the soccer field maybe just a dream. We got to push him for some time off on Sunday so the other doctors can visit their families. Maybe you could suggest it to him that you think he can get more work out of the other scientists if they can see that their families are all right."

Elizabeth replied, "OK Shane, the next time we see him I will mention it to him, right now I need you to hold me because I looked into Dr. al-Sadr's eyes today and he scared me to death. Shane I don't know if we will get away from him or not."

Shane took Elizabeth in his arms and said, "Honey, don't under estimate us and our friends Tom and Bob. I am really sure that by now they are working on a plan to get us out of here and since Dr. al-Sadr brought us our clothes I am certain that Tom knows where we are. Coming on baby, let's go to bed and try to forget the bad guys for awhile. I love you. You know, but of course it's just for your money."

Elizabeth said, "I don't think that you are too concerned about my money right now. I think you are just after my body and you know I only love you for yours."

For the first time since they had been captured they began making love and it felt good. Really good!

CHAPTER ELEVEN

RG called out to Tom, "Dr. al-Sadr's vehicle is back at the ranch. I thought you would want to know that."

Tom replied, "I sure do. Too bad we can't make him stay there until we are ready to get our people out. I would love to get him at the same time that we get our people out."

Bob said, "Well he has never stayed there overnight since we have been tracking him. It's funny we can't pinpoint his vehicle when he is in Paraguay. We know with in a few hundred feet I guess, but than we lose the signal from the tracking unit. I think the vehicle must be going underground that's the only thing I can think of that might cause us to lose him or we simple can't get close enough with our vehicle to pick up the signal from that short range tracking device."

Tom said, "The good thing is that we can at least find his vehicle the next morning. That's sure better than we could do before. One thing is for sure I don't think we can try to get him Sunday morning when we go after our people at the ranch. We don't have a good reading on where he is at night and I don't want to invade two countries that the State Department is going to have to explain what we are doing going into their country with a military force without their help or their permission. That's a good way to have your career end and I been around too long to lose my pension."

Bob said, "You and me buddy! I don't think my family would be to understanding if that happened and I lost my pension!"

Colonel Hayes said, "Let's go over our final assault plan. Charlie Thomas just gave me the location of the hostages and the number of the enemy so I am ready to set the assault plan now. It looks like they have about eighty troops that stay all night at the ranch and perhaps another fifty people that leave between six thirty and seven in the evening. These people must be locals that are hired to take care of the cattle, cleaning the houses and maybe cooks. Our plan is to hit the ranch on Sunday at two in the morning. It appears no one stays overnight in the main house. We know that Dr. Smith and Dr. Browning are in this small house."

Colonel Hayes pointed to the house on his map and continued to use his map to point out the other buildings involved in his plan.

Colonel Hayes continued, "It is designed as "Honeymoon Cottage"; the first of the long barracks is where the other doctors are being held its name is "Doc's House" and the second and third long barracks is the enemy troop's barracks, named "Bin and Laden." The families are being held in a barracks on the other side of the airfield, its called "Family Time."

"We will have a squad of troops in each Blackhawk that are fully equipped for nighttime operations. We will have two Blackhawk's for both "Bin and Laden", landing one at the front and one at the back of each building. A Cobra will be positioned over the front and over the back of "Bin and Laden." Blackhawk's with a squad will land at the front and back of "Doc's House" and at the same at "Family Time." Our troops will shoot anyone that try's to come out of "Bin and Laden." The squads at "Doc's House" and "Family Time" will go in and get the hostages and load them into the Blackhawk's."

"We will have three other Blackhawk's in the air to set down and pick up our three squads of men after the hostages are gone. The Blackhawk at the rear of "Doc's House" will remain on the ground until time to withdraw and the squad that came in on it will go out on the same chopper. We plan to use two Blackhawk's to go to the two other houses on the far side of "Honeymoon House" and capture whoever is in those houses and bring them out in the Blackhawk's. These houses are called "A and Q." A Blackhawk will land at "Honeymoon Cottage" and pick up Dr. Smith and Dr. Browning. When everybody has been accounted for we will return back up the river to the Brazilian airbase with our mission accomplished."

Colonel Hayes said, "OK, Tom what do you think?"

Tom replied, "Jack the plan sounds good. Let's spend more time on some of the details as they say, the devil is in the details. I want to be sure we got so much equipment and troops that these people don't even think about firing a shot and I want those people in "A and Q" alive if at all possible."

Bob said, "I have prepared a list of the people that we should be picking up at "Doc's House" it includes Drs. Anthony Hinson; David Allen; Arden Borland and Charles Van Meter."

"In "Family Time" we have Betty Hinson; Tony Hinson Jr., age 12; Beverly Hinson, age 10; Lou Ann Allen; Lori Allen, age 13; Wayne Allen, age 11; Troy Allen, age 9; Joan Allen, age 7; Dorothy Borland; Lois Van Meter; Tuesday Van Meter, age 12; Charles Van Meter, Jr., age 10; Brenda Van Meter, age 8."

"In "Honeymoon Cottage" we have to get Dr. Shane Smith and Dr. Elizabeth Browning, all together that's a total of nineteen people."

"I have made copies of the list of people in each of the facilities to give to the squads responsible for picking our hostages up." Bob said.

Colonel Hayes took the copies to give to the squad leaders. Than he and Tom again studied the maps of the ranch buildings and discussed the assault on the ranch point by point. They decided to add two more Cobra's to the plan to cover the rear of "A and Q" houses. They also talked at length about if they saw a need to cover the airfield and decided that it would not be necessary since no one was in the area at night. The also talked about the guards on patrol around the fence line of the ranch and concluded that the only guards that could reach the main ranch buildings in time to provide aid would have to come from the ranch's main entrance and they felt with the Cobra's in the air they could take them out if it became necessary.

Tom said, "Let go over the execution of the plan one more time Jack, lead me through it step by step."

Colonel Hayes began, "Beginning about eight pm on Saturday night we fuel all of the choppers and load the chopper's weapons. This task should be finished by around eleven pm."

"At midnight on Saturday we load the troops and their gear including their night fighting equipment, weapons and ammo."

"One am we start the engines on the choppers and check the radio equipment. If everything is OK we are airborne by one-fifteen and precede in formation from the airbase to Lago De Itaipu and cross the lake and than string the choppers out in a line at a low altitude to follow the Rio Parana to the ranch."

"Once the choppers reach the ranch they will regroup in formation and fly to the ranch buildings at a low altitude than each of the choppers will move to their assigned positions around their buildings."

"At two am the choppers will reach the ranch buildings and at "Doc's House" we will have a Blackhawk land with a squad at the front door and a second Blackhawk with a squad at the rear door." The squad's will storm "Doc's House" and remove the doctors loading them in the Blackhawk at the front of the house. The squads will remain in place at the front and back of "Doc's House" until told to withdraw. The squad leader will check the passenger's list to be sure we have all of the doctors aboard and notify control that we have the doctors. Than the Blackhawk with the doctors will be airborne and proceed away from the ranch back to the airbase. The Blackhawk at the rear of "Doc's House" will remain on the ground until it's time to withdraw all of the troops."

"At the same time two other Blackhawk's will land at "Family Time" with one Blackhawk at the front of "Family Time" and one at the back of the building. The squads will remove the hostages and check to see that all of them are loaded on board the Blackhawk's and when they are airborne report to control that the hostages from "Family Time" are enroute back to the airbase. The troops will remain on the ground until told to withdraw and when it's time the two Blackhawk's that have been hovering above to pick them up will land, load the troops and than return to the airbase."

"The two Blackhawk's assigned to "A and Q" will land in the front and the rear of the houses and deploy their squads, storm the houses and capture the people inside the houses and take them aboard. When airborne with their prisoners they will confirm that they have capture them to control and return to the airbase."

"A Blackhawk will land at "Honeymoon Cottage" and pick up Dr. Smith and Dr. Browning and confirm to control when they are airborne and enroute back to the airbase."

"After all of the choppers that have landed to pick up hostages or prisoners have confirmed they are airborne and enroute back to the airbase than the remaining troops on the ground will be picked up in the Blackhawk's and return to base. When all of the choppers confirm to control that they have all of their people loaded and are enroute to the airbase than control will give permission for the hovering Cobra's that are guarding "A and Q" that they can return to the airbase."

Colonel Hayes finishes his step by step plan by adding, "Control will be here in your hotel rooms and I will be leading the raid myself. We will move the necessary radio equipment and a radio operator in here tomorrow to act as control under your command. If all goes according to plan we will be on the ground back at the airbase by three-thirty Sunday morning."

Tom said, "I like it. It's a good plan and we shouldn't take any casualties, but the two things I hate is not capturing these men in "A and Q" and the people on patrol around the perimeter and not getting Dr. al-Sadr. What if we left the four squads on the ground and the two Cobras' around "A and Q" and than get the people inside to die or surrender and pick them up latter in the morning using your C-5's. By using some of the jeeps that are on the ranch we could have the squads from "Family Time" along with a couple of the Cobra's round up the guards around the perimeter and bring them back to go with their buddies or kill them if they didn't give up. Than we could take all of them to Guantanamo Bay and not have to fight them again somewhere else in the future?"

Jack said, "I'll buy that. We can do it while we have them trapped like rats in a trap. What about your buddy Dr. al-Sadr? What can we do about him?"

Tom replied, "Maybe we set a trap for him by just waiting for him to come back to the ranch and grab him when he does. I think we could spend a couple or three more days here without having any problems from headquarters if we could get him or kill him, what do you think Bob?"

Bob said, "I think if we got a chance in hell of getting him we should stay right here. We would need to make everything around the ranch look like it normally does, but I am sure we could do that. Let's give it a try to see if we can get that son of a bitch!"

Jack replied, "Tom you're the boss we will set up to capture him and the other troops if that's what you want."

Tom said, "That's exactly what I want. I want to get that no good bastard!"

Jack said, "You still have a vehicle tag on his vehicle don't you? That should let us know when he is coming to the ranch in plenty of time to have everything ready to grab him."

Tom said, "Yes we do, and I hope he shows up Sunday and we get him. He has killed a lot of people around the world including some of my friends."

Jack replied, "Than Dr. al-Sadr is on our menu for Sunday lunch!"

As Shane and Elizabeth were walking back to their house Saturday night after saying goodnight to Drs. Allen;

Hinson and Van Meter they were stopped by Dr. al-Sadr. He asked them if they would come to dinner with him in the main house. They thought for a moment and Shane told him yes they would join him for dinner.

They were asked to get into the car parked nearby and Dr. al-Sadr's driver soon had them parked in front of the main house. It seemed a long time had past since they were first parked in this location. Could it have been only six days ago. It seemed so much longer, maybe half a life time ago.

When they entered the house Dr. al-Sadr's driver also came into the house with them and Shane noticed that he was carrying some type of automatic weapon. The entrance foyer of the house was spectacular with a huge gold and crystal chandler that looked as if it belonged in a concert hall or a palace. Shane and Elizabeth's were soon to see that the entire house was indeed a palace with elegant décor and furnishings.

From the entrance foyer they went into a large sitting or living room. It too, was very well furnished and decorated using gold trim on white woodwork. The gold trim was a theme though out the room on all of the furniture, lamps and picture frames. Everything in the room had a gold accent applied to it. Even the plush green carpet had gold thread weaved into its rich pattern.

Dr. al-Sadr asked them to please sit down and have some orange juice. He promised Shane that it would not be spilled on him as had happened at the hotel when they first met. A butler dressed in a tux served them very cold hand squeezed orange juice in tall crystal glasses. The glasses had the family crest of the Prince painted in gold on them.

Dr. al-Sadr said, "We should drink a toast to our host, Prince Abdullah Bin Turki even though he doesn't know we are his guests. After all it's a beautiful place to be and the luxury and beauty of his home is unquestionable."

Than Dr. al-Sadr raised his glass in a mock toast and Shane and Elizabeth followed suit. Shane quickly drank down his orange juice and Elizabeth carefully sipped at hers wondering if it was just juice or something more sinister.

Dr. al-Sadr said, "Dinner should be ready in a few minutes. In the meantime Dr. Smith I would like to say that you are doing an outstanding job of getting this project organized and some action on conducting the research. The ranch hands almost have the holding pens complete and Dr. Van Meter has filled the pens that are completed with the cattle he has selected for the experiments. I would say that in less than a week you have done very well."

Dr. al-Sadr continued, "The chemicals should begin arriving here next week along with your computers. The only big problem is the equipment for the feed mill it will take a month, maybe two months to begin getting this equipment. I will try to find us a mill somewhere near here to make up the feed pellets until we can get our own equipment."

Shane replied, "I guess I am not surprised that it would take that long to get the feed mill equipment. Considering the part of the world we are in I am surprised that you would be able to get the equipment that soon."

Dr. al-Sadr said, "I had to make a lot of extra pay offs to get our equipment orders to become the number one priority. Money makes the world march to your tune. I am sure you know this already. I am just assuring you that it's true. American's are not the only ones to know what it takes to get things done. Money! That's the secret."

Just as Dr. al-Sadr finished expounding on the virtue of money, the butler return to pick up the glasses and announce that dinner was being served in the dinning room.

Dr. al-Sadr said, "Shall we withdraw to the dinning room and see what kind of a special meal our cooks have made for you. One thing is certain for this meal no woman that the Prince has brought here for dinner has every match the beauty of Dr. Browning. As I told you Dr. Smith you are a lucky man to have such a beautiful wife. Shall we go?"

The three of them proceeded to the dinning room. This room matched the beauty of the other rooms of the house that they had been in. The same motif was carried out with the plush carpet, the gold trim on every piece of furniture and woodwork. The chandler was even larger and more beautiful than the one in the entrance foyer. The table settings were white with double gold rings around the edge and the crystal matched the glasses that the orange juice had been served in.

The meal began with a shrimp cocktail served in a crystal sleeve insert with ice in the bottom of the main vessel of the server. The shrimp were very large and very fresh and the cocktail sauce was as good as Shane had ever tasted.

Next the main course was served, chateaubriand with béarnaise sauce and pomes soufflés. It was perfection, some of the finest beef that Shane had ever tasted. The red wine served with it was excellent.

Next a small dish of lemon sherbet was served to cleanse the pallet.

In the European tradition the sherbet was followed by a small green salad with a Raspberry Vinaigrette Dressing. Dessert was Crepes Suzette.

The dinner ended with coffee and fruit.

Shane and Elizabeth knew when they finished their meal that the Chef that had prepared the meal was no doubt a world class Chef that was use to preparing meals for people that appreciated fine food. He was surely the Chef for the Prince when he was in residence at the ranch.

After their coffee was finished Dr. al-Sadr suggested that they return to the sitting room and talk for awhile. After they were comfortably seated Dr. al-Sadr began to talk.

He said, "It is a pleasure to have dinner once in awhile with someone that appreciates fine food and is worldly enough to recognize it when it is being served. My current associates wouldn't know fine food from dog food; in fact they would probably prefer the dog food."

Dr. al-Sadr continued, "It's a long ways from how I grew up with wealth and privilege to my association with the people in al-Qaeda. Most of our people have little or no education and have never had the chance to enjoy life as we have. They have only known poverty, poor health, death and conflict. Their lives have been a far cry from Oxford and Harvard where I received my education. My family ask me why I belong to the al-Qaeda, is it because of my religion or because I feel sorry for the plight of our people? Of course I tell them yes that's why I belong, but it's not the truth. The reason is because I enjoy the power I have over people and the thought that just being a part of this organization I can bring terror and fear to the whole world. That's power, like almost no one in the world has ever had before."

Dr. al-Sadr paused and than said, "Just seeing the fear in the eyes of you two brings me pleasure. The al-Qaeda will win the war against the infidelities, because if I tell one or hundred of our followers to take a bomb and blow up their homes they would only ask when, not why. That's the kind of power we have over our followers and for every Arab that are killed by America and its allies we get two volunteers to take their place."

Dr. al-Sadr continued, "We can't win a traditional war, but we can win the type of war we are conducting and when enough Americans are killed in Iraq. The Americans and their lap dogs, the British will go home. They will say look we won the war, but they will be wrong, they only won a few battles. We will win the war; Americans hold their lives as too precious to stay and lose one, two or ten people every day. The American President gave us a great opportunity by invading Iraq it took the pressure off of our leaders and gave us easy targets in a land that you can't protect."

Shane and Elizabeth had sit through his tirade by just holding their breathes. Waiting for him to grab a gun and shoot them both because they didn't know what would come next. Dr. al-Sadr instead became very quite and asked if they would like to have another glass of orange juice or something stronger to drink. Both told him no thank you.

Shane said, "Dr. al-Sadr we have listened to you and I have to say that I don't think you believe a word that you said. In fact I think you miss the life you had and are sorry that you just can't go back to it."

Dr. al-Sadr replied, "Maybe you are right. One thing for sure is I can't go back to my old life and you are one of the few people in the world that would have enough courage to say that to me. You know Dr. Smith if we had met years ago I believe that we would have become lifetime friends. I admire you and your lovely wife very much."

Elizabeth said, "I think we should say thank you for a wonderful dinner and an interesting evening, but I think we need to say goodnight."

Dr. al-Sadr replied, "Please don't go yet. Today is my birthday and for the past several years I have only had members of al-Qaeda with me on my birthday and they see no reason for a birthday celebration. You see Dr. Smith I do miss part of my old life."

Shane said, "OK we will stay for awhile longer if you insist."

Dr. al-Sadr said, "I do insist. Let me show you the rest of the house."

Elizabeth said, "Happy Birthday and OK let's see the rest of the house."

"Wonderful!" Dr. al-Sadr said.

Than he got out of his chair and motioned for Shane and Elizabeth to follow him. As he showed them around the house they could see that the entire house was striking in its design with the same motif used in every room of the house. The rich gold trim on every piece of furniture and all of the woodwork in the house was painted white with the gold trim. The rooms in the house were extra large in size and well appointed with there furnishings. The bathrooms all had both tubs and separate showers stalls trimmed in gold and the light fixtures had the same gold trim of each of them.

The piece de resistance was the master bedroom and bath. The bed was the largest bed they had every seen it was the size of two king size beds. The covering on the bed was a brocade green material with the Prince's family crest in gold thread that covered half of the bedspread. Elizabeth carefully pulled back the bedspread to look at the sheets and pillow cases they were a combination of silk and Egyptian cotton. She told Shane to just touch the sheets. The feel of the material was like what Shane thought fluffy clouds must feel like.

The rest of the furniture in the bedroom had a hand finished appearance like nothing Shane or Elizabeth had ever seen. The bedroom had a huge one hundred inch television screen mounted on one wall of the bedroom with all kinds of DVD's and recorders attached to the TV system. The rest of the walls were mirrors all trimmed in gold. Shane decided that this room alone must have taken a hundred pound of gold just to do the trimming and the bedspread.

Than the bathroom was a wonder in it's self. It had gold fixtures the stool, sinks, and the bidet. The bathtub was the size of a small swimming pool with the Prince's family crest painted in gold on the bottom of the tub. The walls were almost nothing but mirrors.

Elizabeth's said, "The Prince must like to look at himself no woman would ever want that many views of all of herself."

Shane and Dr. al-Sadr laughed in spite of themselves.

When the tour of the house was over Dr. al-Sadr asked Shane if he liked airplanes.

Shane replied, "Yes I do."

"Good we will go down to the ranch airport and I will show you some interesting airplanes." Dr. al-Sadr said.

Dr. al-Sadr, Shane and Elizabeth left the house and walked to Dr. al-Sadr's car. His driver appeared from somewhere and got into the vehicle. The driver was told by Dr. al-Sadr to take them to the ranch airport. Shane was thinking what a break. Elizabeth and he would have an opportunity to look over things at the airport and Dr. al- Sadr was taking them there. This should help them with Shane's plan to escape tomorrow.

When they arrived at the airport the driver parked near the large hanger, but away from the very large sliding door.

Shane was surprised at how large the hanger was from a distance it didn't look nearly as large as it was. The driver got out of the car and proceeded to a small door just to the left of the large hanger door. He took a key out of his pocket and unlocked the door. Next he turned on lights in front of the hanger and also overhead lights inside the hanger.

Dr. al-Sadr told Shane and Elizabeth to come on and follow him inside the hanger. Once inside the hanger Shane couldn't believe his eyes. There set a fleet of World War II fighter planes. He saw a P-40 Warhawk; P-51 Mustang; P-47 Thunderbolt; Japanese Zero; German Messerschmidt; British Spitfire; and a P-38 Lighting.

Most of these planes Shane had only seen pictures of, but had never seen the real airplanes. All of these planes looked like they were ready for combat duty. Perfect in every way.

Dr. al-Sadr said, "It seems the Prince liked the looks of the fighter planes from World War II so he bought them and restored them. I understand he is quite a pilot and fly's one or two of these planes each time he visits the ranch."

Shane asked if it would be OK if he looked into the planes. Dr. al-Sadr told him to be my guest, look them all over. Shane began with the P-38 Lighting and explained to Elizabeth something about each plane used during the Second World War.

After about an hour had gone by Dr. al-Sadr asked, "Shane would you and Elizabeth like to go for a little ride in a plane?"

Shane said, "Sure, but these planes are all fighters and only have room for the pilot."

Dr. al-Sadr said, "No, not these planes I am speaking about the Gulfstream IV sitting outside."

Elizabeth replied, "It's getting pretty late, I think we should return to our house and go to bed now."

Shane said, "Elizabeth how about just a short flight."

"OK, just a short flight if that's all right with you Dr. al-Sadr?" Elizabeth replied.

"Sure, we will just take a flight down to Buenos Aires and back. That won't take too long." Dr. al-Sadr said.

Dr. al-Sadr told his driver to get the Gulfstream ready to take a little ride to Buenos Aires and back. The driver said something to Dr. al-Sadr in Arabic and Dr. al-Sadr replied in Arabic back to him.

Shane asked if there was a problem with the plane or something. Dr. al-Sadr told him no it not a problem with the plane my driver just wanted to know if we should take time to refuel the plane since we have less than half full fuel tanks. He said he told him no that would be enough for this trip.

All of them got into the plane and the driver than became the pilot. Shane was sure that Dr. al-Sadr would be their pilot, but he was wrong. Shane asked Dr. al-Sadr if he was a pilot too and was told no, he never wanted to take the time learning to fly.

Dr. al-Sadr said, "I am sorry, but while we are in the plane I must tie you both up to your seats."

He took out leather straps that were like belts from the pockets in front of the seats and fastened Shane's arms down to the arms of the seat and than did the same to Elizabeth's arms. When she complained that the straps were too tight

Dr. al-Sadr loosed them up a little and than asked if that was all right. She said that it was better, not comfortable, but better.

Dr. al-Sadr said, "I can't take chances with two of you up here in an airplane you might overwhelm me while my man was flying the plane."

The pilot began taxiing the plane out toward the runway and than sent a radio signal to turn on the runway lights. The lights spring to life and the Gulfstream was soon picking up speed down the runway and lifting up in the air. In a few minutes Shane could see the lights from the ranch buildings as the plane circled around the airport and than headed southeast toward Buenos Aires.

Shane and Elizabeth continued to look out the windows of the plane and could see lights of small communities and larger cities as the plane continued on its destination. Dr. al-Sadr had moved up to the right hand seat in the cockpit as his man flew the plane.

Shane couldn't see his watch to know what time it was, but knew that it was getting to be sometime after midnight. They continued on their southeast flight for another hour or so and Shane could hear radio traffic between the Gulfstream Pilot and the airport controller in Buenos Aires. The pilot told the controller at the Buenos Aires airport that they were proceeding to turn around to return to the ranch airport. He said that he had been checking out the airplane for a minor problem, but it had now been fixed and everything was all right. The entire radio conversation had been in English. Shane sure didn't know that Dr. al-Sadr's driver/pilot could speak and understand English.

Dr. al-Sadr returned to the main cabin of the Gulfstream with Shane and Elizabeth and told them they were now retuning to the ranch. Shane asked what time it was and Dr. al-Sadr told him that it was just a few minutes before one-thirty in the morning. Sunday morning. He also told them it would be about an hour before they arrived back at the ranch.

Forty-five minutes latter the pilot began his descend and approach to the ranch airport. The pilot sent a radio signal to the ranch's runway lights and Shane could see the lights come on. The pilot began his approach on the downwind leg to land; next the pilot turned the plane on the base leg and than on final approach to land. The Gulfstream came in hot and bounced one, than twice on the runway than settled down for a nice smooth roll out then the pilot reversed thrust the engines and the Gulfstream came to a stop about halfway down the runway.

The pilot turned the plane around on the runway and headed back toward the hanger and as he was coming up to the hanger area he yelled out something in Arabic to Dr. al- Sadr. Dr. al-Sadr immediately got out of his seat and went up to the cockpit.

Seconds latter the Gulfstream came to a complete stop and began turning back around toward the other end of the runway. The plane now was going down the runway at a high rate of speed.

Shane yelled to Dr. al-Sadr, "What's happening?"

Dr. al-Sadr didn't answer and the plane traveled to the far end of the runway and made a quick turn and the pilot gave the plane full power and they were soon flying down the runway and lifting off. As soon as the plane was airborne again the pilot made a turn to the northwest and Shane could hear the pilot talking on the radio to Asuncion, Paraguay control and advised them they were enroute there.

After they had been airborne for about fifteen minutes Dr. al-Sadr came back to the main cabin and told Shane and Elizabeth that the ranch had a lot of company and they decided that it was best not to stay and greet them.

Shane said, "I don't understand what you are talking about?"

Dr. al-Sadr replied, "The ranch had a whole flock of helicopters hovering over it."

Shane didn't say any more. The next thing he heard was the pilot radioing Asuncion control and advising them that he was having a problem with his magnetic compass and his radio navigation equipment. Asuncion advised him that he was going north and needed to turn back to the southwest. Than the pilot shut down the radio that he had been communicating with them on. The pilot started descending to a much lower altitude and after he had dropped the plane below where the plane had to be pressurized he leveled off the plane and put the plane on auto pilot.

The pilot told Dr. al-Sadr something about what he was doing in Arabic and than a few minutes latter came into the main cabin. He went back into the storage area in the back of the plane and came back with two parachutes. He handed one to Dr. al-Sadr and they both began putting on the parachutes.

Dr. al-Sadr said, "Children I am afraid that we are going to have to leave you in a few minutes. We can't stay on this plane because who ever had the flock of helicopters at the ranch will be able to track this plane when we land and they will be waiting for us. This is our only way to escape capture. I am so sorry to tell you that the plane will run out of fuel soon. Every time I start to like someone they always die. I don't understand why, they just do."

Shane said, "At least take Elizabeth with you. You know you want her."

Elizabeth said, "Shane, I won't go without you. I would rather stay here and die with you than go with him."

Dr. al-Sadr replied, "Sorry, I couldn't take you with me anyway we only have two parachutes. I could never leave my brother he has always looked after me."

Shane said, "Give us a chance turn us loose so we can at least die in each others arms."

Dr. al-Sadr replied, "What a romantic! You are about to die and all you can think of is holding each other."

Just than Dr. al-Sadr's brother said in English, "We must go now.

He opened the door of the plane and held the door open against the wind. Dr. al-Sadr came to the door and just before he jumped he said, "Elizabeth I could have loved you and gave you everything."

Just as he finished saying it he jumped out of the plane and his brother jumped right behind him.

CHAPTER TWELVE

Colonel Jack Hayes radioed control and talked to Tom to advise him that they were airborne and on the way to the ranch on time.

Tom said, "We have some news regarding Dr. al-Sadr. His vehicle is still at the ranch, but Shane's Personal ID indicates that he left the ranch about midnight and must be on a plane. We believe that he is on the Gulfstream that has been parked in front of the hanger because it's gone from the ranch. The plane is flying in the direction of Buenos Aires at the present time. We don't have any idea what's going on or who is on the plane with Shane.

Colonel Hayes asked, "Are we still a go?"

Tom replied, "Roger that lets get everyone out that we can."

Colonel Hayes said, "We are on our way for operation "Dangerous Food."

At two hundred hours the choppers were ready to land at the ranch.

Colonel Hayes gave the orders, "Let's go get them."

The plan worked just as it had been planned. The Blackhawk's were in position in the front and rear of "Doc's House" and "Family Time." The squads stormed into the dorms and woke up all of the scientists and their family members that had not already been waken by the landing of the choppers. In less than ten minutes the scientists were loaded on board the chopper that was waiting in front of "Doc's House." The squad leader for "Doc's House" radioed control to report that one of the doctors was not there, Dr. Borland. He was told that Dr.

al-Sadr shot and killed Dr. Borland when they were first were captured. Twenty minutes later the families from "Family Time" had been secured into the two waiting Blackhawk's at "Family Time." The squad leader reported that Mrs. Borland was not among the families rescued. Mrs. Allen told the squad leader that Mrs. Borland was killed by Dr. al-Sadr the first day they were prisoners.

The choppers at "Bin and Laden" had surrounded the troop's barracks and demand them to surrender. At first the troops inside refused to surrender, but after about an hour the troops began coming out of the "Bin" building with their hands in the air, than the troops in the "Laden" building followed suit. As the troops came out of the buildings their hands were secured with plastic straps and searched for weapons and bombs. When all of the troops were out of the barracks the squads searched the buildings and removed all of the weapons.

Tom called, "Colonel Hayes the Gulfstream has turn around and appears to be heading back to the ranch."

Colonel Hayes responded, "We will have people waiting for the plane at the airport."

Colonel Hayes instructed the squads from "Doc's House" and "Family Time" to move to the airport and to conceal themselves and wait for an incoming aircraft. The squads moved out at double time to get in position to capture whoever was on the plane.

The Cobra's remained in place over "Bin and Laden" buildings.

The Blackhawk's squads assigned to houses "Q and A" hit the buildings right on time and captured Fahd al- Saud and Ahmed Bin Aziz without a fight. The men were so shocked when the squads knocked down the doors and entered their houses they didn't have any time to react.

The Blackhawk assigned to "Honeymoon Cottage" found no one in the house and reported that to Colonel Hayes. Tom Parker intercepted the radio transmission regarding Shane and Elizabeth not being in "Honeymoon Cottage." He advised the squad to check out the main house since earlier in the evening there had been a lot of people in the house earlier in the evening although there was no activity indicated at this time.

A few minutes latter the squad that had entered the main house reported back that no one was in the main house. They said that they found no weapons or anything that indicated there was any thing used in the house for making bombs or anything to do with the al-Qaeda.

In the meantime Colonel Hayes said that the runway lights had just been activated and he could see the landing lights of the Gulfstream approaching the runway. Tom Parker advised everyone to stay back and let them land before getting any closer to the ranch airport with the choppers.

Tom was told by RG that the plane was just touching down and rolling out. Tom told Colonel Hayes to get ready to move in quick because he had a feeling that Dr. al-Sadr was on that plane along with Shane and Elizabeth.

Colonel Hayes radioed Tom to let him know that he was beginning to move his Cobra's toward the hanger right now since the Gulfstream was almost at the hanger. RG told Tom the Gulfstream is moving away from the hanger at a high rate of speed. Now it was turning around and coming back up the runway at take off speed.

RG said, "The plane is airborne and leaving the airport and is turning northwest."

Colonel Hayes said, "My God they must have seen the choppers in the air hovering above the buildings and took off. I would follow them, but there is no way we could keep up with them in the Cobra's. Tom, keep tracking them and we can get some help from our friends at the Brazilian Air Base. We had an escort of a couple of Air Force F-16 Fighting Falcons on the way down and I had them standing by in case we need some help tonight."

Tom said, "We will be tracking every move and checking with air controllers to see what we can find out about the Gulfstream. We will tell them it's one of our company planes and we think it's been stolen. Who knows we might get an idea of where they are headed. We can only pray that Shane and Elizabeth will be all right."

Colonel Hayes replied, "That maybe all that we can do because if Dr. al-Sadr thought that they were agents he would probably throw them out of the plane."

Tom said, "Get those Air Force F-16's on their tail right now!"

Colonel Hayes than instructed the squads from "Doc's House" and "Family Time" to take the ranch jeeps that were parked near "Bin" and "Laden" buildings and work with the Cobra's to round up the guards that were patrolling the perimeter of the ranch. In less than two hours they had captured the guards that were on patrol. They soon had them back at the ranch headquarters to join their comrades.

Shane struggled trying to get his arms out of the leather straps that held him to the arms of the aircraft seat. The more he struggled it seemed the tighter the straps got. He asked Elizabeth if she was having any luck trying to get free from her leather straps.

Elizabeth said, "Not yet, but I am able to turn my left wrist a little. I will keep trying to get my hands out of the straps."

Elizabeth continued to turn her left arm in the strap. It seemed to be getting a little bit looser as she continued trying to get her arm out of the strap.

Shane asked, "How are you doing Elizabeth? I hope you are doing better than I am the straps are just too tight for me to get my arms out. We need to get control of this plane before we run out of fuel."

Elizabeth replied, "I got my left hand out of the strap! I will try to use my left hand to get my right arm free."

Shane said, "Wonderful! Hurry and get me free."

Elizabeth said, "I haven't got my right hand free yet."

"Come on baby you got to save us!" Shane said.

"I'm trying, I got it!" Elizabeth shouted.

"Great now come and get me lose so I can see if we can fly this plane safely to some airport." Shane said.

Elizabeth started trying to take off the leather straps off of Shane's arms and was having trouble pulling the right one tight enough to get the prong out of the hole that had been used by Dr. al-Sadr to fasten Shane into the seat. She thought it was good that Dr. al-Sadr loosed her straps or she would have never been able to get out of them.

Shane said, "You must be making progress getting this strap off because it is sure getting tight and hurting my wrist.

Elizabeth replied, "Sorry love, there I got it."

Shane soon was able to take the strap off of his left arm and took off his seatbelt and got out of his seat. He went first to secure the door left opened by the exiting al-Sadrs and than went into the cockpit with Elizabeth following right behind him. Just as Shane was sitting down in the left hand pilot seat the engines began sputtering and Shane reach down and flipped a switch changing fuel tanks. The engines again started running smoothly.

Shane checked the fuel in this tank and saw that it too was almost empty. He told Elizabeth that we have to find an airport to get this bird on the ground before it lands nose first Next Shane turned back on the radios and found the Gulfstream's registration number posted on the face of the radio. Shane than called Asuncion control this is "Gulfstream xvyl00."

He heard Asuncion control reply, "This is Asuncion control we are glad to have you back."

"Asuncion control this is Gulfstream xvyl00 can you give me our currant position and your frequency for direct approach to your airport?" Shane replied.

"Gulfstream xvyl00 your current position is about 350 kilometers northeast of Asuncion on a northwest heading." Replied Asuncion control.

Shane said, "Roger. Please give me your radio frequency for direct approach to the airport."

Asuncion control said, "Airport approach is 137.2 and squawk 120. Are you advising you now have your radio navigation system back in service and that Asuncion Airport is your destination?"

Shane replied, "Airport approach is 137.2 and we are squawking 120. Affirming Asuncion Airport is our destination we are running low on fuel."

Asuncion control said, "Gulfstream xvyl00 are you declaring an emergency?"

Shane answered, "Xvyl00, we are not declaring an this time."

"Roger xvyl00" Asuncion control replied.

Shane told Elizabeth, "You can sit down in the right hand seat Elizabeth. You won't bother the airplane by sitting down."

Elizabeth said, "Are you sure it's all right."

Shane replied, "It's not a problem and you need to get use to sitting in the right hand seat in a Gulfstream because when we get married we will be using my family's plane a lot."

"Xvy 100 this is Asuncion control."

"Asuncion control this is xvy100." Shane replied.

"We have a inquiring regarding who is flying your plane by officials of your company." Asuncion control requested.

Shane replied, "Please advise my company that Dr. Shane Smith is now in control of the plane."

"Roger, I will pass on that information to your company." Asuncion control replied.

A few minutes latter Shane heard another call on his radio.

"Xvy 100 this is Tom Parker calling."

Shane said, "This is Shane Smith on xvy 100. How are you Tom?"

Tom said, "We are doing OK here at the ranch. Do you have company onboard with you?"

Shane replied, "Dr. Elizabeth is with me and we had two other passengers on take off but they jumped off."

Tom asked, "What is your destination at this time?"

Shane replied, "We don't have a choice we are enroute to Asuncion Airport because we are running low on fuel. Is everything OK at the ranch? Are our people safe and with you now?"

Tom said, "We have our people secured and they will soon be enroute home. Right now they have been taken to an air base in Brazil."

Shane asked, "That sounds like great news. Advise where we should meet you."

Tom answered, "Shane if you feel comfortable in flying the Gulfstream can you come back to the ranch? We didn't know that you were a pilot and were qualified to fly a Gulfstream."

Shane said, "As soon as we get refueled we will be on our way to the ranch. I am fully qualified for Gulfstreams with several hundred hours of experience."

Tom said, "Look forward to seeing you soon."

Shane and Elizabeth continued flying southwest following the radio directional signal toward Asuncion Airport. When they were about 100 kilometers away from the airport they received a radio transmission from Asuncion control.

"Xvy 100 begin descending to 10,000 feet and reduce your speed to 300 knots." Asuncion control said.

"Roger, Asuncion control." Shane replied.

Shane than begin reducing the speed of the plane and the nose began going down as the plane slowed down. At 10,000 feet Shane leveled off and Shane reported to Asuncion control that xvy 100 was at 10,000 feet.

Asuncion control than said to reduce speed to 275 knots and descend to 5,000 feet. Shane acknowledged the instructions to descend to 5,000 feet and was reducing speed to 275 knots. When Shane reached his new assigned elevation he again reported it to Asuncion control.

Asuncion called again a few minutes latter, "Xvy 100 how is your fuel?"

Shane replied, "We are sucking fumes."

Asuncion control said, "We are going to bring you directly in. Reduce speed to 200 knots and level off at 1,000 feet."

"Roger. We are reducing speed to 200 knots and heading for 1,000 feet Asuncion control." Shane replied.

Asuncion control replied, "We are passing you to Asuncion tower on 126.2 for final and landing."

Shane answered, "Roger we are heading to 1,000 feet at 200 knots and switching to 126.2 for Asuncion tower and will contact them. Thanks for your help Asuncion control."

Asuncion control replied, "Goodbye and good luck."

Shane changed the radio frequency to 126.2 and called, "Asuncion tower this is Gulfstream xvy 100 at 1,000 feet and request landing instructions."

Asuncion tower replied, "Gulfstream xvy 100 we have you and will be bringing you in direct. Maintain 1,000 feet and turn to 180 degrees and in a few minutes you should be on the glide slope and be able to see the runway lights. Advise when you see the lights."

Shane replied, "Roger, turning to 180 and can now see the runway lights."

Asuncion tower said, "OK you are cleared to land and you are on the glide slope."

Shane said, "Roger we are on the way down. Wheels are going down now."

A few minutes latter the wheels of the Gulfstream smoothly touched down on the runway. The plane continued to roll down the runway and Shane reversed the thrust of the engines. The plane slowed down and the tower said we are turning you over to ground control at 180.1.

Shane responded, "Thanks Asuncion tower. We are switching to 180.1 for ground control."

"Asuncion ground control this is Gulfstream xvy 100 requesting taxiing instructions." Shane said.

Asuncion ground control replied, "Gulfstream xvy 100 turn right on taxiway "A" to go to the transit terminal hanger."

Shane turned the Gulfstream onto taxiway "A" and acknowledged this to ground control. After making the turn the engines stopped.

Shane called ground control, "We have a problem, we are out of fuel and the engines have stopped and we are dead on the taxiway."

Ground control replied, "We will send a tug to your location to tow you to the transit terminal to get refueled xvy 100."

Shane said, "Elizabeth I guess you know we were really lucky to make it to the airport if we had a few more miles to go we would have crashed."

"Shane that just shows you how lucky we are being together." Elizabeth replied.

A tug arrived and hooked the plane to it and began to tow the Gulfstream to the transit terminal so the plane could be refueled.

When the tug had pulled the plane into the transit terminal and parked it Shane and Elizabeth opened the door of the plane and got out. The question from the tug operator was how much fuel that Shane wanted. Shane told him to put 1,000 gallons in each tank.

Shane than turned to Elizabeth and took her in his arms and said, "We made it and we are free and alive."

Both Shane and Elizabeth began to cry tears of joy.

They walked to the transit terminal to see what they could do to pay for the fuel. Shane realized that he still had his billfold and his Amex Card. One problem solved.

When Shane and Elizabeth walked inside the transit terminal the manager said, "Cutting it pretty close on fuel aren't you. Those Gulfstreams are great planes, but not worth a damn without jet fuel."

Shane replied, "I'll tell you I wouldn't want to cut it any closer."

The plane was refueled and checked over and was ready for Shane and Elizabeth to leave. Shane did the customary walk around inspection of the plane before he and Elizabeth got aboard.

Elizabeth asked, "I have watch pilots do that walk around for years what are they looking for?"

Shane replied as he and Elizabeth were settling into their seats, "You would be surprised how much we can learn by just walking around the plane to inspect it. Things like damage to the skin of the plane, if there was any damage visible on the plane, the tires and if there were any leaks of any kind."

Fifteen minutes after that they were airborne and enroute back to the ranch. Less than an hour later they were on final approach to land at the ranch and Shane pull the plane up to the hanger. When Shane opened the door of the plane standing at the bottom of the stairs of the plane was Tom Parker and Bob Barker.

Tom spoke first, "What the hell are you doing spending the night flying around South America?"

Shane replied, "Elizabeth and I just didn't have anything else to do on a Saturday night down here on the ranch, so we thought we would take a little ride."

Bob said, "You're still joking after being a guest of Dr. Death for a week."

Shane came down the stairs and gave Tom and Bob a big hug. Than he said, "God are we glad to see you guys."

Elizabeth came out of the door of the plane and down the steps right into Tom's arms.

She said, "Thanks for saving us."

Tom replied, "I not sure we saved you or almost caused you two to get killed."

Shane said, "Well I would like to talk to you about that. Dr. al-Sadr's brother saw the lights of the choppers and really took off. I guess you understood my message about having two passengers get out that they parachuted out of the plane saying that if they landed with the plane they would be captured."

Tom replied, "Yes we understood that from your message. We just didn't understand why they let you two escape. We thought they would kill you. What were you doing flying around anyway?"

Elizabeth said, "We were asked to take a little ride after having a birthday dinner for Dr. al-Sadr. It was a little hard to say no to him. Really hard to say no to him after hearing about him killing Dr. Borland and his wife the first day the other doctors and their families were taken prisoners."

Shane said, "How are the doctors and their families?"

Bob replied, "They are doing fine and reunited with their families."

Tom said, "I just want to know if Dr. al-Sadr knew you could fly the plane when they bailed out on you?"

Elizabeth said, "I don't think he was worried about that since he had us strapped to the seats when he bailed out of the plane. As he was leaving the plane he told us that we would soon be running out of fuel."

Shane said, "Elizabeth saved us by getting out of her leather straps and unfastening me. Without that when the plane ran out of fuel we would have gone down with the plane. No doubt about it. We just did have enough fuel to get to Asuncion."

Elizabeth quickly replied, "Getting out of the straps was nothing unless someone could fly the plane, Shane saved us."

Tom said, "It sounds like you two make a good team and are really good together. So what do you think about that."

Elizabeth replied, "I certainly hope so since Shane and I are getting married as soon as we return to America. So what do you think about that?"

Tom said, "I think it's wonderful! We didn't know we were acting for cupid when we put you two together on a honeymoon."

Bob said, "I'll be dammed! I thought you two were really good together, but I never thought about you two getting married. How about it Shane, are you ready to marry this woman?"

Shane replied, "More than ready. I can't wait to get home to Oklahoma to marry Elizabeth. I will tell you one thing my Dad is going to be shocked. I think for several years he thought I was gay or something and he will be shocked to meet this English lady that I am going to marry since her father is a friend of his. Oklahoma will never be the same. My Dad is going to fall in love with her just like I did."

Elizabeth said, "Stop it Shane, you're embarrassing me."

Shane said, "Well it true. I will say for awhile I thought I might have to fight Dr. al-Sadr for her. He took quite a shine to her as we say in Oklahoma. He was having a hard time making up his mind if he wanted to leave his brother and take her when he jumped out of the plane, but she blew it when she said she would rather stay and die with me than go with him. So he took his brother and left her to die with me."

Shane than asked, "Do you have any chance of finding Dr. al-Sadr and his brother in Paraguay?"

Tom said, "The military will be searching for them, but it's really rugged country in the area that they bailed out in."

Shane said, "I hope they can find them, they are bad people!"

Bob replied, "We hope so!"

CHAPTER THIRTEEN

Dr. al-Sadr parachute opened with a sudden up draft and it felt like it had taken him back up several hundred feet. It had been a long time since he bailed out of a plane and he remembered that he never did like doing it. However, he thought I like this better than being captured, tried and put to death for the people he had killed. He was hoping that his brother Muhammad made it safely out of the plane. He certainly couldn't see him in the dark.

Now he had to worry about getting down to the ground without breaking a leg or something worse like his neck.

Dr. al-Sadr began to be able to make out trees and things on the ground. He thought Muhammad picked a great place to have us jump out of an airplane, mountains, trees and big rocks. Another fine day being a member of the al-Qaeda. If only he didn't like the feeling of power he got when people were scared of him so much. When they didn't know if he was going to let them live or was he going to kill them. That look in their eyes gave him more pleasure than sex or anything else that he ever experienced. He loved it. Nothing was power like the power over life or death. Only Allah knew better than he.

Suddenly he didn't have time for any more thoughts as he came crashing into a huge tree. He hit the tree limbs with such force they gave way from the force of his weight and speed from his fall. Luckily he was far enough out from the trunk and the main branches of the tree that he didn't hit any of the really large tree limbs. His parachute lines were tangled up enough in the limbs that he was still six to eight feet off of the ground. He struggled to get the parachute lines loose from the tree limbs and he fell another couple of feet, but than he stopped falling.

He still was four to six feet off of the ground. He continued to jerk and pull on the lines, but got no where. Than he worked to unhook himself from the chute, but he found that hanging there with all of his weight on the chute caused him to have a hard time getting it to release to let him out of the harness and let him fall on down to the ground.

Than all of a sudden pop, crack he was free and fell straight down to the ground as the chute released. He hit the ground hard and rolled a few feet away from the tree trunk. He sat up and tried moving his legs, they seemed to be all right next he looked over his arms they too were OK. So he wiped off his clothes and got up off of the ground. He made it all right. Now he had to find Muhammad.

Dr. al-Sadr began walking northwest the best that he could figure out what northwest was. He figured that the plane was flying on a northwesterly course so it was reasonable to think that Muhammad would be somewhere northwest of where he landed.

The walking was not easy he couldn't see too well yet since the nighttime continued to hang on until almost eight o'clock in the morning in this area of the world. The best he could deicide was that he was about half way up a very large mountain. He hoped that Muhammad was on the same mountain. He had been walking for almost thirty minutes when he heard jet planes overhead and they were low, too low he thought. Maybe they are already searching for the downed plane. Surly it was too soon for the Gulfstream to run out of fuel and already have planes out searching for the wreckage.

He continued walking and he could tell he begun going down hill. Sure enough he was certainly coming down off of the mountain that he had landed on. He thought that he could see the sun coming up, but he knew it was too early for the sun to be coming up. No what he saw was lights from a small hillside village in front of him. That meant that there would be some kind of roads and people.

As he continued walking he could hear dogs barking. He didn't need to find dogs and people right now he needed to find his brother. Muhammad had to be somewhere not very far from were he had landed unless some wind caught him and carried him farther away than what he thought.

Dr. al-Sadr decided that he needed to stay away from this village so it changed his direction back up the side of the mountain. He had now walked maybe another thirty or forty-five minutes. He wasn't sure how far he had walked, but than he saw his brother hanging against a large boulder. He called out to him, Muhammad, Muhammad. No answer. When Dr. al-Sadr got closer he could see blood coming from a wound on Muhammad's head. Than he saw that Muhammad's parachute was tangled up in a tree and that must have swung him against the boulder hitting his head.

Dr. al-Sadr grabbed his brother around his legs and pulled. He pulled again and the lines of the parachute came free dropping his brother to the ground. Dr. al-Sadr checked his pulse he couldn't feel a pulse at all. Next he tried to listen to his heart. Nothing. He checked for any sign of breathing. Nothing. Muhammad was dead.

Dr. al-Sadr checked his brother's pockets for anything he could use for his escape. He took his billfold, compass, watch, large knife and his nine millimeter pistol. He found four extra clips of ammunition in his coat pocket and a road map of Paraguay.

Than Dr. al-Sadr leaned over and kissed Muhammad on the forehead and said to him, "I'm sorry my brother I will see you in paradise where we will have a grand reunion. I will miss you here on earth my friend and companion. I will never find anyone that will look after me the way you have all of my life. I loved you."

Dr. al-Sadr got up off of the ground and again started walking as fast as he could to get away from his brother's body and away from the village. As he walked along in the trees he could hear jets flying low as if they were searching for someone. He was afraid they were searching for him. He had to find a way to get to Sao Paulo where he could contact an al-Qaeda cell to help him get out of South America.

After walking a few minutes he unfolded the map and looked to see if he could tell where he was at. After looking at the map he decided that he should try to reach San Pedro and find an international truck that would be going to Sao Paulo and buy a ride with a driver.

He felt like if he followed a northwest direction he should find a road that would lead him to San Pedro. He checked the compass and began walking on a northwesterly course. It was now well past daylight and he could no longer hear the jet planes overhead. He knew that he had to get out of this area soon before they found the wreckage of the plane or someone found his brother's body.

Four hours latter Dr. al-Sadr came down a hill onto a paved road and started following it north according to his compass. Another hour past as he walked along the paved road and he could see a town ahead of him. Very few vehicles went past him in either direction as he walked along the road. None offered to stop and he never tried to get a ride either. As he approached the town he saw a service station with several trucks parked around it. Some filling fuel and others just parked.

When he arrived at the station he asked the attendant that was fuelling one of the trucks if the driver was around that drove this truck. He was told that the driver was sitting outside of the station drinking coffee and smoking a cigarette. He was the man with a green shirt and dark green pants and wearing a straw hat.

Dr. al-Sadr walked over to where the driver was sitting and asked him where he was going the driver said he was traveling to Asuncion. After talking with the driver for several minutes.

Dr. al-Sadr asked him, "What he thought was the best way for him to go to Sao Paulo, Brazil from here."

The driver told him that going to Asuncion was the best way since there he could get a ride east on the Pan American Highway to Brazil and on to Sao Paulo.

The driver said, "It was too bad he wasn't going to Buenos Aires because the load on his truck was bound for there."

Dr. al-Sadr said, "Are you going all the way to Buenos Aires with your truck?"

The driver told him no that he was meeting a boat that would take his load to Buenos Aires than the load would be loaded unto a ship bound for Rotterdam.

The driver said, "He was sure that he could get him a ride on the boat going to Buenos Aires without any problem."

Dr. al-Sadr told the driver that he would like to go with him to Asuncion and have him help him get a ride to Buenos Aires on the boat. He told the driver that he would pay him one hundred US dollars if he would help him. The driver said it's not a problem for a hundred US dollars he would let him go with him and help him get a ride on the boat.

Dr. al-Sadr knew that the al-Qaeda had a cell in Buenos Aires that he could contact for help. It would be better than trying to get to Sao Paulo since he didn't want to go anywhere near Cidade Del Este since the Pan American Highway ran right through the City and he would have to cross the border into Brazil there. He was sure that whoever raided the ranch would surely be watching the border from Paraguay into Brazil for him.

Dr. al-Sadr paid the driver one hundred dollars when he got into the cab of the eighteen wheeler and told the driver if got him a ride on the boat he would pay him another one hundred US dollars. The driver smiled and said his wife would never believe that he had so much money.

The trip to Asuncion took several hours much too long for no more distances than it was, but Dr. al-Sadr made good use of the time he slept the whole way. When he woke up the driver was backing his truck up to a dock where a crane was waiting to load the large forty foot container off of the truck and onto the boat. After the driver stopped the truck he got out and went to talk to the boat captain in a few minutes he came back to the truck and told Dr. al-Sadr that he was set to go on the boat to Buenos Aires. Just one thing the captain wanted fifty US dollars to take him. The driver said I told the captain that you would pay the fifty dollars. The driver said if it is taking all of your money to give me the extra one hundred I will give the captain half of my hundred dollars to pay the captain.

Dr. al-Sadr told the driver that it was all right I told you that I would pay you the extra hundred dollars if you got me the ride on the boat and I will. I don't have too much more money left, but I can cover the fifty dollars that the captain wants. The driver smiled again and told Dr. al-Sadr you are an honorable man.

Dr. al-Sadr thought to himself that this poor peasant had no idea of how dishonorable he was. He had a vision of how Elizabeth eyes looked at him when he left her to die in the plane and Dr. Smith's. Than he thought about leaving his poor dead brother out in the middle of nowhere without even a proper burial. All his brother ever wanted out of life was to look out for his younger brother and his brother didn't even take care of burying him. Honorable. No, Dr. al-Sadr didn't think so, no he was most dishonorable.

Dr. al-Sadr gave the driver the extra one hundred dollars and thanked him for his help. Than he paid the captain the fifty dollars and the captain showed him were he could rest and ride for the trip to Buenos Aires. Soon after the container was loaded the boat cast off and was underway to Buenos Aires.

Dr. al-Sadr decided that when he got to Buenos Aires he would have the boat captain help him to get a ride of the ship taking the container to Rotterdam. It would be a good hiding place and let him return to Europe where he could get in contact with the al-Qaeda to see where they needed him to go next. One thing he knew was the mad cow project was dead. It was too hard to do and required too many risks and too many experts. It was a great concept, but not practical.

No, he could do much more damage to America quicker and safer than this mad cow scheme. Taking a sea voyage would be just the thing to do. It would give him time to plan many other attacks on America and could do them using their own al-Qaeda people to carry them out. No need for outside experts. Life was good.

CHAPTER FOURTEEN

Shane asked Tom, "OK, what do we do now?"

Tom replied, "First we need to get these prisoners loaded into the C-5 troop transport plane that should

be landing here in a few minutes. Next, we will be flying back to the Brazilian Air Force Base and you can catch up with the other doctors before we leave for America. I also want to introduce you to Colonel Jack Hayes the commander in charge of the military operation that came to save you and your doctors."

Bob said, "I guess someone from the State Department will need to contact Prince Abdullah Bin Turki to tell him that he needs some new managers for his ranch. So far the State Department must have been busy soothe feathers with the Government of Argentina since we haven't been attacked by their military yet. That probably will cost us a few million dollars."

Elizabeth said, "If we are going to be leaving the ranch after while I would like to get my things out of the little house that Shane and I were staying in."

Tom said, "Some of Colonel Hayes people have already packed up your clothes and things from the house along with Shane's. They also have all of the clothes packed up for the doctors and their families. Everything is being transported to the Brazilian Air Force Base right now."

Elizabeth replied, "Great. I won't have to worry about packing them."

Tom said, "Elizabeth you know I will take care of you."

Bob said, "You better watch him Shane, he maybe trying to steal your woman."

Tom said, "I would, but I know I couldn't, she saw him first."

Bob replied, "Yeah, first last and always!"

Everyone laughed at Bob statement. About that time a Cobra landed a little ways away from where they had been standing. Colonel Hayes got out of the Cobra Helicopter and began walking up to where they were. When he got to where they were he said, "You must be Dr. Shane Smith and Dr. Elizabeth Browning?"

Shane reached out to shake his hand.

Colonel Hayes took his hand and said, "I'm Jack Hayes, Dr. Smith."

Shane replied, "How are you Colonel Hayes, I'm Shane Smith and this is Dr. Elizabeth Browning."

The two men continued shaking hands vigorously.

Than Shane said, "Thanks for coming to help us."

Colonel Hayes replied, "I understand instead of helping you and Dr. Browning we almost got you both killed. It's a good thing you knew how to fly an airplane like this Gulfstream."

Shane said, "That was lucky since my family has a plane almost like this one."

Elizabeth said, "Thanks Colonel Hayes, we certainly appreciate you and your troops saving us and the other doctors and their families."

Colonel Hayes said, "I think it was made a lot easier due to your efforts of becoming bait for al-Qaeda. We had it easy, we didn't have to fire one shot, none of our people were injured or killed and we have captured almost eighty members of the al-Qaeda here on the ranch. The rest of the locals that were working on the ranch have been sent home. There were a couple of chef's that worked for the Prince that didn't have any idea what had been going on here. I am sure the next time the Prince arrives here they are going to have some stories to tell."

"That's great news Colonel Hayes." Shane said. "Have you had any luck finding Dr. al-Sadr and his brother yet?"

Colonel Hayes replied, "Not yet, but we have put some troops on the ground in the area that we believe that they should be in. If they are anywhere in the area we will find them don't worry about that."

Tom asked, "Jack how much longer will it be before the C-5's are here to pick up these prisoners? We would like to get going soon so that we can get started back to the States tonight."

Colonel Hayes replied, "Tom the plane should be here any minute now, but you don't have to wait here at the ranch. We can have a Blackhawk take the four of you over to the Air Base."

Tom said, "That's good I will call our pilots to tell them to fuel up the Gulfstream V and come to the Brazilian Air Force Base to be ready to fly us back to the USA. I am sure that the doctors will want to say goodbye to their colleagues before we leave for the States. I know for sure their colleagues will want to say thank you to Shane and Elizabeth for risking their lives to come and save them."

One of the C-5's was turning on final approach for landing at the ranch airport as Tom was finishing his statement. Colonel Hayes radioed his troops that were guarding the prisoners to bring them down to the runway and be ready to load them onto the big plane.

Shane asked, "Where are you taking the prisoners?"

Colonel Hayes replied, "They are heading to join some of their buddies at Guantanamo Bay, Cuba."

Tom said, "That will be a good place for them maybe we won't have to fight them again latter in some other part of the world."

Colonel Hayes said, "Let's hope we get to stop fighting these terrorists one of these days. I would like to finish my thirty years and retire without firing one more shot or writing one more letter to a grieving parent, wife or husband about a lost son or daughter."

Tom replied, "Now you are talking, let's get these love birds on the way to Oklahoma to get married. Jack we forgot to tell you that Shane and Elizabeth have decided to get married as soon as they get back to the states."

Jack said, "That's pretty good you use them for bait and they fall in love. That maybe a new one for the CIA."

Tom answered, "Yeah, I'm not sure how to write that up in my final report for the "Dangerous Food Mission". Maybe I just write mad cow nothing, love one!"

Everyone laughed as they watched the prisoners being loaded into the plane. Colonel Hayes radioed a Blackhawk to come to pick up Shane, Elizabeth, Tom and Bob to fly them to the Brazilian Air Force Base. The four of them climbed aboard the Blackhawk and it was soon on its way.

After an hour ride in the Blackhawk they landed at the Brazilian Air Force Base. As soon as they arrived at the base they were taken to the officers club to be reunited with their colleagues.

Dr. Allen said to Elizabeth, "We certainly didn't know that you and Dr. Smith had been sent to find us. But we are really glad that you did. It was a real shock when the squad of US soldiers came bursting into our barracks this morning. I was never so happy to see American soldiers in all my life."

"Elizabeth on behalf of my family and the rest of the doctors and their families we want to say thank you for what you did to rescue us. One thing we have learned about this whole thing. Be really careful about accepting a deal to speak at a conference if the terms sounds too good to be true. It could cost you your life."

Dr. Van Meter said, "Shane, Elizabeth thank you. I know that without your help we might never have gotten away. I am so happy I don't know what else to say, but thanks."

Dr. Hinson added, "It was too bad you weren't with us when we were first taken prisoners you might have been able to save Dr. and Mrs. Borland's lives. After you arrived you give us hope that we could get out alive with our families we just didn't know you were going to be bringing the American Army with you. You never said anything about being there to save us.

Shane said, "We are sorry, but we thought it would be better not to say anything about that we had been used as bait by our Governments to help find all of you and to get you out of there."

Than each of the doctors proceeded to hug Elizabeth and Shane and introduce their wives and their children to Shane and Elizabeth. Each of them thanked and hugged them. Everyone was so grateful to be free and to know they would soon be on their way home. Than the tears started following. Tears of joy. Even Tom and Bob's eyes became teary.

Shane saw that and knew that it was time for them to leave. Shane and Elizabeth started telling each one of their new friends goodbye.

When they got to Dr. Allen he said, "We will never forget what you did for us. If we can help you in anyway just tell us how."

After the four of them left the building they went to the operations center to check to see how much longer that it would be before the Gulfstream V would be arriving from Rio to take them back to the USA. They were told that air control had been in contact with their plane and it should be arriving within the next hour or so.

Colonel Hayes came into the operations center to say goodbye to them and he told Tom. It was great working with you again. It was almost like old times except he thought that Tom must be getting old because he seemed far too mellow.

Jack said to Tom, "Well boss, I guess I have to say goodbye to you again and at least you didn't have to carry my body and throw it on a chopper to send me home like you did the last time we worked together."

Tom replied, "No, you did good this time I didn't even have to fight my way out of a mess like you left me in last time. You're getting better. Take care of yourself and don't let the bad guys get you!"

Shane and Elizabeth's luggage was sitting on the tarmac waiting for the Gulfstream V to arrive and even though it seemed like it took forever for it to get there. It finally did.

Captain Martinez and Lieutenant Wheatley congratulated them for finding the missing scientists and their families and helping to rescue them. They welcomed them aboard and asked if they were ready to go back to America. They assured them they were more than ready. After the plane was airborne both Shane and Elizabeth were soon fast asleep. Tom and Bob were not long behind them. The four of them slept for the entire flight to the States. Shane woke up when he heard Captain Martinez talking with Miami Flight Control Center.

Soon Elizabeth, Tom and Bob were awake as well and asking where they were at. When they heard they were two hundred miles southeast of Miami a small cheer went up. All four of them were ready to go home.

Shane asked Tom, "Do you think I could make arrangements to buy Elizabeth's engagement ring and our wedding bands from the CIA?"

Tom said, "I am sure they would be happy to make a present of those rings it's a wonder they didn't get lost or stolen while you were prisoners of the al-Qaeda. I not sure they weren't, are you Bob?"

Bob said, "I am pretty sure that somebody stolen those rings."

Shane said, "No, I really want to pay for them."

Tom replied, "OK doc. We will have them deducted from your salary."

Shane said, "Thanks Tom. These rings mean a lot to Elizabeth and I and I am sure she would rather have them instead of another set."

Elizabeth replied, "You damn right. I'm not giving up my rings. For now I will take off my wedding ring and Shane can take off his. I will keep his ring and he can keep mine until the wedding vows are said."

With that said Elizabeth took off her wedding band and gave it to Shane and Shane gave her his ring.

Than Elizabeth said, "I am only letting you hold my band for a little while because I want it back real soon."

Shane replied, "Whatever you say my love."

CHAPTER FIFTEEN

As the Gulfstream V was on final approach at Andrews Air Base Tom got a call on his cell phone from Colonel Hayes.

Colonel Hayes said, "Tom bad news we found Dr. al-Sadr's brother Muhammad al-Sadr, but not the doctor. Muhammad was dead from parachuting into a huge tree that swung him into a big boulder and cracked open his head. Sorry, we looked everywhere, but couldn't find your doctor. Tom I am sorry to say that it took us longer to find where they landed because they were farther away from where they should have been based on our tracking of the plane. The wind must have blown them farther northwest than we had projected. Sorry. Anyway the doctor was nowhere to be found. We did find some tracks for a little ways away from his brother's body, but the mountain was pretty much just hard rock and so no footprints for us to follow."

Tom replied, "Thanks Jack. I am sorry you couldn't find the doctor, that's bad luck on our part. I would have sure liked to have found him and got rid of him forever. Now we will still be plagued by him somewhere in the world. You can bet we have not seen the last of that son-of- bitch. He's a killer and one of the worst kinds of killers, he likes it."

After they landed Tom told Shane that he would make arrangements for him and Elizabeth at the Park Hyatt Hotel in Washington. Also, he would have the Air Force provide a car and driver to take them there because Bob and he were going home and we will talk to you sometime tomorrow.

Shane and Elizabeth arrived at the Park Hyatt and the desk clerk said, "Hello, Dr. Smith it's nice to see you again."

Shane replied, "It good to be back here again. I been too many miles since I saw you the last time and I hope you have a wonderful room for Dr. Browning and myself."

The desk clerk said, "We certainly do have a lovely suite all ready for you."

A bellman took their luggage up to their suite on the ninth floor and Shane used the keycard to unlock the door. This suite was as beautiful as their suite in Rio. But Shane and Elizabeth could only think of a warm bath and going to bed.

As Shane was giving a tip to the bellman Elizabeth was already taking off her clothes. The bellman asked if there was anything else he could do for them and Shane said you can hang the "Do Not Disturb" sign on their door.

By the time the door to the suite closed Elizabeth had taken off her blouse and her pants were on there way to the floor. Next the bra and panties came off and she was on her way to the bathroom. Shane was quickly off with his clothes as Elizabeth had started filling the extra large bathtub. She poured in a goodly amount of bubble bath into the tub. As the water was rising, so were the bubbles. The bubbles kept rising until they were almost to the top of the tub and when Elizabeth stepped into the tub the bubbles began spilling onto the floor.

Shane said, "Elizabeth you are going to have to let out some of the water from the tub before we flood the room below us."

Elizabeth lifted the bathtub stopper and the water went down and the level of the bubbles receded below the top of the tub. Shane quickly took a large bath towel and wiped up the overflow of water and bubbles from the floor and placed the very soaked towel in one of the sinks.

Elizabeth leaned back in the tub and told Shane that this water feels wonderful come on and get into the tub with me. Shane told her to move forward so that he could get in the tub behind her. Elizabeth moved forward in the tub and Shane got in the tub behind her and as he sat down the water and bubbles again started pouring over the top of the tub. This time Elizabeth quickly pulled up the plug and the water went down again so that it was no longer pouring over the top of the tub.

Elizabeth than leaned back against Shane body and the two of them stayed in the tub soaking for over an hour. With Elizabeth letting out water and than filling the tub back up to keep the water warm. When they finally got out of the tub they had wrinkles where they never had wrinkles before. They just laughed and made their way to the king- size bed, pulled back the bedspread and sheet and lay down and stayed in the bed without moving for the next ten hours.

When Shane finally did wake up it was because he need to go the bathroom and discovered he was hungry. As he got out of bed he woke up Elizabeth who had the same needs.

Returning to the bedroom Shane found a room service menu and asked Elizabeth if a hamburger and French fries and a coke would be all right for her or did she want breakfast. She replied from the bathroom that a hamburger would be fine for her. Shane picked up the phone and dialed room service and ordered their hamburgers.

Elizabeth returned to the bedroom wearing a Park Hyatt bathrobe. Shane asked her where she found the robe and she told him that she found two of them hanging on the back of the bathroom door. Shane got the other robe and put it on so that he could answer the door when they brought their meals.

After putting on his bathrobe he took Elizabeth into his arms and began kissing her. He asked her if he had told her lately that he loved her. She told him no and that he needed to do it early and often because she could start worrying that he didn't love her any more. Shane told her that's one thing in her life she would never have to worry about.

The kissing continued until there was a knock on the door. Oh ha, their food had arrived. Shane opened the door and the waiter brought in a silver cart with their food and drinks on it. He sat up the table in the combination living dining room with their hamburgers, French fries and their cokes. Shane signed the bill and added a twenty percent tip onto the already extra charge for the room service.

As they ate their hamburger and fries they talked about what they should recommend to Secretary Ridge to safeguard against the possibility of mad cow disease ever being spread in America. They made a list of recommendations. Their list included:

1. Positive electronic identification and tracking of every cow from birth to the slaughter house.
2. Testing of every cow slaughtered in the USA.
3. Development of a test for BSE on live cattle.
4. Increased budget for development of a vaccine to prevent BSE in cattle.
5. Ban of all spinal cords, brains or spleens in feed pellets.
6. Increased inspections of all plants manufacturing feed pellets.
7. Ban of all waste from chickens used to make feed pellets.
8. Rigid inspection of all imported feed for cattle or a ban on all imported feed pellets.
9. Increase in the number of inspectors hired by the Government for meat processing plants.
10. Development of a computer tracking program that uses the worldwide web to keep track of each cow in American.

Shane said, "I think that is about enough if we could get a fourth of these things implemented it would be a huge improvement for the safety of the America's food supply."

When they finished their meal and were beginning to think about making love and calling people the telephone rang.

Shane said, "It could only be Tom calling. He has this knack of calling at just the wrong time."

Shane answered the phone, "Hello."

"Hello Shane this is Tom. Have you heard the news?"

Shane said, "No we haven't had on the TV or anything. So what's the news?"

Tom said, "They think that got a cow in Washington State that has mad cow disease and they want you and Elizabeth to go there as soon as you can to see what you can find out. I told them you were planning to get married right away.

They said that would be OK to getting married before you went to Washington. Is that all right?"

Shane replied, "I guess we can honeymoon in Washington State or where ever this leads us."

Shane hung up the phone and told Elizabeth what he had just been told by Tom.

Elizabeth said, "I don't believe it. I think we better call my Dad and let he know that we are safe and back in the States and that we are going to get married in Oklahoma as soon as we can."

Shane said, "Let's call him, than call my Dad and tell him, than we have to call Logan and Molly to tell them."

Elizabeth got her Dad on the line and told him that she and Shane were going to get married in Oklahoma as soon as they could make arrangements. He was thrilled.

Next Shane called his Dad and after trying several locations Shane got him on the phone in the plane.

Shane said, "Dad I have something that I am going to tell you that may come as a surprise. I'm getting married as soon as we can make arrangements. Her name is Elizabeth Victoria Browning. She is your friend Dr. Clive Browning's daughter."

John Paul said, "That's a real surprise I was beginning to think you might never get married. Logan told me that Clive had a daughter that he only found out about her recently and she was working with you on your project. So where do you plan to get married and am I invited to the wedding?"

Shane replied, "Dad you are not only invited, but you are my best man. Elizabeth wants to get married in Oklahoma on our ranch. What do you think about that?"

"I think it wonderful. What can I do to help?" John Paul asked.

"A lot I am afraid we need to get married quickly, because we have been asked to go to Washington State as soon as we can to investigate the reported BSE in some cow there. I didn't tell you but Elizabeth is a research veterinary too. Can you see what you can do about the three day waiting period before a wedding license can be issued?" Shane asked.

John Paul said, "I'll call one of the county judges about that. Do you want me to make arrangements with our preacher?"

Shane said, "Yes Dad, do whatever you can do to get us set up to get married. I want to marry this English girl before she finds out what kind of a family she is getting herself into."

"All right you leave everything up to me. I'll get one of those wedding planners out of Tulsa or Oklahoma City. I'll ask around to find out who is the best one in Oklahoma. You're going to have the best wedding held in Oklahoma in the last forty years maybe fifty. You leave it to me. What about Logan and Molly and Clive do I need to have someone take the plane and pick them up in Ames? John Paul asked.

"That would be great. Just have them picked up as soon as you can so we all have sometime together before the wedding." Shane replied.

John Paul said, "I am on it right now I will have the plane take me home and than send it to Ames to pick up the rest of the folks. By the way where are you?"

Shane replied, "Elizabeth and I are in Washington, DC staying at the Park Hyatt we just returned from a mission in South America for Homeland Security."

John Paul said, "I knew you and Elizabeth were in South America because Logan called me about the plot to develop a super BSE by the al-Qaeda. I glad you are both back safely in America. Don't worry about the wedding it will be great. See you soon."

Shane and Elizabeth both called Logan and Molly. Molly couldn't believe that they were going to get married so soon, but sounded happy for them and Logan couldn't have been happier for them. Shane told them that his Dad was sending the plane for them to come for the wedding. Shane told them he didn't know how long it would be before the plane got there but it would be soon. He suggested that they bring something to wear for the wedding and plan to stay three or four days.

After all of the telephone calls Elizabeth told Shane I need to get a wedding dress maybe we can go shopping here in Washington to see what I can find. Shane said that he needed to find out when they would be able to meet with Secretary Ridge so he called his office and spoke with Sue Barrett. She told Shane that the Secretary was out of town making a speech in New York, but would return latter tonight. She set up an appointment for him and Dr. Browning for ten am tomorrow morning. Shane thanked her for her help.

Than Shane told Elizabeth that they could go shopping for her wedding dress. Shane checked the telephone directory for shops that sold wedding dresses and found that many of them would be closing before long. Than he saw an ad for a shop at Montgomery Mall in Rockville, Maryland that was open until nine pm. Shane told Elizabeth let's get dressed and go see what we can find at the Mall.

After dressing they got a taxi and had it take them to Montgomery Mall to look for Elizabeth's wedding dress. It took them awhile to find the wedding dress shop but walking around this three story Mall they found several stores that carried wedding dresses. Elizabeth started her search for her wedding dress in the store that Shane had read about in the telephone directory.

It didn't take her long to find it. It was an old-fashioned white wedding dress covered with English Lace over white satin. The train of the dress was detachable so that it would be easy to wear at the reception and dance after the wedding. The salesclerk was very good insisting that this dress was made for an English bride and Elizabeth just had to try it on. Shane could see when she came out of the dressing room in the dress that the salesclerk was right it was made for Elizabeth. She looked like an angel just sent down from heaven in the dress.

Elizabeth agreed it looked OK on her. Shane told her it looked better than just OK it was beautiful on her. The dress set off her black hair and brown eyes. They bought the dress, now they only had to worry about packing it up to transport it to Oklahoma. Shane didn't know that wedding dresses could cost so much, a dress to wear only one time. Elizabeth's wedding dress was seven thousand five hundred dollars and all the time the salesclerk was writing up the ticket for the dress she kept telling them that Elizabeth was getting such a bargain.

Elizabeth said after they left the store, “It’s a good thing I am only going to get married once because I don’t think I would ever pay that kind of money for a dress again. I did thought didn’t I?”

They got a taxi back to the hotel and when they were back in their suite Elizabeth began to cry. She had big tears rolling down her cheeks and she tried to hide the tears from Shane.

Shane softly asked, “Elizabeth what’s wrong? Why are you crying is there something wrong with you?”

Elizabeth replied through her tears, “My mother, she wanted to see her daughter get married so bad and I kept telling her I was never go to get married and here I am getting married. Now she not going to be here when I get married.”

Shane replied, “I think your mother would be very happy for you that you found someone that you wanted to getting married and I think both of our mothers will be watching over us at our wedding.”

Elizabeth said, “Oh Shane, I’m sorry. I had forgotten about your mother not going to be at the wedding either. I think you are right our mothers will be with us at our wedding. Oh Shane I love you so much.”

Elizabeth wiped her eyes with a tissue that Shane gave her and reached for him to hold. Shane held her and gently pulled her toward the bed and than down on the bed.

Elizabeth said, “Make love to me.”

Shane replied, “I thought you would never ask.” As he began pulling up her skirt and running his fingers around the edge of the waist of her panties.

Elizabeth whispered, “Just pull them down I want you right now.”

The rest of the night was spent making love and holding each other as close together as they could get.

Before they were to meet with Secretary Ridge they telephoned Logan and Clive to ask what they had decided about the capabilities of actually developing a super strain of BSE. Their thoughts were that it was not possible to develop such a strain of BSE. This confirmed Shane and Elizabeth’s thoughts on the subject.

Tom and Bob picked them up to met with Secretary Ridge. Arriving at his office they passed through security without any problems. Sue

Barrett told them to please go into the conference room and she brought them coffee and rolls. She told them I know you will all be shocked but Secretary Ridge will be here for the meeting on time. No call to the White House this morning.

Secretary Ridge arrived promptly at ten and was introduced to Dr. Elizabeth Browning he than started the meeting by congratulating the team for a job well done. He was pleased to hear that the opinion of the leading experts in the United Kingdom and the United States believed that it was not possible to devise a formula to develop a super strain of mad cow disease. He told Shane and Elizabeth that he was sorry that they turned into bait to find the missing scientists, but was pleased that the plan worked to free the scientists and their families.

Secretary Ridge told them that it was very important for the team to go to Washington State as quickly as possible to find out as much as they could about the reported case of mad cow disease. He wanted to be sure that there was nothing that indicated that this was caused by al-Qaeda operatives. He said it certainly has had some of the same effects that we had been concerned about when we heard about the plot of the al-Qaeda. People worried about eating beef and countries banning the importation of our beef.

He said, "We can only hope that this is the only cow that has been affected by the disease and that no person had contacted the disease from eating any of it."

Shane and Elizabeth delivered their recommendations to the Secretary regarding the steps they thought the government must take to safeguard America's beef supply and the people who ate beef.

Secretary Ridge thanked them for their suggestions and said he would speak with the President and ask him to pass their recommendations on to the FDA and the Secretary of Agriculture. He told them that he understood that they were almost killed by al-Qaeda and he just wanted to say that he was pleased that they were able to escape safely. Also he said the President knew of the danger they had been exposed to and he wanted to give them a token of appreciate from the White House for a job well done. Secretary Ridge presented Elizabeth with a White House pin for her jacket and Shane a pair of White House cufflinks.

Before he left the meeting he told them that he understood they planned to make a stop in Oklahoma to get married on their way to Washington State. He congratulated both of them and wished them all the best.

He said, "I guess something good came out of this plot of the al-Qaeda. You two met and fell in love that's something good.

Do a good job for me in Washington State and let's hope that the cow with mad cow disease just slipped through the cracks somewhere and it something we can fix quickly."

After they left the meeting they went back to the Park Hyatt to get Shane and Elizabeth's bags. As usually Tom and Bob already had their stuff in the car. Tom said its back to Andrews to get our plane to head to Oklahoma to get you two hitched.

Less than two hours latter they were enroute to Oklahoma. Captain Martinez and Lieutenant Wheatley were again up front flying the Gulfstream V. Captain Martinez asked Shane, "What's the name of this town we are going to again?"

Shane replied, "Enid, Enid, Oklahoma. Just head for Tulsa and than just keep flying the plane a little bit northwest for a few more minutes."

Captain Martinez said, "OK I found it. You sure they have an airport that can handle this plane?"

Shane replied, "It can take my families Gulfstream IV OK, so I think you will be all right."

Bob said, "I guess you know that we're going on your honeymoon with you. Didn't we just do that a little while ago?"

Shane said, "I guess you will be going with us or meeting us in Washington State after the wedding. You know that all of you are invited to the wedding don't you?"

Tom said, "I certainly hope so after all who else has played cupid for the two of you?"

"Only you guys." Shane replied. "We couldn't have done it without you."

When the plane touched down at Enid. Shane could see his dad's plane parked over by the fixed base operator's hanger.

Shane said, "Captain Martinez just park over by my dad's plane at the fixed base operator's hanger."

"OK, Dr. Smith we'll try to get parked right next to it if they let us." Captain Martinez replied.

As soon as the plane was stopped Shane took Elizabeth's hand and was out the door of the plane before anyone else could even move.

Shane could see his dad coming out of the office of the hanger. Shane let go of Elizabeth's hand and ran ahead to greet his father.

The two men hugged and kissed each other.

Than Shane brought his dad to where he had left Elizabeth standing.

Shane said, "Dad this is Elizabeth. Elizabeth this is my dad, Dr. John Paul Smith."

John Paul reached his arms out and took Elizabeth into his arms and off of her feet. Elizabeth didn't know that John Paul was like her dad six foot six, but built like a slim cowboy. The ones that she had seen in the movies years ago. He kind of reminded her of John Wayne. Seeing John Paul she knew what Shane would look like in thirty years. He would still look pretty good.

John Paul released her from the bear hug that he had her in and let her stand back down on the ground.

Than John Paul said, "Elizabeth, welcome to Oklahoma and welcome to the family. I've waited a long time for my son to find someone to love and I can already see why he loves you. You are beautiful and probably way to good for my son but I hope you will have him anyway. The Smith's have a habit of marrying above their class."

Elizabeth replied, "Thank you Dr. Smith for the welcome and after that hug I not sure I'm marrying the right Dr. Smith. Shane you never gave me a hug like that. Whew!"

Tom, Bob and the pilots walked up to where Shane, Elizabeth and John Paul were standing and Shane introduced each of them to his father. John Paul told them that he had made arrangements for them to stay at the Holiday Inn and that he had a car brought here for them to use during their stay. He also told them that he had taken care of all of their food and drinks and their hotel rooms while they were here.

Tom said, "Thank you Dr. Smith, but that's not necessary the Government will take care of our expenses all right."

John Paul said, "Hell I'll just pay for it now instead of paying it latter in income tax. Besides you're in Oklahoma and you are my son's guest. I'll just take it out of his allowance."

Everyone had a hardy laugh at John Paul's statement.

John Paul said, "Elizabeth we need to get on out to the ranch your daddy is getting pretty concerned about you. It's not bad enough that you go off with these men chasing al- Qaeda than you came back telling him on the phone that you are marrying my son. Your dad probably thinks they drugged you or brainwashed you while you were in South America. If you were my daughter I would have never let you go on such a mission."

"Shane, I have something to show you and Elizabeth in the hanger. It's yours and Elizabeth's wedding present." John Paul said.

Shane, Elizabeth and the rest of the group followed John Paul into the hanger. When they got inside the hanger sitting out in the center of the hanger was a new Gulfstream V painted white with blue striping and lettered with the brand of the Smith's ranch. Diamond Bar S and under the brand was painted "Smith Ranches; Enid, Oklahoma USA and on the left under the cockpit window was painted Dr. Shane W. Smith and under the right cockpit window was painted Dr. Elizabeth V. Browning Smith.

John Paul said, "Well son what do you think of yours and Elizabeth's wedding present?"

Shane said, "Dad I can't believe it. It's beautiful! Elizabeth can you believe it?"

Elizabeth replied, "No, I can't believe anyone would give such a present."

John Paul said, "Come on and get in and take a look around."

Shane opened the door to the plane and let Elizabeth go aboard first Shane followed right behind her than John Paul. The interior of the plane was beautiful. Walnut trim and off white leather was the design through out the plane. This plane had everything. A galley, bathroom and one of the seats was a couch style seat that converted into a queen-size bed.

Shane said, "Dad you shouldn't have done this. It's way too much!"

John Paul replied, "Why not. What else do I have to spend my money on? Besides half of the money now days is yours any way! So you just bought yourself half of your own wedding present!"

Elizabeth said, "This present is unreal. Are we sure we need such an airplane."

John Paul said, "You damn right you need such a plane, because if I'm every going to get to see my son and daughter they need a way to get here fast and this is it. Besides if I ever have any grandchildren I want to have them here as much as possible and God only knows where you two maybe next."

Shane and Elizabeth thanked John Paul and than they got him between them and hugged him as hard as they could.

John Paul said, "Come on let's go to the ranch we got a wedding to finish planning."

They got into John Paul's car and off they went to the ranch. Thirty minutes latter they arrived at the entrance of the ranch. The entrance had a cattle guard between the road and the ranch road and a pole type of sign holder over the entrance to the ranch with the ranch's brand hanging over the entrance. It looked just like all of the ones that Elizabeth had seen in the old cowboy movies.

Once they arrived at the ranch house Elizabeth saw a rambling ranch style house that looked a lot like Shane's house in Ames except this house was smaller. The ranch also had several bunk houses that looked like smaller versions of the ones that were on the ranch in Argentina. In addition three other smaller houses sit on the other side of the main ranch house. Shane explained that these houses were for the ranch foreman and the ranch manager. The other house was used as a guest house.

All of the property was well maintained and when Elizabeth got out of the car she saw at the back of the house was a huge deck that was a two level deck that could hold more than one hundred people. Shane explained that they used to have barbeques all of the time out there for half of Oklahoma when his mother was living. Now his dad only used it when he had meetings for the employees of the ranches.

Clive opened the door of the guest house and was soon at his daughter's side grabbing her and picking her up and swinging her around.

Clive said, "Let me look at you, are you all right?"

Elizabeth replied, "I'm OK dad, I'm just fine but between you and Shane's dad I can't keep my feet on the ground."

"Darling a woman in love is not supposed to have her feet on the ground." Clive said.

"Well I must sure be in love, because since I've landed in Oklahoma I can't get my feet on the ground." Elizabeth replied.

Clive sat Elizabeth feet back down on the ground and than picked up Shane and said, "So you're going to make an honest woman out of my daughter are you?"

Shane replied, "Yes sir, if she hasn't changed her mind by now. You know I love her don't you?"

Clive said, "It would be pretty hard not to love someone as beautiful as she is wouldn't it?"

Molly came out of the guest house and gave Shane and Elizabeth several hugs and kisses. Than she said, "Congratulations to both of you I think you two are going to have a wonderful life together. Just like Logan and I have had."

"Thanks Molly." Elizabeth said.

Shane joined in with his thanks.

Elizabeth asked Molly would you be my maid of honor for the wedding.

Molly didn't know what to say except, yes. She would love to be Elizabeth's maid of honor.

Logan came out in his new power wheelchair and greeted Shane and Elizabeth. Shane told Logan that he was thrilled to see how well he could get around with his power wheelchair. It's wonderful to be able to do something for myself Logan told them.

After dinner they discussed the plans for the wedding. It would be tomorrow night and John Paul had made arrangements for the Governor of Oklahoma to officiate at their wedding as well as the

Smith's minister. John Paul said the Governor owes me a few favors even if he belongs to the wrong political party. He can take care of waving the three day waiting period and I made arrangements for your blood tests in the morning and for a county judge to issue your marriage license.

John Paul said, "The food, flowers, live music and everything else is being handled by the wedding planner from Tulsa. He is to take care of everything else and for his cost he should. I was told that he is the best in Oklahoma. If you want anything different from what he has planned you can tell him tomorrow morning. I think from here on out this wedding is up to Elizabeth and maybe she can enlist Molly to help her."

Elizabeth said, "Would you help me Molly."

Molly said, "I wanted a daughter so bad to have a chance to help her with her wedding and here I get a chance to help Clive's daughter with hers. Thank you so much you honor me."

John Paul said, "Well that's settled. If there is anything wrong with the wedding on your fifty wedding anniversary you can redo it. Let's all have a glass of champagne to toast the bride and groom."

After champagne it was time for bed since they would have a long day tomorrow. Shane and Elizabeth went to Shane's old bedroom that he had all of his life. After they were in bed Elizabeth told Shane she loved his father. Shane told her his dad was going to love her like the daughter he never had.

Shane asked, "Elizabeth can you believe the wedding present that my dad gave us?"

No she thought it was unbelievable.

Morning came early, by six am Shane could hear people in the kitchen fixing breakfast and as he looked around his old room he thought about all of the mornings he had woke up in this room. One thing that he never would have dreamed about back than was having a beautiful young woman sleeping in his bed. Well maybe in his dreams.

CHAPTER SIXTEEN

Activity in the main ranch house was at a fever pitch by the time Shane and Elizabeth made their way into the kitchen. Shane and Elizabeth saw a small army of workers carrying in food, preparing various dishes for the reception, chairs and tables being unloaded onto the deck. They could see people erecting a giant white tent a few feet away from the deck. A short ways from there was another crew of people unloading flowers and serving trays.

In the middle of all of the activities a slender built man with a black tux's was directing all of the people that were working on the preparations for their wedding. Than he spotted Shane and Elizabeth watching all of the activities and immediately stopped what he was doing and ran toward them.

He said, "You two must be my bride and groom. I am Robert Van Sheldon, your wedding planner."

Shane replied, "Yes, I am the groom, Shane Smith and this lovely woman is my bride, Dr. Elizabeth Browning."

Robert took both of their hands in his and said, "I am so pleased to met both of you and want you to know that in spite of all of this confusion and mess I want you to know that your wedding will be the talk of Oklahoma for the next ten years.'

Elizabeth said, "Oh I am sure it will be."

Shane said, "It looks like you have a small army of people working to get everything ready."

Robert replied, "An army for just a small country."

Shane said, "I glad it's only a small country."

John Paul came out of the house and told Shane you two need to go to the hospital and get your blood test and than over to the courthouse to pick up your marriage licenses.

Than he stopped and said, "Good morning son and my soon to be daughter how are you two this morning? Also it would be safer I have found out already this morning if you get out of Robert's way and let him do his thing."

Both Shane and Elizabeth assured him they were fine and they would get out of Robert's way and take care of the things they needed to do to get ready for the wedding.

John Paul said, "I had your old jeep cleaned up for you if you want to take it to town or you can take my car if you want to."

Shane replied, "Thanks dad we'll take my old jeep."

On the way to the hospital and courthouse Elizabeth asked, "What are you wearing for the wedding?"

Shane said, "You know with all of the rush and everything else going on. I guess I forgot that I needed something to wear."

Elizabeth replied, "I think unless we change the venue of the wedding to a nudist colony it would be traditional for you to wear something."

Shane said, "I guess I will buy a tux in town, will that be all right?"

Elizabeth thought for a minute a replied, "That will be fine, but only if you wear a pair of cowboy boots. After all if I'm marrying an Oklahoma cowboy he has to look something like one."

Shane said, "OK you got a deal, but on our wedding night you have to help me take them off."

Elizabeth answered, "No problem cowboy."

Shane and Elizabeth took care of getting their blood test and marriage license and than Shane had to buy a new pair of boots. After some looking he found a pair of black ostrich boots that fit him. Elizabeth was fascinated with all of the different style and materials that cowboy boots came in. Next they went to a Formal Renting Company on the square and after a short time they found a black tux that fit him perfectly and all of the other items that he needed for the tux. The clerk tried to sell him black patented pumps for his tux, but Elizabeth told the clerk he was wearing his cowboy boots. Another problem solved.

Shane said, “Before we go back to the ranch let’s go by the airport and take our wedding present for a little try out.”

Elizabeth replied, “OK if you want to. Do we have time to do that?”

Shane said, “Let’s take time.”

They drove out to the airport and Shane talked to the folks at the fixed base operator’s office for a few minutes than they pulled the plane out of the hanger. Shane and Elizabeth got into the plane and took seats in the cockpit. Shane started the right engine and than the left engine. He let the engines run for awhile as he checked over all of the instruments and radioed the tower for take off instructions.

A few minutes latter they were airborne and Shane flew straight for the Smith’s Ranch. As they flew along Shane was explaining everything he was doing and what each of the instruments in the plane were for.

When they reach the ranch Shane flew a circle over the area of the ranch house and when the people on the ground stopped to watch the plane circling around. John Paul came out in front of the house and yelled to everybody that was his son Shane and his new wife’s airplane. All of the people started waving at the plane and Shane wiggle and waggled the wings of the plane acknowledging the workers on the ground that were waving at them. Shane made one more circle around the ranch house even lower than before.

As he leveled off the plane and started back to the airport.

Shane said, “I guess we better get back to the ranch.”

Forty five minutes latter they were back at the ranch. Elizabeth decided that she needed to have her wedding dress pressed.

Logan and Clive met them in the yard of the ranch and said that they wanted to give them a wedding present.

Clive said, “Children we have made arrangements for you to stay your wedding night in Colorado Springs at the Broadmoor Hotel. Than when you finish your work in Washington State we have a trip for you to Tahiti for two weeks.”

“Wonderful!” Elizabeth and Shane said at the same time.

"We talked to Tom Parker and he said they would take the government plane and go onto Washington State and begin checking on things there and for you two to take a couple of days coming on out in your plane." Logan said.

By six o'clock everything was ready for the wedding. Crew by crew the workers began leaving. The food service people were now all dressed in their serving gear the men in black tuxes and the woman in black short dresses with crispy white aprons. The wedding cake sat waiting for it to be cut by the new bride and groom. The cake was a marvel seven layers high and the bottom layer was the size of a small washtub. Flowers were everywhere, flowers of all kinds and colors. Throughout the décor for the wedding Robert had used white and gold for his theme. The plates were sparkling white with gold edges and the stem wear had the same gold trim around the rim of the glasses. Ribbons of gold and white dressed up the chairs and the flower arrangements were all in gold and white vases.

The Governor arrived with his entourage including four highway patrolmen. He was escorted into John Paul's office to wait for the ceremony to begin. Musicians arrived in a group and Robert directed them to an area on the deck that he had reserved for them.

By six-thirty Elizabeth and Molly were dressed. Molly couldn't believe how stunningly beautiful Elizabeth looked in her wedding gown. She told her you were beautiful before, but in that dress you are sensational, movie star sensational. It's no wonder Shane wants to marry you. You're too good for him.

Elizabeth thought back to her first conversation with Molly when Molly had almost told her that she wasn't good enough for Shane. What a change.

Shane and John Paul were dressed in their black tuxes and both had on a pair of cowboy boots. It seems John Paul had recently bought the same pair of boots that Shane had purchased this morning.

Clive also was wearing a rented black tux, but no cowboy boots for him.

He said, Putting on a tux for my daughter's wedding is bad enough, but killing my feet in cowboy boots is not for me. I'm a civilized Englishman you blokes know."

Even Logan had been put into a black tux against his will, but Molly insisted. So what else could he do! Shane getting married was like having his own son get married.

John Paul said, "Son, I am so sorry that your mother couldn't be here to see this day. She would have been in tall cotton with all of this going on in her house.

Clive said, "Elizabeth's mother would have been right there in the middle of all of that cotton with her. She loved weddings and having her daughter as the bride would have been the highlight of her life."

Shane asked, "Why do you think that a wedding is such a big deal to women that they plan them there whole lives?"

John Paul replied, "I don't know, but if you ever have a daughter don't ever asked that question."

The Smith's minister arrived and came to meet with Shane and John Paul. He wanted to ask if there was anything special from the bible that Shane would like him to read or if he knew of something that the bride would like. Shane suggested that he read the passages from John, chapter two, verses one through eleven. The minister said that he would include it in his portion of the wedding ceremony and now he would go meet the bride and than speak with the Governor to talk about how the services would be done between them.

The minister did meet with Elizabeth and she asked him to say something about Shane and her missing their mothers on this joyous occasion. Than she asked him to include the Lord's Prayer as part of the service.

Next the minister meet with the Governor to decide how they would work together to perform the wedding ceremony. They decide that the minister would begin the ceremony and than the Governor would take care of the legal issues of the state and the minister would close with a prayer for the bride and groom. Than the Governor would invite the guest on behalf of the bride and groom to the reception. That settled, the two of them went to the grooms dressing room to await the beginning of the wedding. Guest had been arriving for sometime by now and being seated as they arrived.

The orchestra had been playing for quite awhile, but than they started playing the bridal march at exactly seven o'clock.

The minister asked Shane and John Paul if they were ready to go and they assured him they were. Clive had already gone over to the bride's dressing room. As soon as the minister began the approach to the aisle the Governor fell directly behind him. John Paul was next followed by Shane.

The minister positioned the men in front of a small altar that Robert had built for the wedding directly in front of the seating for the guests. The minister had the Governor standing next to him on his right. The men were all in place waiting for the bride.

The orchestra again started the bridal march and Shane and John Paul were facing the aisle waiting for the bride. Molly began her walking down the aisle and took her place on the left side of the men.

Clive and Elizabeth appeared at the back of the aisle and they began their trip down the aisle. The guests all stood to see the bride and her father coming down the aisle. Whispers of how beautiful the bride was and her dress could be heard over the wedding march.

When Clive and Elizabeth reached the altar Clive raised her veil and kissed her than placed her hand in Shane's. The minister began the wedding ceremony by stating that marriage was a serious matter and should be not taken lightly or without fore thought and that he and the Governor were here to conduct the marriage of Shane and Elizabeth. He asked if there was anyone present that had a reason that these two people could not be married. Than he said hearing no objections to the marriage of Shane and Elizabeth we shall proceed. He asked, "Who gives this woman to be married?"

Clive replied with a strong voice, "I do."

The Governor stepped forward and asked, "Elizabeth Victoria Browning do you take Shane William Smith to be your lawfully wedded husband, to love and cherish him, to have and to hold, to honor and obey, in sickness and in health, for richer or poorer, keeping yourself only to him from this day forward till death due you part?"

Elizabeth replied, "I will."

"Shane William Smith do you take Elizabeth Victoria Browning for your lawfully wedded wife, to love and to cherish her, to have and to hold, to honor and comfort her, in sickness and in health, for richer or poorer, keeping yourself only to her from this day forward, till death due you part?"

Shane replied, "I will."

The Governor said, "As Shane and Elizabeth have pledge their love for each other in the present of this company. As Governor of the State of Oklahoma I here by pronounce you husband and wife."

The minister than took over the rest of the ceremony. He offered a prayer for Shane and Elizabeth for guidance and faith in the future and in each other. He read John chapter two, verses one through eleven.

Than he said, "Traditionally the giving and receiving of rings are a symbol of a never ending love. The ring is a circle with no beginning and no ending. Where as Shane and Elizabeth have been joined in holy matrimony they have chosen to exchange rings as a symbol of their love. Shane place your ring on Elizabeth left hand and repeat after me, with this ring I thee wed and give it to you as a token of my everlasting love."

Shane placed the ring on Elizabeth's left hand and said, "Elizabeth with this ring I thee wed and give it to you as a token of my everlasting love."

The minister than said, "Elizabeth place your ring on Shane's left hand and repeat after me, with this ring I thee wed and give it to you as a token of my everlasting love."

Elizabeth took her ring and placed it on Shane left hand and said, "Shane with this ring I thee wed and give it to you as a token of my everlasting love."

The minister said a prayer for the guests and the family and friends that were present and for them that were unable to be with them on this joyous occasion. After the prayer the minister told that Shane and Elizabeth faced a very sad time during this wonderful happy occasion for them because both of their mothers never lived to see them find the love that all mothers wished for their children.

Than he said, "Somehow I know that Shane's and Elizabeth's mothers are happy and together watching the union of their children. I know, because God is a kind and thoughtful God."

Than the minister asked everyone to join him in repeating the Lord's Prayer.

The minister completed the service with another short pray for Shane and Elizabeth. Than he told Shane you may kiss your bride.

Shane raised Elizabeth's veil and kissed her very hard and whispered to her I love you my wife now and for always.

The Governor announced that Shane and Elizabeth wished all of their guests to honor them by attending the reception and dance here at the ranch starting immediately after the wedding.

After Shane and Elizabeth left the altar and walked back up the aisle their family and friends gathered around them congratulating them on their marriage.

The newspaper reporters were present in force taking pictures of Shane and Elizabeth and their guests. Robert had the ceremony recorded using a camera that could produce a DVD of their wedding and reception.

The reception and dance after the wedding was a spectacular event that would not soon be forgotten in Oklahoma. The party lasted till the next morning and ended with breakfast being served. However, by ten o'clock with their fathers help Shane and Elizabeth slipped away and made it to their new airplane and took off for Colorado Springs.

When they were safely in their suite at the Broadmoor Hotel and the door had been closed Shane and Elizabeth sat down on the side of the bed and took a minute to realize that they were indeed married. The last few days had been a whirlwind that swept them up and dropped them at the Broadmoor Hotel.

Shane was still in his tux and Elizabeth was still in her wedding gown minus the long train that had been detached a long time ago.

Shane said, "OK Elizabeth, you said you would help me take my cowboy boots off so get started wife."

Elizabeth replied, "All right husband, but what do I do?"

Shane said, "First you get up off of the bed and turn around and take my foot between your legs and pull on the boot until it comes off."

Elizabeth got up off of the bed and faced away from Shane and pulled up on her wedding gown trying to keep the gown up high enough to see Shane's boot. No luck she couldn't hold up enough of her gown to be able to find Shane's boot.

Than Shane said, "I don't think that's going to work we are going to have to take off you gown first."

Shane got up from the bed and reached up and unzipped the gown and let it fall to the floor. Elizabeth carefully stepped out of the gown. Next she took off her slip and she was left with her bra, panties and her panty hose on.

She turned back around and reach down and took hold of the right boot and began pulling and getting nowhere. Shane took his left boot and put it on her rear end and gave her a push. The boot came off and Elizabeth ended up on the floor.

Shane rushed over to her to help her up off of the floor and to make sure she wasn't hurt. She was laughing so hard

that Shane was having a hard time getting her up off of the floor.

After Shane helped her up he had her sit down on the bed and he removed his other boot. He started taking off his tux and when he was down to his white cotton briefs.

Elizabeth said, "Wait, I can take those off all right."

She put both hands on the briefs and pulled them down to the floor. Shane stepped out of the briefs and turned his full attention to helping her off with the rest of her clothes.

When the last article of her clothes had been removed.

Elizabeth said, "Shane, my husband come and make love to me because you know I only love you for your body and how you make love to me."

Shane replied, "Yes, my wife. I know that, and I only love you for your money."

Tom and Bob left the wedding of Shane and Elizabeth to go onto Yakima, Washington to investigate the report of mad cow disease to be certain that it was not caused by the al-Qaeda. They believed that the freeing of the five scientists in Argentina had stopped the al-Qaeda's plan to introduce a super strain of mad cow disease into America's beef supply and could not even think that this report of mad cow was somehow tied to the al-Qaeda.

Drs. Smith and Browning were to meet them there after a couple of nights at the Broadmoor Hotel in Colorado Springs. Tom and Bob felt they would only be in Yakima for a short time before returning to Washington, D.C. for new assignments.

They were fortunate to still have Captain Martinez and Lieutenant Wheatley and the Gulfstream V flying them

to Yakima after Shane and Elizabeth got their own plane for a wedding present from Shane's dad. Without the two doctors they would lose their "Juice" in Washington, which meant without them they would soon be flying commercial. Having their own plane and pilots was a real luxury and they decided that they could get use to this kind of service real easily. The plane went when they wanted to go and where they wanted. Nice.

As they were arriving in Yakima in the very early morning and the sun was just coming up they could see the top of Mount Rainer sticking over the clouds below it. It was a breath taking sight.

Tom said, "Bob sometimes our jobs do have some advantage. Just look at that beautiful mountain. It's a beautiful country we live in it's too bad we don't get to stay in it more."

Bob replied, "Tom, I think when we get back to DC. I going to put in my retirement papers and leave the FBI to the younger folks. Virginia and I bought a place ten years ago in the Ozark Mountains down in Arkansas and I am going to pack up my family and go sit on top of my own little mountain for about a year, than sit up my own law practice. What do you think about that?"

Tom replied, "Well if I had someone like Virginia to sit on that mountain with me, than I might just join you. Since I don't, I guess I'll keep working until they throw me out of the company or one of the bad guys kills me off."

Captain Martinez said over the intercom, "Better tighten your seatbelts it's going to be really rough coming down through these clouds."

Tom and Bob heard what he said and pulled their seatbelts tighter. Captain Martinez didn't lie they were being tossed all over the sky. All they could see outside the plane was cloud and snowflakes blowing in a sideways motion. Finally, they broke through the clouds and the plane settled down from its pitching and yawing. The rest of the landing went smoothly.

After they landed they rented a car and got hotel rooms for each of them at the Holiday Inn Express and made reservations for Shane and Elizabeth. After they had time to clean up and have breakfast. Tom and Bob drove to the ranch near Mabton that had the cow reported with mad cow disease had come from.

Interviewing the rancher he told them that he had purchased the cow along with some other cows a few years ago. The rancher told them that the cow had been injured giving birth to her third calf and he thought that's caused her to be a downer. He explained that a downer was a cow that had problems standing or walking and that was why he took her to a processing plant.

He was able to give them the ear ID tag number that the cow had on when he bought her and the name of the sale barn he purchased her from. That was about all that he could tell them about her. Gleaning as much information as they could, they drove back to Yakima for the night.

The next day they traveled to the sale barn where the cow had been purchased several years before. Although the owner of the sale barn was anxious to help them he told them it would take sometime before he could go back through his records to see who had previously owned the cow.

Shane and Elizabeth were due to arrive sometime tomorrow and although Tom had Shane's worldwide cell number, even he was reluctant to call them the second day after their wedding.

The next morning Tom's own cell phone began ringing at six am. He woke up enough to find the phone and than when he was a little more awake he found out how to open his phone to answer it.

He said, "Hello, this is Tom Parker."

At the other end of the call he heard, "Hello Tom, this is Shane and Elizabeth. How are you this morning?"

Tom replied, "Obviously not as good as you two. Where are you?

Shane replied, "We are just getting ready to take off for Yakima, but first we have to get the plane refueled."

Tom said, "You are still in Colorado Springs than."

Shane replied, "Yes, but not for long. How is the weather in Yakima?"

Tom told him that it was too dark to see much outside yet this morning, but it had been cold and snowing yesterday.

Elizabeth took the phone from Shane and asked, "Tom, Shane had to go check on fueling the plane. What have you found out so far about the cow with BSE?"

Tom replied, "Not much so far, but I am sure that this cow with BSE never had anything to do with the al-Qaeda. I would already bet my army pension on that with what we know right now."

Elizabeth said, "You sound pretty sure of that if you are willing to bet your pension on it. Just what have you found out?"

"We've interviewed the rancher that owned the cow and he gave us her ear tag ID number and the name of the sale barn that he bought her from. We talked to the owner of the sale barn and he is looking through his records for the name of the previous owner of the cow that he sold her for. All sounds pretty straight forward to me and these guys are about as far away from being any kind of al-Qaeda agents as you could get." Tom replied.

Elizabeth said, "We don't know where she got the disease from though. I guess someone is checking out the mills that supplied feed pellets to the rancher that owned the cow."

Tom replied, "Well Bob and I never thought about asking that question, but I am sure the FDA and the Department of Agriculture agents that were here before us must be all over that by now."

Elizabeth said, "I'm sure you're right, they would certainly be all over that. Did you tell us where we are staying in Yakima?"

Tom said, "No I didn't, but you have reservations at the Holiday Inn Express where we are all staying."

Elizabeth said, “I’m giving the phone back to Shane now. I’ll see you in Yakima in a few hours.”

Shane took the phone and said, “Tom, we are fueled up and ready to go. So we should see you before too long. Do you want us to meet you at the airport or where you are staying?”

Tom said, “Why don’t you pick up another rental car at the airport when you get here and come to the Holiday Inn Express where we are all staying. That way we can go in different directions if we need to. We need to try to eliminate any possibility that there is any link to mad cow disease here in Washington State and the al-Qaeda as quickly as we can, so you and Elizabeth can go on your honeymoon to Tahiti.”

Shane said, “OK Tom, we’ll do that and see you at the hotel as soon as we get in. Bye for now.”

Shane and Elizabeth boarded their new Gulfstream V airplane, that Shane’s father had given them for their wedding present and were soon on their way to Yakima to check on the only case of mad cow disease ever reported in America.

Arriving in Yakima they rented a car and drove to the Holiday Inn Express to meet Tom and Bob. After they checked into the hotel and went to their room they tried to call Tom’s room, no answer. Shane called Bob’s room, no answer. Shane than called Tom on his cell phone and found they were just coming into the hotel’s parking lot. They made arrangements to meet in Shane and Elizabeth’s room.

After the four of them had exchanged greetings and Tom and Bob had their fill of ribbing the newlyweds they got down to the business at hand. Tom had gotten information from the owner of the sale barn of who he had sold the cow for. It was a rancher from Moscow, Idaho. They had tried to reach him by phone, but found out he was gone on a Christmas vacation and would not be back for a week.

They all looked at each other in a bit of a shock. Tomorrow was Christmas! They had been so rapped up fighting terrorist and having a wedding they didn’t even realize the date. That meant Shane and Elizabeth had gotten married on December twenty second. They hadn’t even thought about the date of their marriage before. They were just so happy to be alive and to be able to get married that dates had meant nothing to them.

Poor Bob, here he was stuck on assignment out in Washington State and his family was back in DC. He was going to miss Christmas with his wife and four children. He along with the rest of the team had not bought one present for anyone.

Bob said, "This is going to be my last Christmas away from my family. I told Tom on the way here that I was thinking about putting in my retirement papers when we got back to DC and that was before I realized that I was going to be missing another Christmas with my family."

Shane said, "Tom, I'm so sorry that you can't be home for Christmas. Aren't we kind of stuck here with nothing much to do until our rancher from Idaho gets back from his vacation?"

Tom replied, "Yeah, there's not much we are going to be able to do here until he gets back or we can find him."

Shane asked, "Why don't we get Captain Martinez, Lieutenant Wheatley and the rest of us loaded up in the Gulfstream and Elizabeth and I will take all of us back to DC for Christmas and we can come back the day after Christmas. What do you think?"

Bob said, "No, you can't do that just for me."

Elizabeth asked, "Why not. It will be a present to all of you for bringing Shane and I together."

Tom replied, "I think you would have to give more credit to the al-Qaeda for bringing the two of you together than us."

Shane replied, "Let's not give those guys any credit for anything that happened for the good. Besides, aren't I still the boss of this operation?"

Tom said, "Yes sir you are, so we will do whatever you say."

Shane said, "Ok let's go and by taking our plane it won't cost the taxpayers any money."

They made the trip to DC for Christmas and Bob and Virginia had a huge Christmas dinner for all of the team. The next day they flew back to Yakima to finish their investigation.

After they returned to Yakima they traced the rancher that had previously owned the cow and found that he had gone to Sun Valley for his vacation. After tracking him down in Sun Valley he told them that he would call his accountant and ask him to check on the cow's ear tag number to see where that cow had come from. Two days latter Tom got a call from the accountant who told them that the cow had come from a ranch up in Alberta, Canada.

The big surprise that they got when they talked to the rancher in Alberta was that the cow in question was over eight years old and must have gotten the contaminated food before the use of brains, spleens and spinal cords to add protein to feed pellets was outlawed. Before talking to the rancher every one though that she was only about three or four years old.

The FDA had sent a sample of the cow's brain tissue to England for testing and the lab there confirmed that the cow tested positive for mad cow.

No there was no al-Qaeda involved in this case, but the bad news was that a lot of damage had been done to the American beef industry. Sales of beef in America were down some, not too much; thirty countries had banned the importing of America beef and sales to the far eastern countries that were the big buyers of the brains, spleens and spinal cords were lost.

The good news from this was that no one in America besides the few people involved in the investigation would ever know that the al-Qaeda had targeted America's beef industry by trying to develop a fast acting strain of mad cow disease that could had potentially killed thousands of Americans. Dr. Logan Price and Dr. Clive Browning's experiments concluded that it was not possible to develop the super strain of BSE that could affect the normal cuts of beef consumed in America.

Bob Barker told the team that when he returned DC that the first thing he was doing when he got in his office was to file his papers for retirement and make arranges to move his family to his mountain top in Arkansas.

Captain Martinez and Lieutenant Wheatley took Tom and Bob back to DC and were soon assigned to duty in Iraq flying visiting government officials in and out of Baghdad.

Tom Parker was given a new assignment to find Dr. al-Sadr. After the CIA found out in Argentina that he had come down the river on a boat from Paraguay and than on a container ship bounded for Rotterdam. He had paid too much money to the locals they bragged about their new found riches and that information was soon picked up by local police and told to the CIA for a small fee.

Shane and Elizabeth took their honeymoon trip to Tahiti and during their stay made plans to do research to develop a test for BSE that could be used to test live cattle. They thought they would work six months in England and six months in America.

The last night of their honeymoon Elizabeth asked Shane to come and make love to me.

Than Elizabeth said, "You know I only love you for your body."

Shane replied, "Yes I know dear, and I only love you for your money!"

The End

Milton Keynes UK
Ingram Content Group UK Ltd.
UKHW041836171124
451242UK00012B/202/J

9 781964 982793